# Riverson

*In loving memory*

*Eric Duenas*

*Always with love as the sky remains blue.*

# Table of Contents

# For my dad,

*Thank you for teaching me to be strong and mature, while always being someone I can lean on.*

*Su Nasha Tus*

# *Prologue*

1...2...3...4...5.
Time is all about counting. Count the seconds until the school bell rings, until you get your lunch break, until you finally fall asleep—or don't. Counting until the day ends. Until it all ends.

All I did as a kid was count. It helped the time move faster. 6...7...8...9...10. Each second that passes is one you will never get back to. Some people don't have enough time. Others waste what they have. I think I always knew, even back then, that time was fragile. Destructible. Something that could collapse under the wrong kind of pressure.

I used to count on keeping myself still. Now I am writing to remember what I shouldn't forget.
11...12...13...

October 4th, 2014.

Fourteen seconds left on the clock.

Fourteen seconds until we knew if we were walking champions, or if we'd carry this loss with us like a scab, we couldn't stop picking. I remember the gym's lights humming, the way the court squeaked under every step, and the shout that cut through it all—Coach's voice ringing in my ear like a fire alarm.

"I don't care if you must push her to the ground—do not leave your opponent unless you want them to score on you. Are we clear?!"

I was sitting on the bench when he said it, sweaty palms pressed against my shorts, heartbeat racing in sync with the bouncing ball. My teammates all turned toward me. Shaya, who sat next to me, gave me that same look we always traded—half amusement; half *is this guy for real?* I mean, it was the elementary school basketball championships, not the NBA Finals.

But Coach didn't care. He never did. Winning was winning, no matter what the stage.

The whistle blew, and Shaya and a few others jogged onto the court. The crowd was a loud blur—cheering, stomping, chanting. I could feel the noise vibrating inside my chest.

That's when the Coach pulled me aside.

"Charli," he said, "I haven't coached anyone like you before. You can win this game. This is your team. Lead them— on and off the court. I'll give you the plays, but you control the ball. So, control it."

He meant it. He always did. I've known Coach Milowski since I was five years old. I am eight now. He hadn't changed. Just the words.

So, I stepped on the court.

Everything felt distant. The crowd, the court, even my teammates. Like I was underwater, peering out from a glass bowl. But I locked it in. Fourteen seconds. We were down two. 34–32. Just enough time.

Shaya was guarding the point. My teammate pressed up to the right. The left stayed back with me in case they tried to rush. And our best defender shadowed the top scorer—the one with nearly as many points as me. *Nearly.*

The ball flew across the court—exactly as I thought it would. A high pass. My teammate intercepted it. Timeout. Smart play.

The coach huddled us up. Drew the next move. Gave us the layout like we were clockwork soldiers.

In those few seconds, I looked up at the bleachers.

There they were.

My dad's arm draped around my mom, who looked— gorgeous. Always. She had that kind of beauty that wasn't about looks. It was how she *was doing.* Elegant and gentle. She made life look light, like it never weighed her down. I wanted to be like her. I still do.

She was smiling down at me. That smile—the one that always cracked the lock on my fear. In that moment, I knew exactly what to do.

The whistle blew. Shaya inbounded the ball to me. I waited. Drew the defense close—then cut past them in one clean move. The screens my team set confused the rest of their defense. I faked left, went right, and scanned the court.

Shaya was posted low, but she was too small for the matchup. We locked our eyes. I gave her a signal.

She bolted to the opposite wing. Wide open. I drew the defense under the basket, then whipped the pass out to her—clean. She caught it. Set. Shot.

The world held its breath.

And then...*swish*.

The place exploded. Our team swarmed each other. We were elementary school basketball champions of Nevermore. Families rushed to court. Photos were snapped. Shouts rang out.

I ran into my parents' arms.

"My beautiful girl, I am so proud of you!" Mom beamed.

"You were born to lead, Charli," Dad said. His arm still wrapped around her like she might float away.

"Let's take a picture!" Mom shouted. "Come on, come on—one with all of us, then one with you, Shaya, and Lio!" She pulled out this ancient camera—no home button, no screen, just film printed on a white strip. We took so many pictures they had to kick us out of the gym.

Outside, the cold breeze made us sweat. It felt *perfect*. My mom held my hand, firm and warm. Dad walked on the other side, cheeks red from yelling during the game— or the wind.

"So," Mom said, crouching beside me near the car, "what's next for my little champion? How should we celebrate this win— and the many more to come?"

I shrugged, flushed from all the attention.

"Can we make brownies?"

"That's *all*?" Dad called out from the trunk, laughing.

"Can we watch *Home*? On the big screen?" I shouted, grinning. Mom raised an eyebrow, smirking.

"Okay, how about this," she said. "You go with your father, wash up, maybe build me a new house on *Sims*…" She paused, wiggling her eyebrows before launching into a tickle attack. I squealed, squirmed, laughing too hard to breathe.

We laughed so loud, our voices filled the whole parking lot. Dad's laughter drifted from the trunk while Mom kissed me all over my face.

Eventually, she picked me up and buckled me in, kissing my forehead one last time. And in that quiet second, something in my chest tightened. I didn't know what it was.

I looked at her longer than usual—like I was trying to memorize her. Her eyes sparkled, but not from leftover game-day adrenaline. There was something else. Something quieter. Heavier. Tiredness, maybe. She worked hard.

Dad returned from the trunk, wrapped his arms around her waist, and lifted her off the ground. Mom squealed the whole time, laughing until he spun her and set her back down.

"You're crazy, Lloyd," she said, laughing.

"For you? Possibly," he replied, kissing her again.

"That's disgusting," I groaned. They both turned to me, exchanged a look—and then attacked me with kisses again, calling me "our little champion" and "my baby all grown."

We drove home to the sound of old-school R&B—Aaliyah on the speakers; the windows cracked just enough for the wind to hum along. We sang like we didn't have any care in the world.

Dad was my protector, my motivator. He pushed me to do my best, always.

When we got home, I tried to bolt the computer—my *Sims* world wasn't going to build itself.

"Yeah, no, Charli. Upstairs. Shower. You stink."

"But I almost reached a new lev—"

"I don't care," he said, looking up from his phone. "You stink. Go. Or I'm taking the computer away."

So, I did. Because *Sims* meant that much to me—and I'd already done my homework.

I had just made a whole *Gravity Falls* world. Mystery Shack and all.

I walked into my room. Posters covered the white walls. My desk overflowed with books. I pulled open the drawer and grabbed a CD. Popped it into the player. Pressed play. Music filled the space, covering everything else.

I picked out fresh socks, sweats, and an oversized tee. Laid them on the bed. Then I walked into the bathroom, steam already curling out from under the door, and turned the water up just enough.

And I sang along with the music like nothing in the world could go wrong.

~~~~~~~~~~~~~~~~~~~~~~~

When I reached downstairs afterwards all I saw was red and blue lights outside the window, I go into the kitchen to tell dad, only to see two police officers sitting at the kitchen table with him. They all turned to me once they noticed I was in the room.

"What's going on dad?"

"Go upstairs Charlotte, I'll come up right after, okay?" My dad said, but I saw something. He is usually laid back and charismatic. But now? He looks scared, like something bad happened.
~~~~~~~~~~~~~~~~~~~~~~~

"Where's mom?" The moment I asked this question, I saw the two officers looking down. Pain was all over their faces. "I'm not going upstairs," I declared, feeling something weirdly twisted in my stomach.

My dad sighs and nodded as he pulled out a seat for me to sit in, right across from the officer who has honey blonde hair and black mustache. Who told him that he looked good?

Dad took my hand and squeezed it. I looked at him scared about what was about to happen. Was my dad arrested? If so, what did he do? Where is Mom? Is she okay? Can I still play my Sims game after this?

"This is about your wife, Astrid Riverson, Mr. Riverson. Are you sure you want your daughter to be here?" Officer Blonde asked. I don't like this tone; I don't like this conversation.

"Whatever you have to say, you can say in front of my daughter, I taught her to be strong when life tests her." My dad said, looking down at me and nodding. With that I sat up and faced whatever was about to be thrown at me.

"There is no way to say this easily, Mr. Riverson. We found your wife dead in front of a lake. It seems she has committed suicide due to the intensive search that was conducted, and we are sorry for your loss…"

I tuned everything else out. My mother? Dead? *Suicide? What is suicide? Something you have genetics for.*

What was that? I cannot breathe; it is like nails are being swallowed every time air hits my lungs. I have to go. Anywhere. Anything but here.

"What the fuck do you mean *intensive search?!* What happened to my baby? No, she would not choose this. We just saw her about an hour ago, who the fuck hurt her?" My dad yells out, pulling out my thoughts.

In an instant the blue table with the lacy white cloth, the one my mom picked out, was thrown across the room. Dishes broke and chaos entered the room.

I could not move, I could not blink, and I could not breathe. I was stuck, frozen, because I wanted to. If I move, then that means I must face the reality that my mother is dead.

I felt an arm grab me and I could see my dad getting pinned to the ground, but nonetheless he was too strong. The officer, blondie, that was grabbing me by the shoulders set me down in the living room that was attached to the kitchen only to return to help his partner. From the living room I see two officers pinning down my father, his screams ringing in my ears. It's too much. I need to go, so I do.

I run out the front door, as fast as I can. I need to find my mom. I yell louder at each step as I run.

"Mom! Mom!" My ribs hurt; my lungs and my heart ache, reaching for something not there.

"Mommy, please! It's scary, dad is going crazy!" I was getting out of breath, my footsteps never slowing their pace. I can hear and see my neighbors coming out their doors, mumbling and my dad yelling at me. All I hear is my name. Charlotte. Charlotte. Stop Charlotte. But none of them sound the same. So, I push faster and faster until I am out of the block.

My legs were almost falling off, but I couldn't stop. The pain from my chest down to my feet was the only thing distracting me, distracting me from the fact that-

No. I need my mom. I ran so much that I ended up at the basketball court, where my dad taught me to dribble the ball, and my mom took a picture. Where she made sandwiches for us to eat after a workout, smoothies too. It was where a park was attached with swings and a playground, a table, and my family bonded with the sun beaming on us.

Now it is dark, the clouds covering the stars and nothing but the streetlight glowing over the empty court. I was breathing so hard that I could barely breathe. *No. No. My mom is still here. No, those officers are lying. They always do.*

I didn't realize I was pulling my hair until I felt the headache forming towards my front temple. I go to the bench and sit down, rocking back and forth, legs tapping, and hair grabbing. It felt like some sumo wrestler was sitting on my chest and would not let me get up. Worse than that.

My breathing stopped the moment I felt a hand on my shoulder. I looked up to see Dario, one of my closest friends. He carries a look like he was crying, seeking a place to redeem just like me.

"Why are you crying Charlotte?" He asks sympathetically. His hand stays on my shoulder until he sits next to me. There it is again. My name: the one where my mom called me Charlotte baby, always her Babygirl.

"Why are you, Dario?" I asked back, seeing the tear stain on his face and his puffy eyes.

"If I tell you, will you tell me?" Dario asks, his dark green eyes lingering on me waiting for my answer.

"I promise." I said, trying to force a smile, voice cracking.

"You don't have to be fake with me River," Dario breathes out. "It's okay I can hold you up until you're ready."

Dario puts the rest of his arm around my shoulders as I lean on his chest. Sniffles exchange between the two of us, both of us at the same time at certain points. We see cars passing by, but they don't see us by the bench with the tree blocking.

"My dad told me officially he never wanted a family and does not want a relationship with me anymore. It has only been a month since my parents separated, but it feels like it has been a year," Dario says, still looking ahead but now his face is like stone. What happened to my friend? Dario is always laughing and making jokes with Lio.

"I'm sorry Dario." I say as I squeeze his hand, that's hanging off his shoulder.

"It's--it is okay, Charlotte. I'm--I am okay," he pauses as he takes his arm off and turns to me. "You do not have to tell me if you do not want to. I want you to be comfortable."

I face him, trying to find the words of what to come next. Thinking of the whole afternoon. Three hours ago, I was getting ready for my basketball game with my mom, now her soul has been taken. How can time be so deceiving?

"My mom is dead," I said bluntly, trying to fight the tears from my eyes. The remaining question keeps popping in my head repeatedly. I sense Dario's eyes on me that I try to avoid.

"Dario, what is suicide?" I asked. Clinging onto his answer as I waited.

"Charlotte, come here," he tried to pull me into a hug, but I rejected. I just want an answer.

"No, Dario, please tell me and if you don't know it's okay, I just need to find someone who does," I say as I get up from the bench. I maybe got up two centimeters before I was pushed down by Dario.

"No Charlotte, I will tell you. I am here for you though Charlotte, always." Dario responds before hesitating to continue. "Your mom took her own life by killing herself Charlotte." He just stares at me as I stare at him.

It must've been minutes, maybe more before I realized I was crying silently. Dario wiped it away but kept falling more, eventually he pulled me into the tightest hug I can imagine, that is when the silence turns into sobs and then turned into screams, and Dario just held me.

The person who gave birth to me, the person who carried me, and the person who loved me unconditionally are dead. My mother is dead. What I didn't know at the time was that I lost two parents on the same day.

I became an orphan.

# *Anchor* Novo

## *Amor*

October 4, 2023

All colors must fade eventually; everything in life loses its spark until there are only shades and hues of what was left initially. A reminder of the life that was once present soon turned dark and dreary.

The end of a rainbow doesn't always reward gold and fortune. What was once purple eventually turned red when all the blue was gone. But people do not know if red means anger or love until they are met with their circumstances.

I stopped writing as I dropped my pen on top of my notebook and picked up the rose beside me. As I am picking off the petals off the flower, I see the dried blood on my fingers as the stem pricks my skin. I throw each petal into the calm lake, which causes little ripples into the stillness of the water. Rupturing the peace and quiet that took so long to happen.

"Mom, every year I come here and every year I am left with nothing. No answers, no clarity, no you," I huffed out, feeling dread rise on my chest.

"Life is not getting easier nor better, yet I still look for change." I said softly as I took the last petal off the flowers. It flows through the air as I toss it into the water, once again showing the act of cause and effect.

I stood from the ground and stared off into the lake. This is where my mom died, supposedly, but for some reason I cannot wrap my mind off the fact that she chose to die.

To take her own life and leave the life she had. To choose a lake underneath a bridge that connects two worlds. To choose to shoot herself in the head as she dropped in the lake, where trees are drowsy all over. Yeah, my mother "chose" that.

It has been nine years since she left me and everyone in town ignores the death of Astrid Riverson. They don't just ignore it — they swallow her name mid-sentence, as if it burns their tongues.

People look at me with pity in their eyes but glance away when I stare back at them. It is almost as if they cannot handle the product of a motherless teen in their world.

"Bye mom. I'll see you after school, okay? We'll spend the evening together. I promise." I said as I stared at the petals flowing through the water. I am met with silence. Waiting for an answer that never comes, constant despondency engulfs me like a blanket.

I walk back to the empty road as I take my headphones and phone out of my pocket. The time shows 6:30 in the morning and school starts at 7:45 as the walk is about 20 minutes from my house. If I can get home before my dad realizes I am out of the house early, then it is an upside to this foreboding day.

I walked the road home. The cold October air is biting my skin, creating bumps to form on my arm, but I don't mind. They are just a constant reminder that I am still alive and that I can feel it. Sometimes I feel prone to pain, that is the only feeling I can endure. I tried to talk to school counselors about how I felt, therapists as well, but none of it worked. *Even professionals can't help my ass.*

The gust of wind pulls me out of my thoughts. The road was eerie quiet, even with my headphones blasting music. I look at my surroundings and see the sun coming up, saying good morning as the moon says good night. The beautiful image of life being brought to the cold, drastic world settles me. My mind wanders: memories resonate.

*"Mommy why does the sky go dark?" I said as I was kicking my feet off the car seat.*

*"Sometimes the sun needs its rest too baby. Don't worry, you'll see it again tomorrow, I promise." My mom says while smiling from the mirror. I always wanted her to smile.*

*"I don't want to wait until tomorrow; the dark is scary mommy. What if it is always dark?"*

*"Charli, where there is dark there is light. You must look and be patient, okay? I want you to look for the moon, okay? Can you do that for me?*

*"Okay, but why mommy? "*

*"The moon will help you be able to see it at night, Babygirl. It will shine its light on the darkest parts of life and guide you until you can find the sun again."*

*So, I look for the moon.*

*I look for my light.*

The familiar smell of my front yard pulls me into reality. It only took me about 10 minutes to walk from the lake to my house, especially with my speed walking, damn near running. When I reached the door, I paused, hoping my father wasn't home. I creak the door open slightly only to see pitch black. I open the door fully to reveal the depressing living room. The couches are sunk in, the paint from the walls is chipping, and there are empty spaces from which pictures used to be hung. Daunting.

I move around the glass table and head upstairs to my room. Once there, I took a black shirt with baggy army cargo from my wooden chest. I look in the mirror and see the nest that lies on top of my head.

"Leave it to curly heads to put their hair through hell," I sighed to myself. I go to my drawer in my closet and take out necessities. My hands are shaking as they rummage through lotions and smell of goods.

*He's not here Charlie; it is okay, breathe.*

*Or maybe he's hiding like before to catch you off guard. Never be off guard.*

*Charlie, no, he is not here. You know he is never here in the morning.*

*Remember that one time Charli? Yeah, he's never here in the mornings my ass.*

My breathing picks up. It gradually increases and soon I can't even feel the air hitting my lungs. The idea seems to be very foreign to me, if only it was. I look in my mirror and see my eyes hung low, my chest going up and down rapidly. My vision starts showing black dots and my mouth gets dry instantly. I decided to lay on the floor and bring my knees to my head, and I counted.
1...2...3...4...5...6...7....7...6...5...4...3...2...1. Repeat.

~~~~~~~~~~~~~~~~~~~~~~~~~

I made it to school, kind of. I missed homeroom and first period, but all that matters is that I am here now. I walk through the crowded hallways and tune out everyone's conversation. When people walk alone through crowded places, they often use music to blur out everything. Although
~~~~~~~~~~~~~~~~~~~~~~~~~

I am a victim of that assumption, sometimes I don't even need music. Whatever is going on inside my head creates its own distraction for me to fade out of reality.

I eventually got to my locker and hit shuffle on my playlist. When it comes to music, my taste is very bipolar as it rummages through several genres. Everything is included in my playlist, going from R&B to Heavy Metal to Soul music. Anything and everything but country music, do not put any country music-

"Hey Charlotte, how are you?" Rola asked, dragging me out of my thoughts. A girl on the dance team who is very "popular" by standards. She beats the stereotype to be honest. This is reality, she is not a bitch who just peaked in high school. Though her friends on the other hand can be said otherwise.

"Rola, really?" Quinn asked. Quinn Valley, now there's your stereotypical high school bitch.

"Quinn, shut up," Rola rolled her eyes as she continued, "Hi, Charlotte would you like to-"

"No." I stated firmly.

"I didn't even say anything yet-"

"And my answer would still be no." I exclaimed still not facing her. I grabbed my notebook and red pen. I love this notebook to be honest. It has red mushrooms on top with plants surrounding it. It has a black background and the pages inside it are white. And the red pens, they're just a plus side-

"Earth to Charlotte, did you hear me?", Rola asked.

"Charli." I uttered.

"What?" Rola questioned me.

"I said Charli, don't call me Charlotte."

"But your name is Charlotte-" Quinn laughed off.

"I don't fucking care, don't call me Charlotte." Can they just leave? I just got into school.

"We can call whatever you want. I don't care what you prefer. Is it not the name your disaster of a mother called you?" She clapped back. I just look at her. Today, really? Of all days? My face is calm, and my fists are tight; my lips are hard.

I smile and she smiles. I laugh and she laughs. Like a person to cobra. Copying off one's move in a trance. I can feel my hands bleed from my nails digging deep in my skin. Just one swing-

Just as I was about to step up to Quinn, someone pushed me back to the locker. I look up to see Emilio holding me back and someone else between Quinn and him.

Emilio, Lio for short. Best friend since diapers. Literally. Our mothers were practically sisters, just without blood in their veins.

"What the fuck is going on?" Thea says while in arms with Cameron. I fuck with them to be honest. They are a cool couple; I had no problems with them. They just have weird taste in their friends.

"Charli, chill. Calm down." Emilio hissed out.

"I'm calm. Move." I stated. He didn't budge, earning a laugh from my mouth for a moment. Emilio just glared at me.

"Move Lio. I'm not going to do anything." I said again, this time slowly as I pushed him aside. He moved over and I headed into my locker and grabbed my headphones.

Yeah, I'm not going to class right now; I'll just go after lunch, which is fourth period. It's second period now, which means I have two more to wait for. I turn around and see everyone looking at me. I put my headphones on and grabbed my bag; pushing past Lio and some other person, I took a right and then a left, now I'm in front of a huge gym, with nobody in it, and two hoops.

I look around to see if they have a basketball anywhere, but of course not; someone like me would just take it. However, people are lazy so there's probably one behind the bleachers.

Just as I imagine, there is a Spalding ball sitting in the crook of the left corner. I picked it up and sat down. Looking at the ball in my hands I felt the grooves indented in the ball. The grip is peeling, soft, and worn. Too slippery to handle. I push the ball to feel the ball deflate a little bit.

Everything is so wrong with this ball, but ultimately it is the best; it holds the most memories. I look up to the hoop and can see the ball flowing through the air while dropping into the net. The swish sounds satisfying yet short. Most best things are.

I get pulled out of my thoughts when I feel a presence beside me on my left. I look to see D.J. looking at me and then at the ball. D.J. Black, short for Dario Jr. We don't have any bad blood with each other; we just don't speak to one another. Friends to strangers with memories. *Good, don't have to ruin his life like you do to others.*

He finally looks up at me again in the eyes. He nods and then sits back on the upper level behind him. He puts headphones on but doesn't play anything. I just stared at him for a few seconds and then turned my head to the basket ahead of me.

A few minutes passed and we still no talking. Nothing but silence. It's deafening, strangely for someone who likes quiet.

"What are you doing here D.J.?" I whispered.

I don't know if he heard me or not, but he doesn't say anything. He just gets up and leaves. Footsteps that fade away one by one. 1...2...3...4...5...6...it stops. It usually takes about 11 steps for someone to get out of earshot.

I turn my head to see D.J. waiting for me by the door.

"Come on." he uttered before heading out the door fully.

My body gets up without my consent and follows.

*Stay away. Leave. Alone. Alone.*

*Don't go with him. Stop. Stop. Stop. STOP.*

My brain is screaming to stop but my body argues against it.

~~~~~~~~~~~~~~~~~~~~~~~~~~~~~~~

Flashes of colors pass by the window. I see green, blue, gray, brown, and so much more. I looked to the side and D.J. focused on the road. I put my headphones on, without playing anything, and took out my notebook and pen. In the beginning of the notebook, there are pages torn out. I ignored them and turned to the next empty page. The lines running across the page correlate to the red ink that is being bled into a single slice of a tree.

"What happened to the first few pages?" D.J. asks while his eyes are still on the road.

"Where are you taking me D.J." I turned to him and asked.

Nothing. No response, just the motor from the vehicle making the noise and the endless road we have seemed to partake in. His one hand is firm on the steering wheel while the other rests on the arm rest next to the gear. Lefty; not many people I know are lefties.

"D.J. I'm serious, do you not have a football game later? You can't skip classes." I spit out while still looking at him.

"For someone who does not like or care about anyone or anything, you sure ask a lot of questions." D.J. says
~~~~~~~~~~~~~~~~~~~~~~~~~~~~~~~

sarcastically, taking his eyes off for a split second only to look at me.

"Who said I didn't care?"

"Who said that you did?" And that was the end of the conversation. The rest of the drive was hushed and almost irritable. *Like everything that has become our norm.*

After about an hour, we pulled off the main road into a closed community. I see houses pass by looking the same, almost like Nevermore. D.J. parks the car in the parking lot and gets the car out. I do the same and follow his long strides into what looks like a main register building.

"Hi, D.J., back again this week?" The receptionist greeted him warmly.

"Yes, but just here for an hour though. I must get back soon." D.J. answers without looking up as he signs his name on a clipboard and then passes it to me.

I signed my name and looked up to see D.J. typing on his phone.

"Ready?" D.J. asks.

"No."

"Tough luck."

And with that he put his hands behind my back and pushed me towards a pair of double doors. I pushed his hand off me and started walking beside him, glancing up only to see a hint of a smirk.

We open the doors and see tables set up with food and baggies. Areas are filled with peanut butter and jelly, bread, packaged snacks, and so much more.

"Come on." D.J. states as he leads us to the middle of the table.

"Have you ever done this before?" He asks.

"I don't even know what this is."

"I know you are not stupid Charli." D.J. says slyly. *If we were still friends, I would've gut-punched him for that remark.*

I look around again and that's when it connects; this is a service. One of which was volunteers making food bags and give them out to people in need. *Why did he take me here?*

Without having the second to process it, D.J. hands me a loaf of bread, a jar of peanut butter, and jelly. He also gave me a pair of gloves, and I put them on instantly. No talking, no awkward silence, just two people with distinct lives making sandwiches.

I look around the room to see diverse types of people. I do not know anything about them, yet they welcomed me as if it was no problem. I'm not going to lie to anyone, whenever I saw closed communities in my neighborhood, I automatically thought they were stuck up and narcissistic. That's not the case here. This reminds me of my mother, as does everything else. But this specifically gives me clarity as she was always in her organization finding ways to help her community. I would come home sometimes to see mountains of food, being jealous that I could not eat anything.

*"Charlie, we have a roof over our heads, food on the table every night, and you specifically have two loving parents. You have the bare minimum not everyone was granted,"* my mom would explain to me every time I had my seven-year-old bitch outs.

She had a beautiful soul, one of which I would not see in an exceedingly long time.

~~~~~~~~~~~~~~~~~~~~~~

True to his words, we wrapped up all the bags we made and put them in a pile. In each bag there are two PB&J sandwiches, a Capri sun, a bottle of water, about 4-5 bags of variety snacks, and a phone number and address in which people can contact the local shelter.
~~~~~~~~~~~~~~~~~~~~~~

"So, did you like it?" D.J. speaks up as he holds eye contact with me.

"Precisely." I responded. Truly short and simple. He smiles smugly and starts to walk towards the doors we entered before.

"Excuse me miss!" a random lady announces. I turned around to see the full image of her. She has red hair and looks like she is in her mid-60s. Her small frame mirrors mine, haunting me with a look of optimism while I return it with despair. Nonetheless, she does look great.

"Can I help you?" I asked. I noticed the snark in my statement when she physically recoils with her facial expression. I heard D.J. chuckle a little bit, which led me to side eye him.

"I'm sorry to bother you, but is this your first time here?"

"It is. I'm sorry is there a problem?"

"No, no, of course not. I was just asking because you look...familiar is all. Maybe it is just me getting old," the lady asks as she chuckles. "I'm sorry, my name is Wilma. You are?"

"Charli. Nice to meet you." I forced out a smile, something that made my face ache.

"You as well Charli, sorry to intrude but I must get going now, have a good rest of your day. And D.J. please take care of this girl, will you?" Wilma responds with laughter in her eyes, but a bit of resilience. I look between D.J. and Wilma, seeing the tension rise between the two of them.

"I will Wilma, have a good day as well." D.J. replies with a tight smile. We exit the building, leaving Wilma in the lobby.

As we approached D.J.'s car, I tried to open the passenger door. Keyword: tried. That is, before D.J. himself only unlocked the trunk to grab a basketball.

"What are you doing? Are we not heading back?" I questioned, crossing my arms. A chill from the wind runs up my spine, making me pull my jacket closer.

"No, that is what I tell the people inside, otherwise we would have been there all day." D.J. states as he closes his trunk. He looks at me up and down before walking away.

"Come on, River." As he wanders deeper into the community.

"River?" I asked, making my way beside him. I had to run to catch up with his big feet. His one step is about three of my own.

"What is wrong with River?" The breeze hits us both from the parking lot.

"It's not my name."

"Charli is not either, yet you prefer that name."

"I can say the same about you D.J." I remarked as I glanced up at him. He returned his eye contact, and for a moment, we were kids again. The kids who always stuck around each other, the kids who shared pain with one another.

For a moment, I am reminded of why the little girl had to step away from friendship. Now we are teenagers who live our lives near each other but never involve one another.

"Here," D.J. breaks the silence as he passed me the basketball.

A few minutes passed by, and we stopped in front of a basketball court. A very upkept court, but the rims look as if they are double-rimmed. Though the upside is they have chain nets. The ground has black floors that grip every step I take. I look around for a spot to sit and see benches against a shared black gate with a playground on the other side. I take a seat and feel the ball in my hands, D.J. following the same steps.

"Will you not get to play in the game since you skipped class?" I asked.

"I can care less about some football game in all honesty." D.J. responds as he looks up in the sky. I do the same; noticing clouds come in all shapes and sizes, evolving within the wind.

"Why did you bring me here D.J.?" I speak up.

"Why did you come Charli?"

"Must you always answer a question with another question?"

"Must you always ask questions?"

I looked at him with a dull expression only to meet with his charismatic one.

"D.J.?"

"Yes River?" He responds smoothly. His black sweater ruffles when the wind hits it. He has black Jordans, specifically black cats to match it.

"Why did you bring me here?"

He smirks at my question as he shakes his head. "I would want someone I know to reach out to me."

"But why?" *Why now?* I can feel irritation rise to my throat.

He turns and faces me now. His eyes captivated mine and his face turned serious.

"Ask me your real question."

I just stared at him for a couple of seconds to figure out what he meant. Is he dumb?

"River." D.J. expressed his gaze softens, but his voice is still stern.

"What changed today?" I ask as I look back at the clouds.

"What do you mean?" D.J. pulls me back as I stare at him. Blankly, unrecognizable. *Here he goes ignoring my question.*

"What made you want to help me D.J.?"

D.J. smiles at me for a few seconds, like he is toying with me on purpose. For a few seconds I haven't thought about what is going on with my life. I'm just waiting for his response.

"I wanted to help someone I once knew." He just stares back, recognizing me from a mile away.

# *Gilded Lily*

## *Cults*

October 6, 2013

The sound of my dad's laughter rumbles through the car, aligning with the bass of the music coming from the radio. Beat after beat, the song fills the car, diminishing the silence that the world sometimes gives out. We are parked outside of Checkers, the most delicious oily food you can ask for, especially the fries. So much for a healthy diet. My dad only allows me to sit in the front for purposes like these: late night food runs and debrief sessions. I just won my game with Shaya, but we dropped her off earlier. I reminded her the whole ride to facetime— my sim's world isn't going to show itself.

"Charlotte, I have no idea where you came up with these things. Why would you like to try pepper and cream cheese together?" My dad laughs out.

"Especially with hot Cheetos? Goodluck kid, you're going to be on the toilet all day." My dad laughs at me as I join in, loving how he laughs. My dad never fails to make me happy, even when I am down. He would say things like "if you are able to smile you should because it is too short of a life not to." Mom will get annoyed sometimes if we laugh too much, but she always joins after acting mad. I knew she would never be fully mad at me, like I would never to her.

"Dad, you have to eat it with me, I know you want to," I said as I ate my mozzarella sticks. I wish I liked fast food burgers like my family did, but they always make my stomach hurt.

"I will if you choose to do your laundry this weekend and not have mom or I do it for you," he explained as he took a sip of his milkshake. He put it in the cupholder only for me to take a sip a second later.

"Deal." I stuck out my fist to my dad who returned to it soon later. We both twist our wrists and pull out the pinkie and thumb to interlock with one another. A deal is a deal.

Silence falls with Bruno Mars playing in the background. I look outside the window and continue eating my food. I can hear my dad munching on his food as we fall into each other's presence.

"Dad?" I announced as I turned towards him.

"Yes Charlotte?"

"What is love?"

He looked at me and was confused. He swallowed his bite before continuing, "The feeling you get from when you see me or mom." I turn back to the window and just let my thoughts go wild. Everyone talks about love, but no one ever explains it to me when I ask. Am I not capable of love?

Shaking my head I ask, "What about the love you and mom have for each other? You are always kissing, it's nasty." I can hear my dad laugh, making me look away from the window yet again.

My dad puts his food down on the dashboard and turns to me.

"Charlotte, listen to me, one day you will find this love you are looking for the meaning of. I want to tell you what it is, but the truth is love comes in assorted sizes, shapes, and times." My dad clears his throat and rubs his hands together, getting the crumbs on his lap.

"Love cannot be defined and most certainly cannot be measured. What me and your mom have is love, but a lot of it comes from memories." My dad says with a serious face. The laughter that vanishes from his eyes is now replaced with sincerity.

He continues, "One day, a day very far from now," he pauses and gives me a look with his eyebrows raised before starting again, "you will meet someone who does not question love. Love is not easy; it is a journey. You will ask yourself what love is, but you will not have to question the feeling itself. It is all complicated now, but you don't have to worry about this until *much later." He stops and grabs his burger. He smiles at me before taking his bite.*

*"Come on, eat your fries before they get cold." My dad demands as he puts the radio higher. I think about what he said and picture who my ideal love will be only to realize that I don't want anyone else if I have my parents, maybe a sibling or two, but my parents have already shut my idea down. Three times, straight. Sad case really.*

*"Dad."*

*"Hm?" He responded while looking at his phone.*

*"I love you dad," I said as I took more of his milkshakes.*

*"I love you too Babygirl," as he took the milkshake right back.*

*Just me, my dad, checker fries, and too many milkshakes.*

The memory ended when the bell yanked me back to fluorescent lights and blank stares. I close my notebook, and I look around to see that my English teacher, Mrs. Cailo, waiting for me once again. No students were left except for me, which means I completely tuned out the first bell. Great.

"If you want to stay in my room all you have to do is ask, you know that right Charli?" Mrs. Cailo asks, giving me a look that seems all too familiar to me. She seems to want to question me about something she always asks about.

With her big brown glasses, she takes them off and takes a seat at her desk. It is filled with paperwork, one of which she wanted to assign students anyway.

She smooths down her white, ruffled blouse and lifts her head up waiting for my answer. I stand up from my desk and start grabbing my items. Phone, bag, notebook, red pens.

"And what about the time I'm here Mrs. Cailo? Sit and stare at each other until your free period is over? Besides, I have study hall now."

"This can be your study hall room, I'm sure the principle would not mind a student staying with a teacher. Especially if you are studying or writin-"

"I'm going now Mrs. Cailo, thank you for the offer though," I announced. As I was putting my headphones on and sling my side bag on my shoulder, I started heading towards the door. It only takes about four steps from my seat to the door. One step, two steps, three steps...

"Charli, wait."

I turned around to see Mrs. Cailo holding a notebook and pen, along with a single slice of paper.

"No," I responded and was about to head back but before I knew it Mrs. Cailo was beside me and closed the door.

I can hear the shuffle of students on the other side, desperately wanting to join them and get away from what this conversation is about to bring.

"Now Mrs. Cailo, if you just wanted me to stay you could've just asked." I said as I gave her a deadpan look.

"Now I have been patient enough with your remarks, but now it is the end of that. The faculty is talking about you, especially when you have made no plans since the first year to work towards your career." She huffs out.

"Charli, you have talent. I hate watching you shut everyone out. You don't work towards anything but your schoolwork and do not do anything outside of school-"

"Are my grades good?" I interrupted.

"Well, you are a straight A student, but that does not mean any-"

"Have I not been out of trouble within the school, specifically fights, since my sophomore year?"

"Well, yes but with the time outside of school-"

"Is not any of your business or the school's. I'm a straight A student like you said and do not get into fights anymore. I did all the detention and suspension days, so I do not understand why you are keeping me here Mrs. Cailo." I snapped back.

I'm getting tired; I just want to spend my free time alone. Kind of goes against the situation occurring now, however.

"Charli listen; you used to love writing when you were little. Even in eighth grade you would still write and even make it into the high school newspaper. I see you still write in your notebook, but you do not want to share with anyone." Mrs. Cailo announces while pointing to my notebook. I clutch it as close as I can when she hands me the book and pen, along with the paper.

She continues, "The least I want you to do is take the new notebook, yours is falling apart my dear. Please take it. And the entry submission to the essay contest." Mrs. Cailo stops for a second, not wasting her breath.

"You can win a full-ride scholarship to a few colleges if you win. It would not hurt to get away from this town, filled with tragic memories. They will only haunt you my dear." She continued, holding my stare.

I just look at her. No emotion, no reaction. She holds onto my expression as if she is trying to read me. Her light brown hair covers her forehead, hiding her eyebrows when she raises them, questioning me about my next move; like playing chess, or even checkers.

"My mother's life was not a tragedy. Especially if this place is one of the few things I have left of my mother. You know what? Go lecture to someone else. I'm done." I spit it out. Anger fills my blood, and I just want to get out of here.

I headed out the door, almost bumping into other students as they walked to class. As soon as the door shut, the words tasted like rust on my tongue. *So sinister, she was just trying to help you bitch. No wonder everyone hates you. You only have two friends after all.*

I shoved the notebook and paper in my bag as I head down the halls, the walls being burgundy and a huge banner promoting the football game today. I turn the corner and see the cheerleaders heading to the locker room. One of which turned around and just gave me a nasty look. In response, my middle finger is always the way to go, especially when her eyes widen and she rushes back to her teammates. Bitch. *Like you?*

Further down the hall, past the locker room, I approached my locker. I open it with ease, grabbing my small black bag. I placed it in my olive-green side bag on my shoulder and started walking towards the door that leads to bleachers on the football field. Music is blasting in my ears, and the wind instantly pushes my hair out of my face once I step outside. Luckily, my free period is my last one and then I can finally get out of this hellhole. I can smell the fresh air instead of hallways that reek of champagne toast and sweat.

It only takes me a few minutes to reach the bleachers. I headed under and walked to my chair, the one that I purposely hid so that no other teenage delinquent like me took it. I grab my metal chair from the back bushes, next to a shed that holds most of the sports equipment. I carry the chair down the long black concrete behind the bleachers until I meet with the last one.

I open the metal chair and place it in the corner, where each side of the bleacher covers me with its bars. I sit down and open my bag. It is filled with my notebook and endless red pens. Some used tissues piled up and my small black bag. Opening the zipper to reveal three joints and a lighter. Grabbing one and placing the rest of the items next to me, I start lighting the joint. The reddish-orange color spreads as more heat travels to the joint.

Once fully lit, I take my lighter off and take a hit. Smoke fills my mouth, and I inhale all of it, slowly breathing it back out again. I waited for the instant effect to take place, but nothing came. I took another big pull and could hear the crackling sound coming from the spark. The smoke blow upwards, looking at the cloud exit my lungs as warmth returns to my legs sitting on this cold ass chair.

As I was about to take my third pull, I heard a coughing sound to the right of me. Instinctively, I did not put my shit away; instead, I just looked to the right and took my third hit looking at the person right in front of me.

"I have no fucking clue how you do that shit without coughing your lungs out. I do it, and I might as get the security to bust my ass myself." Emilio exaggerated, still coughing like he is a 60-year-old smoker.

"Technically, coughing makes you higher so you're the real one winning here if you think about it. Doesn't mean you got to bitch about it though." I responded as I let out the third hit; I ash the piece that is about to fall before it lands on my clothes. No way I'm trying to have this smell on me. I took another hit and looked back at Lio, who was also taking another hit with his joint.

"I don't know who ruined your mood to make you want to smoke, but don't ruin my high because you have a pissed temper." Emilio said bluntly, jokes aside.

"I'm good. No worries." *You're always annoying everyone; they would be happier without you.*

"Mrs. Cailo?" He tries to spit out without coughing. I'll give him credit for making through the "sentence" without the lungs giving out, but it didn't take a second longer after hearing the elderly in him again.

"Same old, same old." I say it with a dull expression.

"So why let her get to you if it is the same topic?"

I ash my blunt that I was letting burn and took a hit before responding.

"It was the way she brought up the subject. I don't like being reminded that I do not have the same life as others, especially if it points to being a "tragedy," I breathe out along with the smoke that was trapped.

"What happened to you was tragic Charls." Emilo acknowledges.

"My mother's life was not tragic Lio. Don't piss me off now."

"No one said it was Charls, but what she did was. It's okay to let more people in, besides me and Shaya. One day you will have to you know." He ashes his blunt before taking a pull, coughing like a bitch he is. Love him but he still is a bitch. *You fit right in yourself, Charli.* Shut up.

"One day is not today, most likely won't even be this year."

"Never say never Charls."

"I didn't say never dumbass." I retort, rolling my eyes and taking a big ass pull as Lio chuckles. Not allowing my lungs to exhale for at least seven seconds, making it cramp. I inhale harshly, forcing me to cough my whole lung out. This is better than thinking. *I'm still here you fucking moron. You can never do anything right.*

I saw Lio from the corner of my eye, who was still standing in the corner, coming close and sitting on the ground. His free hand wrapped around his knees that is pulled go his chest. We smoke in silence for about 10 minutes until we hear the bleachers making noise.

Instantly, Emilio and I look at each other for a mere second before putting our blunts away. By the time we were done, the people who were walking down the bleachers were already making their way to the back of the bleachers, exactly where both of us were sitting.

"If we get caught just act like you're sleeping, and I'll do the same." Lio would say the stupidest shit. Before I responded, someone beat me to it.

"Who the fuck sleeps in the back of the bleachers when it is windy as hell?" A dark-skinned girl appears, with her locs tied back into her grey hoodie.

She has her hands in her dark red leather jacket pocket. She wears black tinted sunglasses and sniffles every few seconds, showing the wind's effect on her body. Shaya Jones. My found family, my sister. This hoe is high as hell right now. I'm always reminded of how she and Emilio are together. I can't blame her though but shit I wish I didn't put my roach out, honestly the best part of the blunt.

Besides her was D.J., who is smoking as well and staring directly at me. I stared right back. The last time I saw him was when he brought me back from the expedition he led. A ghost smirk forms as fast as it disappears when he takes a hit. He holds it out for me to take, in which I do. I take a hit smoothly, feeling the effect of the drug flowing into me, my eyes get heavy, my arms start to feel dull. *This is some hard ass shit.*

"Babe now is not the time. Your brother over here won't pass me the blunt." Emilio grunts.

"I prefer you not to cough on the blunt." D.J. says while typing on his phone. He holds his hand out, and I hand it to Lio before D.J. can grab it. "Besides cannot let the parents know we partake in drugs." He looks up in amusement, locking eyes with mine before looking at Shaya.

"Please, Calista will always be cool with us smoking. It's more my dad that will have our heads." Shaya takes her hood off and approaches me. She sits on my lap and wraps her arms around my neck.

"Anyways, Charlssss." My gaze breaks from D.J. and turns towards Shaya.

"No." I responded instantly. I move against Shaya, who does not budge whatsoever with her athletic build.

"You didn't even let me finish. I was going to say that we're having a sleepover at Emilio's house. Me, you, Lio, and I guess D.J." Shaya announces while rolling her eyes over D.J.'s name. D.J. on the other hand pays no mind and smokes the rest of his blunt while typing away on his phone. I can hear the short clips that come from Lio's phone as he scrolls through his feed on Instagram.

"Okay, no." My response made Shaya pull my face with both of her hands. I am now forcibly looking eye to eye at Shaya. *It could be worse. I could deal with Lio's hot breath.*

"Yeah, no Charli, you're not spending another Friday night doing absolutely nothing in your household. It's not like your dad is strict, when we were little, he always let you come over." Shaya exclaimed. *He's not strict because he doesn't give a shit about you anymore, maybe he never truly did.*

"Yeah Charli, Shaya can pick you up from your house when she goes to the game tonight and then back to my house," Emilio added.

"No. I don't want to go to a football game. Besides, I got a tattoo to do tonight," I continued, trying to push this conversation. *You're such a fucking wet blanket. You don't deserve friends.* Yes, I do. *They probably don't even like your ass on the low.*

"Charli, listen to me," Shaya states now serious, "I'm not going to let my best friend drive herself crazy in her boring ass room. You are coming and your "client" can come to Lio's house to get the tattoo and leave right after." Shaya demands, her hands still on my face, making it squish together.

"Philo is a real client if he is the one supplying the weed we both smoke in exchange for tattoos." I keep my face blank. She watches anyway, like she's trying to read a page I haven't written yet.

"And if I say yes, will you leave me the fuck alone about this?" I ask, desperately want them to shut up about a stupid sleepover that I know damn well is a party. A high school fucking party, where kids drink cheap shit and get drunk to regret it the day after. I'll stick to my weed and my memories. *Don't forget about me like you are trying to forget your mom's suicide.* I just really want to turn my brain off sometimes. *Try a gun like your mother did.*

"Yes." Shaya, Emilio, and D.J. all answered. We all look at D.J. confusingly, especially when we all forgot he was there. He was leaning against the bar with his arms crossed. His eyes don't look low, but his arms are slouching, which shows that the weed is affecting him. Maybe not as much as Emilio, who only smokes here and there, but still impactful. Whatever he smokes is still strong but not enough to not think. *Can't drive me away like you drive everyone else away. Like your dad.*

"I bet you love that high with your greedy ass," Lio spits out. D.J. only responds by blowing him a kiss before throwing out the roach.

"We have been out here for about 30 minutes. She said she will go; can we go home now, or I can leave you guys," D.J. spits out. He heads away from the bleachers towards the parking lot. All the way up to 13 steps until D.J. was out of earshot; mine would've been 20 steps.

"So, which one is going to drop me off home since you guys are dragging me to a football game and a party tonight." I asked as Shaya got up from me after I nudged her. I put my things in my bag before getting up from the chair. I fold it up and start bringing it back to my hiding spot before walking up towards the parking lot as well. I hear Lio and Shaya pull up to the side of me, his arm over Shaya's shoulders.

"What party are you talking about?" Emilio asks, his voice is going on an octave higher than usual.

"Your voice crack just told me all I need to know," I stated as Lio nudged me. I exaggerated a winded push, acting like he just punched me with full force.

"You're such a clown," Emilio chuckles.

"I'll drive you home but only because I want to come over if that is okay so we can get ready together. I already have my stuff in my car and that way we don't have to rush." Shaya chimes in. One thing about her is that she is a planner; she will break it down to you if you have no clue but will punch the shit out of you if you ask her to repeat herself.

"Okay." I said, tuning the world out and letting my thoughts run freely. *What if dad is there? What if he yells at me for bringing company without him knowing? What if he is drinking?* What if he's not even at home?

All three of us made it to the parking lot, which is now filled with students leaving early, especially those who also have a free period since they allow us to leave 10 minutes earlier than the rest. My sophomore year was brutal when I had chemistry last period, and my teacher would purposely keep us an extra ten minutes to "go over" what he "forgot" in the lesson. I think he was just lonely to be honest, but because of that a lot of parents complained and he eventually got fired. Sad.

As I wait for Shaya to come open her door, she is making out with her boyfriend, who in fact she will see in about three hours. I love my friends and their relationship but sometimes I just want to shave their lips off so they wouldn't be able to kiss every five seconds.

It took 10 more minutes until Shaya finally detached her second pair of lips and unlocked the car door. She is just lucky it's not cold as hell outside, otherwise I would've just dragged her ass like she is doing to mine.

~~~~~~~~~~~~~~~~~~~~~~~~

It's about 4:50 in the afternoon and the game starts at 6:00 p.m. The drive home was nice; stopping to get coffee
~~~~~~~~~~~~~~~~~~~~~~~~

and ranting about new books as they were bought. Shaya treated me even though I tried fighting her for it.

Now, we are in my room, listening to music as we get ready. Shaya fixes her hair, framing her face as she fluffs out her outfit. My beautiful friend, one with the beautiful locs that she decorates with charms hanging from it.

I got up from my bed, massaged my temple and put my book back in the bookcase. Heading towards my desk, I open my notebook and grab my red pen. I can hear Shaya from behind me coming out of the conjoined bathroom in my room and sit on my bed. She wraps her arms around me, squeezing me until there is basically no air left.

"What do you always write in Charli? You are always writing, especially with a red pen." Shaya asks while chuckling.

"Just things to keep my thoughts in check. Therapist recommended it," I said, remembering the intense therapy my dad put me through the first two years after my mom's death.

That is probably the last thing he did for my wellbeing, after that he just points to drinking and gambling his problems away, one of them being me as a constant reminder of what he lost.

Many people say I grew into my mom's looks, which makes me feel worse as people only wanted her for her beauty. I tried anything to get out of my mother's grasp; even dying my hair auburn, getting rid of the natural hair color. Over the years I really did everything to look less like her, no one can compare to her beauty, not even me. That's when I got my nose piercing and started getting useless tattoos. Nonetheless, it didn't help with my low grey eyes that matched my mom's.

"You can always talk to me Charli," Shaya spoke softly. The hug lasts more than a minute, feeling the warmth of an embrace.

She continues, "I always bother to invite you everywhere because I only see glimpses of the Charli I used to know, one where something that happened to her did not define her." She steps back and belly flops on my bed, keeping the energy light. With Shaya and Lio around, it's always like having siblings you can't get rid of, even when they worry about you.

"Charli you don't even have pictures of your mom anywhere in this household." *If only she knew that my dad would get heated at any sight of my mother.* "It takes time, I wouldn't understand how that feels for you, but I don't want you to segregate yourself because you feel you must. You have a village around you," Shaya finishes off.  I turn around and stand up only to see her staring to see my reaction. *She thinks despicable and desperate. So. Do. I.*

"Lead the way, cheerleader." I force a smile, hinting at Shaya's outfit. I'm used to lecture after lecture when it comes to today. A reminder of someone who is a ghost in her own story.

~~~~~~~~~~~~~~~~~

It would be embarrassing for my friends to throw a party if they lost; it's a good thing they didn't. As Shaya and I pull into Lio's driveway, I can see the white door surrounded by grey bricks, all of which are different hues that blend nicely. His lawn is well kept, and he has an automatic garage door that is black.

We got out of the car and headed into the house; the music wakes up the house that is surrounding us and is packed with teenagers. Some of the people I can see are already smoking on the balcony. Flashing colors come from all over the room, and multiple conversations are made ranging from condoms to drugs.

I nudged Shaya to tell her that I'm going to set up my tattoo things in Emilio's room, reminding her to tell Philo to find me. She nods, only to dart into the kitchen the moment the words left my mouth. I would never trust jungle juice
~~~~~~~~~~~~~~~~~

again after Lio's 15th birthday party. Costumes and liquor do not mix.

As I made my way up the stairs, I elbowed to more people than I wanted to. The stairs leading upstairs is just universal code for sex. In any other movie or book, I've encountered it anyway.

Eventually, through the sea of people, I made it to Lio's room, opening the door tentatively. For my sake and my damn eyes, I should've fucking knocked. I'm looking at D.J. and Quinn making out on the desk. It felt like ages of hearing them kiss, D.J. sitting in the chair and Quinn on his lap. It took her slow headed ass to finally look up and notice me at the doorway.

"What are you doing here *Charlotte?* Stalker much?" Quinn slurred her words, laughing afterwards. *I really hate this bitch.*

D.J. was sitting in the black chair while wiping his mouth, staring at me, catching a smirk before he covered it. One side of my mouth curled upwards before looking at Quinn. I tilt my head to the side and pout before straightening my face.

"Get out. I'm doing a tattoo." I said bluntly, giving her a cold hard stare, paying D.J. no mind. I walk into the room, flickering the lights on in the process. I put my supplies onto the bed, crossing my arms as I waited for them to get out.

"And what if we don't want to leave." Quinn lazily places her arm around D.J., who is trying to set her still and stable. She laughs out loud, barely holding her eyes open behind her lashes. "Who are you to tell me to leave?" The words barely left her mouth.

I open mouth to say something, only for D.J. to beat me to it, "I think we should, considering you cannot even stay up." He stands up as he guides Quinn to do the same. "Besides, I need a drink."

I still have my arms folded, standing in the same place as they walk by. Quinn holding D.J.'s bicep for dear life and giving what I think is a death stare. I don't know, she looks fucking constipated. They walk out the door, before D.J. turns back for a second. We look at each other, silence ranging over us as usual. Seeing a stranger, I shared memories with is…numbing. We don't say anything; we just live near each other.

Thea and Cameron broke the tension, pulling D.J.'s attention away. Thea and Quinn hold each other up, repeating the words 'shots' over again. Cameron slings his arm around D.J., pulling him towards the staircase.

Laughter is what I hear from the halls as the friend group walks away. The music is felt through the floorboards, like a heartbeat trying to break free. I dug in my back pocket for my phone, looking at the time immediately.

11:08 p.m.

# *Do I Wanna Know*

## *Hozier*

October 6, 2023

It's hard to have a goal—to have something to fight for, only to lose it. It's like writing; you have it for so long until it becomes foreign. You put words on a page to build your story, but if you don't explain enough, no one will understand but you. And if you don't explain, then you're just selfish.

Your goal is supposed to motivate you to do better, to achieve something. Not everyone wins in this lifetime, though. Sometimes people must lose to see themselves win. I lose, but I don't see the better outcome; I lose, knowing how to get better, yet choosing not to. I'm in a conundrum of destruction.

This motherfucker never showed up. It is now 1:30 am while the party inside is still going on. Shaya dragged me outside after a few failed attempts to go smoke. That is what we're doing now. We smoke outside on the porch sitting on the steps. I take a hit, feeling the smoke enter my lungs. Nothing unusual. Shaya took the blunt out of my hand instantly, her arms wailing all over me.

Shaya chuckles, "I *love* weed," as she takes a hit. My drunk best friend, who I took drinks away from a while ago until she sobers up a little bit. I take a sip out of her cup, tasting the liquor as it chases the weed's taste away.

"I know you do Shay," I smirk into the cup. Shaya passes me the blunt back, and we stare out at the pebble stone path. It leads up to the steps with a small patch of grass on one side with the driveway on the other, where Shaya's car is parked behind Lio's. I took another hit before the door opened and the hard base from the music poured out of the house.

I turned around to see D.J., leaning against the railing to the stairs. I passed him the blunt, in which he took willingly. I can feel warmth across my chest, the weed and liquor in my system intertwining with one another. Like two colors blending for the first time to make a beautiful color, like purple. I feel purple. *Oh god what is Shaya drinking. I only drank two of her cups.*

D.J. breaks me out of my thoughts with a nudge on my shoulder. I turn to see he's passing me the blunt back. I took it only to pass it right back to Shaya, who is now leaning her back against the railing.

"D.J., what are you doing out here? Go back," Shaya says, side-eyeing him and taking a hit.

"Smoking like both of you are. The "sleepover" is ass," D.J. snarks back, lighting another blunt in the process, makes sense since Shaya finished off mine. He takes a hit and then passes it to me, then I pass it to Shaya. Perfect rotation. D.J. finally sat down, two steps behind Shaya and me.

"Got tired of making out with Quinn's fast ass?" Shaya chuckles, blowing smoke in D.J.'s face. D.J. just stared back, unfazed. I look down at my cup, taking another sip harshly.

"I have better things to do," he responds, as he takes the blunt from Shaya's hand. I can feel his eyes on me as I stare at the driveway. My vision starts to blur as I lose concentration on what I was looking at.

I focus on Shaya and D.J.'s continuous bickering. Even though they're not related, it's still nice to have people you can be annoying with. I like hearing them say countless things to each other, fighting like their life depended on it. Ever since I was a child, Lio and I would just sit there and laugh. Or at least I was since Lio got annoyed easily by it.

"River," D.J. said as he was trying to pass the blunt to me. I looked up to him and took it, not breaking eye contact with him. I took this chance to fully look at him, not noticing the features of the little boy I once knew. He had a sharp jawline, one that twitches when he clenches his teeth too much. I can see the dark purple streak in his hair, so dark that unless it is hit with light you can't see it.

"Where'd Shaya go?" I said as I looked across me to see her gone. That girl just disappeared.

"Bathroom." D.J. announces, taking the blunt out of my hand. I look at him with a questioning look.

"If you are not going to smoke it and just let it burn, I am going to take it back," he said, smirking. I rolled my eyes as I took another sip of Shaya's drink.

Silence fell upon the two of us as we passed the blunt back and forth, a couple of sips between. It was nice not talking, not thinking. I breathe deeply, feeling my body.

"D.J." I announced, breaking the silence.

"Yes Charli?" He huffs out. He glimpses at me before looking at the blunt in my hand. I passed it willingly.

"How come you have been talking to me recently?" I asked, my back against the cool railing. I feel my fingers starting to mess with my nails, picking at the dead skin next to it.

"What do you mean?" D.J. asks, taking another hit before passing back to me.

"You know what I mean D.J." I said, staring right at him. I hate it when people act clueless. He stares at me through the night. His eyes haunt mine, trapping me like I have no other choice. Always having my attention; a blessing in sheep clothing disguised as a curse.

"It does not matter, let us not dig up old wounds," he said before passing the blunt before getting up. It took him six steps before he opened the door. Only four seconds until I hear the door close behind me.

Now I'm alone again. I would like to take comfort with the fact that I'm by myself, but everything just goes back to that night; the night I lost my mother, the night police officers tackled my dad, the night D.J. and I cried in each other's arms. Only then was the last time I felt anything but sadness or anger.

I take another sip, looking down at the cup and the blunt in opposite hands. Before I can take a pull, I can feel a presence, making me look up in the process. The energy shifts gradually, picking up in the moments.

"Never would have thought you would show up?" I say, taking a hit as I look up to Philo. I see his brown hair with blonde highlights even in the dark, his brown eyes matching.

"And get to miss my favorite customer? No chance in hell." He responds, taking a seat next to me. He holds his hand out, asking for the blunt, which I gave reluctantly.

"I thought you wanted a tattoo dumbass," I said, nudging him to the side. "I brought my shit and all, I could've skipped this party and just went home," I continued as I took my blunt back.

"It's a good thing I did come; the fuck is you smoking?" Philo said as he coughed up.

"You know it's good, you just want me to smoke your shit dumbass." I laughed out. Philo then joined in, smiling, as he put his arm around my shoulder.

"You know, you can still get the weed Charli, I just don't want the tattoo," he said, now by my ear. I take a sip of the mysterious drink as I can feel Philo's arm moving off my shoulder and now my back. Typical.

It's not the first time Philo and I messed with each other; most likely it won't be the last either. I could feel my mind getting foggy, and with that I finished the rest of Shaya's drink, took Philo's hand off me only to place the cup in it and got up from the steps.

"Let's go Philo," as I reach out my hand for him to take it.

We entered the house, music at once hitting my ears. The smoke blinded my vision, music creating a heartbeat in my ears. Purple and white lights are flashing all over the house as they align with the beat. I look around and see bodies on top of bodies. We headed towards the kitchen, trying at least. As Philo's hand is still mine, I see everyone in the kitchen.

We walked through the bodies, Shaya being the first to notice. I can see her nudging Lio's arm wrapped around her, considering he is helping his drunk girlfriend.

"Charli!!! I missed you, why did you leave me?" Shaya pouts, taking another sip of her drink.

"You left me, since you want piss and shit," I returned, holding a smirk. Shaya laughing hysterically in response and then trying to make a straight face. Failed miserably.

"Charli! Take a shot with us," Emilio said as he is pouring shots for the group. I look around the kitchen, seeing Thea and Cameron making out in the corner, nothing new. In the corner of my eye, I see Quinn going up to D.J. and wrapping her arms around his neck, pulling his attention from Philo to her. I turn my focus back to Emilio, who is giving me a shot already.

"No, I'm good. I'm about to smoke with Philo-."

I could barely spit out my words before Lio insisted again on taking the shot. I can feel Philo's hand climbing up to my waist. I look back at him, seeing him look at me with such lust. I tried returning the look, especially in this moment, but nothing.

Shaya breaks the tension by passing Philo a shot.

"If you're going to fuck her might as well make it good." She says, earning a death glare from me. She completely ignores me as she heads back to Lio. *This bitch really said that only to walk away.*

He stares at the three of us with boredom. "Are you guys ready to take the shot now?"

I shake my head, raising my shot towards Lio. On three, we all chugged down the harsh alcohol, sort of. Shaya almost puked it out, and Lio took it as a sign to bring her to the bathroom. *As he should.*

Before Lio left the kitchen, he looked back at Philo and me. He gives me a concerning look only for me to give one back, saying that I was okay. He nodded in response, and that's when I took the chance to leave. I took Philo's hand and pulled him to the other side of the kitchen, the one that has a door that leads to the backyard.

As we entered the backyard, I went down the stairs to reach the couch in the middle. I take a seat and capture the environment around me. Emilio has a nice house, but his backyard is not as big as the others in the neighborhood. Looking around, not much has changed. He has a grill near the umbrella for the summer to cast a shadow. On the other side, near the fence, lies a hammock, behind the full set couch that surrounds a small fire pit. I remember him and his dad, Mykel, invited me to clean up the backyard for $20 each, and that was the same day we planted the fake grass under the couch set.

I saw Philo sit right next to me and he instantly grabbed my legs to rest on his. He takes a blunt from behind his ears and light it.

"What are you thinking about Charli?" Philo asks. His relaxed demeanor pours into me as the light hits his face.

"Nothing," for once in my life.

"I don't believe that." Philo said as he took the first pull. Smoke clouds in the frigid wind and I watch them disappear into the thin air. Philo passes me the joint, and he leans back; his arm wrapped around my shoulders once again.

"You don't believe anything I say," I retorted, taking a pull off another blunt in the last 20 minutes.

"That is because you always lie to me Charli," Philo responded, now taking my chin to make me look at him. I smirked as I blew smoke into his face. Thank Shaya for that move.

He smirks back through the smoke and takes the blunt out of my hand. He ashes it out and puts it behind his ear again, never taking his eyes off me.

"Why did you light it only to put it out after two hits, wasteful if you ask me."

"It's a good thing I didn't ask you." Philo responded with him licking his lips like he needed some ChapStick.

Before I get to respond, Philo pulls me into a kiss, his hand still on my chin. I kiss back instantly, tasting the mix of lemon and weed. My heart thuds, mind buzzing, but my lips move anyways.

I move my hands to his torso, feeling his body under the thick sweater he is wearing. He responds by letting my chin go only to grab my hips. He then lifts me up, sitting me down on top of him. I can feel the bulge that is basically begging to be freed from his pants. I move my hips back and forth, teasing Philo, who only deepens the kiss. His hands travel from my hips to the lower part of my back.

His fingers singularly go up my spine until it reaches the crept of my neck, in which he grabs. With reflexes, my hips go further down, now feeling the unsurprised guest between my thighs. I can feel Philo moan, making me pull away. I see we're both panting and my mind is still hazy. *It takes more than that to get rid of me. I can see you already following in your mom's footsteps.*

"Where's your car Philo?" I said as I felt Philo kissing my neck, getting closer to my chest. I just desperately need to get my mind on something else, anything else really.

"Philo."

"Hm?"

"Car Philo," I said as I tried to get up only for my hips to stay in place. Philo finally looks up, his eyes low but full of lust. I saw this look before.

"I don't have my car; it's in the shop."

"So how the fuck did you get here?"

"I walked." *No wonder I waited three fucking hours.* Philo is still kissing my neck; his hand is on my chin while the other rests on my hip. I pushed back slightly, gaining his attention.

"I'm not fucking you in my best friend's backyard. Do I look that easy?" I said, playing with the hair on the back of his neck. I stare into his eyes and see that he really does not give a fuck. He takes the back of my neck into his hands once again, this time with more force.

"Come on Charli don't be like that. We can have fun." Philo whispered close to my ear as he started kissing again. *Yeah Charli, don't be a tease, it's not like you're good for anything else.*

Philo makes his way up to my mouth again, with more force and declaration. His hands dropped from my neck only to grab my waist more aggressively, guiding it against him. I can feel him panting against my mouth, and I use it to my advantage. I keep kissing him, biting his lower lip. My hands go from his neck to ear to hair. As my hands glide through strands of soft curls, I can feel his hands loose around my waist, allowing me to take a shot. Within seconds I grab a fistful of hair and pull his head to the side to break the kiss. I then bring my lips to his ear, kissing his neck on the way up.

"Fuck me when you have the ability to do so," I said, instantly throwing his head back and getting up. Philo tried to grab my hand as I walked away, only for me to instantly snatch it. I walk up the staircase, leaving Philo in the cold backyard and a hardon that he will probably get rid of either by his hand or some random ass girl in this shit of a party.

Once I opened the door, I saw an almost empty kitchen. D.J. and Emilio are laughing and pushing each other towards the left, looking up to me as I step in. Passing them, I opened the fridge, revealing bottles of liquor of all sorts. I grabbed the bottle of apple Cîroc and tried moving towards the other end of the kitchen, only for Lio to grab me by the wrist.

"I thought you were good? What he do?" Emilio said, turning around as he stared out the window at Philo. *I could only imagine what he was doing in that chair.* I smirk at the thought, knowing I left Philo in dismay.

"I am good, Philo is just stupid to think I'm going to fuck him outside." I slurred it out, feeling the effects of the alcohol and weed finally taking over. Nevertheless, I opened the bottle I was holding and instantly took a sip, and with that Lio turned towards the back yard, finally registering what I had just said to him.

I took Lio's spot, looking out the window. I smile at a very disturbed Lio, who is yelling at poor Philo. I laugh softly as I take another sip.

"Wow," D.J. announces himself. He is leaning against the counter opposite of me.

"And here I thought the image would never exist again," he continues. His body heat gets closer as he studies me before looking out the small window. I took his appearance over me, and saw he too is feeling the effects of alcohol and weed. Only I don't know if he had as much as me, if not more.

"What are you talking about?" I asked, now turning my body towards him, leaning against the counter. I can hear music through the other kitchen door.

"Your smile River. Whatever you did to Philo must have been good to get Emilio that worked up." D.J. laughs, an actual laugh, as he took a sip from his cup. He turns from the window and looks down at me before his cup.

D.J. lifts his chin towards me, "Mind giving me some of your bottle, River? Or do you plan to get alcohol poisoning?" He chokes out, smirking, and locking his eyes with me. I rolled my eyes and poured some of the clear liquor into the red cup, having to use two hands to make sure I didn't spill shit; it didn't work.

"Thank you." D.J. said as he took a sip, still never breaking his eye contact.

"Yeah, no problem," I said, breaking eye contact to look at the door behind him.

"I'm going to bed; can you tell them not to bother me?" I tried not to look at D.J., wanting to get as much space between us as possible. He huffs out above me, causing me to look up. Far enough for a whisper to connect us.

"Sure." D.J. voice hardens. He finishes his drink, before leaning forward, his body close enough to mine. He throws his cup behind me before coming back in front. He doesn't move, neither do I. Two bodies, inching towards one another, but neither makes a clarifying move. I just see the person in front of me, as does he.

"Goodnight Charli," he continued before turning around and leaving the room. I wait around for about 10 minutes before entering the loud room, full of drunk teenagers who have no idea what they look like when they dance. I pass everyone, making my way to the stairs that lead to the guest bedroom in the basement. Before I took my steps to descend, I could feel a stare burning a hole against the side of my head. Though I choose to ignore it, just like I choose to ignore the incoming headache. I need to sleep.

With all 14 steps, I make it to the basement living room. I walked further down, familiar with the place I basically grew up in. As I passed the couch, something caught my eye on the coffee table. Something sparkly enough for my crossed ass to get distracted from. I look down at the golden knobs on the table. Two drawers, only one has a lock. My fingers trace it before opening the top drawer.

Inside it, papers and sticky notes are everywhere. I rummaged around, not knowing what I was looking for. I grab it from the brown tray it lays on, revealing the little charm that hangs from it. My fingers travel freely, until it is met with something hard and cool. I pulled it out, revealing a gold necklace.

It took a few minutes for my vision to focus, but once it did, I was able to depict the charm: a small, gold cherry blossom to match the gold necklace it hangs from. I instantly put the charm in my pocket and left the living room, stumbling to the bedroom that was no more than eight steps away from me.

The moment the door opened I crashed into the bed I was so familiar with. My mind is everywhere, but nowhere at the same time. Sleep threatens to take over as everything spirals through my head. Only one thought keeps breaking through the haze.

My mother's favorite flowers were always cherry blossoms.

# *People Help the People* Birdy

October 12, 2023

It's hard to reciprocate hate, at least for me. I dislike a lot of things, but to truly hate a person takes more tolls than love; and love hurts like a bitch. Anyone can be stripped away and come back as a whole new person. Many can change right in front of your eyes, and you won't notice until it's too late.

Those are the worst situations; imagine, just think about them. To have a person by your side for as long as you can remember, seeing your difficulties, only for them to no longer support you. To no longer be there for you, listening to your struggles, or even worse, endorsing the pain that you suffer from.

It takes a lot for people to truly hate, to truly be broken enough to inflict pain on another. Nonetheless, the world is filled with hateful people. Love takes less but takes so little to turn into hate. People have killed for love, and many have died from it. There is indeed a thin line between love and hate, I for one hope to not be caught in the middle of it.

"For fucks sake!" The yelling pulled me out of my sleep. Drowsiness lingers, though I still hop out of bed, feeling my grey rug instantly warming my bare feet compared to the cold wood that connects my room. I can hear glasses being thrown, more yelling coming from my dad's voice. Random words, more like curses, fill the household, like water that is trying to suffocate me.

"Stupid fucking bitch! Always creeping on me and never respecting my space. Charlotte Riverson! I can hear your loud ass elephant steps!" I didn't say a word. Just suffocating tranquility stretching long after I hear my name. My hands instantly get sweaty and my breath catches.

"Get down here this instance!"

My dad screams. I was silent; I hadn't even opened my door yet. I can feel my heart pounding as I look over my alarm clock; it's 4:18 am. *Fucking four in the morning.*

I can hear the heavy footsteps hauling up the stairs, making me dart across my room to lock my door. *He's not supposed to be here tonight.* Yesterday was Wednesday, lotto night and beer; he never comes back home since he is God knows where. Why is he here? *To get rid of the only nuisance left in his life.*

It takes five steps for me to reach my door, only five, but inevitably not fast enough. Just when I reach down to lock the door, it swings open hard. Hitting right into my nose, I stumble backwards while keeping my balance. My hands find my nose instantly, trying to mediate the throbbing that occurs. I can just see the darkness in my room as tears start to build. I look up, horrible decision as my dad grabs a fist of my hair and drags me out of my room, my only illusion of a sanctuary.

His hold is getting tighter; I can hear him grunting as we turn the corner to the hall that leads down the stairs. The rings on his finger rubbing against my scalp hard as I look down at the brown steps that almost look black, like coal.

"You don't want to listen?" My dad slurred. "Huh?! Fine, let's do this my way," my dad spitting angrily, letting go of my hair only to place his hold on my upper arm, tight enough that I'm sure I will bruise tomorrow morning. *It's already morning, dumbass. Welcome to the new day you desperately deserve.*

The tightening grip on my arm loosened only to feel a hard push that made me fall. I am by the stairs, gripping on the edge of it to steady my breathing. *Breathe Charli, breathe. Let go, just like your mom, just let go. Did mom think this as well? When she left? Or had she already chosen to leave me with him long before that?* No, she didn't. She didn't choose this.

I can hear my dad yelling at me telling me to get up, but I just stay. I try to inhale but it feels like I am allergic to air, as if I have gills and flopping around like a fish waiting to be caught, waiting for the end. I force myself to breathe, but the air does nothing to ease the headache forming.

I tune out my dad, only hearing the static noise in the background as my thoughts are juggled in my mind. *Why can't you listen to him? Why does he hate me? What did I do? Mom, why not me? I must get up.*

The last thought lingering in my mind as I use my arms to steady my balance. I managed to grab the white railing on my left, sharing the same wall as my bedroom. I can feel needles stabbing my side as I try to breathe more.

Flashes of memories come to play in my mind. My childhood reels by, a film burned at its edges. Moments of my dad's talks after games, sneaking downstairs to get chocolate after bedtime only to see my parents snuggled on the couch, crying from falling off my bike and my dad coming to the rescue, the pain from laughing too much on my sides when my dad impersonates his favorite movie lines. They all blur together, like a trailer for an upcoming attraction.

Instantly, I felt a hard kick to the left side of my ribs, thankfully not hearing an internal crack. I stumble down the stairs, not being able to balance and catch myself despite the railings that pass by like pillars until my back hits the wall. I look up to see the grey popcorn ceiling, like bugs trapped behind the paint that is waiting to crack open.

Hearing my dad come down the stairs, slowly, mumbling. I close my eyes waiting for another blow. But it never came. I open my eyes only to see him face to face. His cold, icy blue eyes pierced through me. Making me hold my breath, I don't dare say a word. I see my father that once adored me but is now causing unrecognizable pain. I feel his hot ass breathe that comes from the alcoholic mouth, surrounded by the desert of his stubble beard.

"Don't spy on me again," he said.

Only then does he hold my eye contact before stepping down the last two steps and opening the door to leave. I just stayed there.

On the charcoal wood that feels cold and isolated.

I waited ten minutes, maybe more.

Until I knew he wouldn't come back.

Only then, and truly only then, do I scream.

Mourning what it was. And what it is.

Mourning the curse of remembering.

~~~~~~~~~~~~~~~~~~~~~

Hours later, the bruises still throb under my clothes, but no one notices as I drift through the halls, half-asleep behind my locker door. I open the locker, seeing the empty pens that lay on the bottom. My black composition notebooks pushed on one side; one threatening to spill over.
~~~~~~~~~~~~~~~~~~~~~

Moments of the earlier inconvenience are still making their marks as I clutch to my side. I have been going through school the entire day, dissociating in most of my classes, catching up on sleep at lunch while Lio and Shaya ramble about whatever movie they watched on Facetime last night. My mind goes through my day, waiting for it to end, wishing to not wake up the next day. *Your dad wishes that every day as well.*

Breathing hard as I grab one of the notebooks and toss it in my grey satchel next to my mushroom one. I rummage around, looking in the sea of red pens to see a usable one. Just as I sink deeper into those thoughts, I feel a presence next to me, hair prickling around my neck.

I close my locker to see Shaya trying to surprise me, holding a ridiculous face that looks like someone just punched her in the stomach; hands stretched out and her tongue sticking out. Her eyes popped out and one side of her face was lifted. I just stare at my weird friend, wondering what the hell is wrong with her.

"If that is your idea of trying to scare me, it worked, I'm disturbed." I said nonchalantly.

Shaya fixes her face as she rolls her eyes. She tosses her arm around my shoulders, and we start heading towards the end of the corridor. Her hair is tied up and she is wearing her team's practice uniform, while carrying two bags.

"Charls, you should come support me at basketball practice." Shaya says enthusiastically.

"No." I respond, lifting one side of my beats towards Shaya's side so I can hear her better through the constant music. It's a miracle my headphones or phone did not die at any point of the day. *Another lifespan, waiting for its termination.*

"Well then instead of the support of your best friend, what about seeing if the new point guard is good enough. Or at least to give me pointers on how to help her, she is a new first-year student, and the coach thinks it's my job to guide her." I listen to Shaya rant more about the team, about how there's a distance this year compared to the team last year before the seniors left.

"It is your job to guide them. That's kind of the point of co-captain." I rolled my eyes. In response, Shaya side-eyes and nudges my head with the arm wrapped around my shoulders.

We reach the end of the corridor; one way is the exit, the other leads to the gym. The same gym where I get away from everyone. We stopped in the middle of the crowded hall; people bumped into us. One person even grunted and said "move," which only resulted in gaining the middle finger from the both of us. Shaya lets go of my shoulders to face me, her eyes pleading.

"Please Charlsss," Shaya screeches, while giving me the fakest puppy look.

"I'll go if you promise never to give me that look again. Save that for Emilio, someone that it works on."

"It worked on you," Shaya says grinning.

"Touche. Doesn't count though, I wanted to gouge my eyes out." I said, smirking.

I roll my eyes, but the corner of my mouth lifts — and against my better judgment, I let her pull me toward the gym. It takes about 23 steps before we open the door and head inside. The familiar basketball gym that brings me to a haven; if only I can love the sport again like I did in the past.

"I have to go into the locker room, but just sit in the bleachers, and smile. Stop scaring everyone away," Shaya said before bringing her hands to my mouth, forcing a smile only for it to drop once her hands are away.

Shaya turned around and ran towards her team. Only a few seconds pass before I head over to the bleachers. I look around to see the empty gym, settling on the seat that overlooks the entire room. By the third row on the rigid wood, I take a seat and place my satchel to the side. I reached into my bag, pulling out my notebook and pen.

The page barely opened before my hands took advantage of their own. The red ink started bleeding once again, letting my emotions run its course while staying content. My ribs on fire, as my hands scribbled through the page that was once empty, blank. I had my headphones on fully, ignoring the world around me. It is just me, my music, and my words. My story goes unsaid.

A few minutes pass by before I am disturbed again, feeling an aura shift beside me. I looked to the side only to see the basketball coach. Coach Lawson, dark black hair is brown if the light touches it. She always has it tied back to a short ponytail with a cap covering the top, or at least from what I have seen of her. Her deep brown eyes land on me holding a look of concern as she rests poised, her athletic body showing no signs of restraint. I can remember her running the track with the junior team of girls in middle school, one Shaya and I were a part of.

"Hey Coach Lawson." Looking up to her only to bring my attention back to my notebook.

"Surprise to see you here, especially with people here," Coach says with determined eyes. As if on cue, groups of girls start making their way out of the locker room, Shaya among them. I hear voices roar in the gym, bouncing off the walls as the girls are warming up.

"A surprise indeed." I said nonchalantly.

"Is there a reason for the surprise visit?"

"Just supporting a friend from the side. Would that be a problem Coach?"

She looks at me like she is trying to read to me. My face stays neutral, like a wall, not letting anyone see anything under a content face.

"I was only wondering if you were looking for a different purpose here. That's all dear."

"No, sorry to disappoint you Coach." I was about to get up, to leave and hear Shaya's bitch out later. But I never did.

"You could never disappoint me Charli, just surprise me is all. I do have a question for you however," Coach announced, making me look it up from my notebook. Raising an eyebrow, starting for her to continue.

"Do you remember how we would run three miles before practice and everybody would complain?" I nodded as she spit out the question, confused about where she was going with this.

"You were the only one who didn't complain, the only one who was truly disciplined enough to see that the energy being used before practice was only to increase stamina." Coach Lawson huffed out. She looks out to her girls on the court, who were now doing ball-handling drills.

"I would practice with you constantly on your ball-handling and every time you messed up you didn't pick up from where you started, no, instead you started from the very beginning every single time." She announced painting a picture I can share with her. I remember the days like it was yesterday; having frustration in my chest until I got the ball exactly where I wanted, like a string connected to follow my every move.

"What is your question Coach?" I breathe out, feeling the pressure on my side immensely. *Only a fraction of the pain I feel.*

She pauses for a moment. Looks at me deeply with wondering eyes. Probably wondering what happened to that same determined girl that died a long time ago. *Should've been you instead, now you're just a ghost waiting.*

"Why are you running from moving forward if you know the steps to get better?" Lawson looks at me deeply. Looking for something I have been searching for. The question lodges like glass in my chest. Before I can answer, she's already gone, her whistle echoing in place of words. She goes down the bleachers, 17 steps, before I decide to open my mouth.

"Maybe I don't want to take the steps that I know. Might lead me to hell instead of the heaven you think of," I announced only for Coach to hear, my fist clenching constantly with the notebook still in my hands.

She turns around smiling, almost like a smirk before blowing the whistle and rounding up her girls, a team that I was once a part of but is now a figure in the empty crowd. I then saw a glimpse of my past, a coach and a player united momentarily.

~~~~~~~~~~~~~~~~

Practice ends before I realize it, and the echo of bouncing balls fades. The only reason I stayed at all was because of Shaya —and because I didn't want to go home. I can feel the dread as minutes pass by until the practice is over.

I sit in silence for a moment longer, staring at the empty court, the echo of the practice still lingering in my head. The thought of going home weighs heavily on me. I stand up, taking one last look at the gym, and see Shaya step out of the locker room, wiping sweat from her brow. It took only eight steps for her to reach me, covered in sweat and chugging her Gatorade bottle.

"I'm surprised you stayed, usually you leave." Shaya says, in and out of breath. I smirked, nodding towards the court before returning my gaze back to her.

"You need to work on your footwork when you're on top of the key. And you're point guard needs more confidence, she's good just doesn't think she is." I said, taking off my headphones and placing them in my bag, along with my notebook. During the duration of the practice, I managed to fill three pages worth.
~~~~~~~~~~~~~~~~

"I'm surprised you paid attention at all. Every time I look up, I see you writing, at least one passion of yours is not gone." Shaya said, intentionally trying to uplift me. I love her, but sometimes her words cut deep even if she didn't mean to.

We start walking out of the gym, towards the door that leads to the parking lot instead of the school. Feeling the chilling breeze, I tug my jacket closer. The coach's words still cloud my mind.

As if Shaya can read my mind, she breaks the comfortable silence between us.

"What was coach talking to you about?" She asked.

"The same thing you tried to guilt trip me about. Look out for the new point guard, use my advice and pass it along to coach."

I can tell Shaya didn't believe what I said, the conversation was in fact anything but. I do in fact miss basketball, but not remotely enough to continue it without my mom. Especially with the relationship I have with my dad now, the chapter of the young girl who thrived in basketball became an inconvenience.

That little girl, the one who poured everything into basketball, disappeared the night D.J. consoled his friend on my childhood court—the same court where I used to feel unstoppable. Now, basketball only reminds me of what's gone, what's been lost.

A honk pulled me out of my thoughts, making me look up and Shaya jump. A slick, black Chevy Camaro pulls up. The tinted rolls down on the passenger side revealing Lio and D.J. on the driver's side.

"You are fucking assholes, you could've caused a heart attack," Shaya remarked, holding her hand to her chest, breathing heavily. I rolled my eyes towards the boys and opened the door. Shaya heads to the other side of the car as we both enter our seats. Not even five seconds after getting into the car and D.J. takes off, making the vehicle roar throughout the parking lot.

"God damn D.J., can I get in first without losing a leg?" Shaya nudges the back of D.J. seat. I smirk and lay my head towards the back of my seat.

"Charli! I'm surprised to see you here." Emilio announced enthusiastically from the front seat. He tries to turn around only D.J. to push him back.

"Stop blocking my mirror with your big ass." D.J. hissed out.

"I didn't have a choice; your girlfriend here gave me those stupid ass puppy eyes." I said looking at Shaya, she nudges my side in response. I silently wince, my teeth grinding together to make the pain pass by. I mask it all with a smirk, ignoring the throbbing sensation.

"Besides, I'm going home now. I want to sleep."

"What? No, you should come over. We're all having a movie night at my house." Shaya announces, earning a scruff from D.J. up front.

"No offense, all offense, I am not watching a movie with you guys and feeling like a third wheel," D.J. announces as he turns the corner. I look out the window, past the tint, and see the road of houses blur by.

Only a few more seconds later and I see the park where Shaya and I beat the boys in a basketball game, having them claim that they let us win at the ripe age of 11. Lies.

I look towards the front of the car, seeing Lio and D.J. both wearing their football uniforms as well, at least part of it. They wear their sleeveless spandex shirts, just opposite colors. I realize I'm the only one that is not wearing sports gear as I look down on my outfit.

I'm wearing a pair of oversized Levi jeans; the cuffs frayed at the ends. My black spaghetti strap shirt clings to me, a sharp contrast to the brown leather jacket that hangs loosely over my shoulders. A brown belt with a gold buckle matches my sneakers, the Pumas that somehow feel like the only piece of me still grounded, still real.

"Yeah, no, I just want to go home and sleep. Thanks for the offer though but hard pass." I said, feeling a stare. I glance up and catch D.J.'s eyes in the rearview mirror, his gaze lingering on me longer than necessary.

My heart skips a beat, a mix of unease and something else I can't name. I quickly look away, but his stare hangs in the air like an unspoken question. The closer we get to my block, the tighter my chest feels. Emilio's voice breaks the silence just as the car slows outside my house.

"Are you going to be, okay? It looks like your dad isn't home." Emilio questions, turning around as we pull up to my house, the white and brown house that slowly looks like it is decaying compared to my friends, though the color is still holding up.

"Yeah, I'll be fine. He's just working more so that I'm able to go to college," I swallow the lie, trying not to choke on it.

"Don't wait up though, I'm going to be sitting on the porch for a few before going to sleep."

I hate lying to my friends, and I guess D.J., but it is better than telling the truth. I don't want to be stripped away from the house where my mom's footsteps once were taken.

From the curb, my house looks almost normal — white and brown paint still clinging to it. But as I step onto the porch, dread coils in my stomach. I heard D.J. unlock the door and said goodbye to everyone. Walking against the cobblestone path that leads to my door, I could hear the car behind me roar off once I made it to my porch. Only twelve steps to the door — each heavier than the last.

Before opening the door, my hand hovering over the knob, I held my breath. I can feel my body starting to get hot despite the cool air that surrounds my neighborhood. The middle of October air hitting my skin like a splash of water, feeling refreshed compared to the piercing ice that soon comes to follow.

After a few moments to control my breathing, I open the door in front of me. Feeling the heavy presence of alienation welcomed me with open arms. The door creaks as I push it open, the familiar scent of old wood and stale air hitting me. My hands are sweaty; my breath is shallow.

Each step feels heavier as I cross the threshold. The house is silent—too silent. It's like the walls themselves are holding their breath, waiting for something to fill the empty space. I walk up my stairs, looking at the same charcoal stairs that have existed in my mind from earlier today.

I passed by the spot I laid until my ribs stopped aching momentarily, I can see the marks on the wall where pictures used to hang, where a family used to live in a home. Where a house felt more than just walls put together with screws. I reach my room after slowly stepping upon each step, feeling some sort of relief only for despondency to gloom over me like my own personal cloud that rains all day.

I don't need sleep. I never did it if I always wake up with tired eyes. To wake up day after day only to never fulfil constant dread as sunlight pours into the room. To cling to the hope of warmth that never comes because of the heart that is manipulated to stay cold.

The mental battle of a person where they sleep is the only revelation to feel some sort of comfort only to be followed with horrific nightmares that can even reach the deepest parts of the mind. So yes, I always wake up with tired eyes. I don't need sleep.

I need answers.

The veracity of the black hole punctured my life.

# *Keep the Rain*

## *Searows*

October 17, 2023

Silence is never empty; it always holds a tension that many reject, even shy away from. Silence is a reminder that the world can be quiet when its inhabitants shut the fuck up. It holds so much without saying anything. The world can be beautiful, really, without the opinions of others. It's not wanted; silence is.

To hold tension, a power that can make people feel scared, concluded, serene, and most of all optimistic. Though when someone opens their mouth, the truth yearns to change the story, to change the subject of a matter.

Silence is wanted, but does that mean it's needed?

An hour and 34 minutes. That's how long I have been on the bus, carrying my bag that is filled with random snacks and water, along with my notebook as always. An hour and 34 minutes of me sitting on the bus, looking out at the steamy windows with raindrops sliding down, and the sound of the engine of the bus taking me from one spot to another.

I got off about 10 minutes ago and now I have finally reached my destination: the community where D.J. and I gave peanut butter and jelly sandwiches. I wanted answers so I was determined to get what I wanted.

I look up at the building in the light drizzle coming from the clouds, my grey hood covering me along with the same brown leather jacket. The building has an arch that connects to the entrance, pillars on each side that look like marble, and a sign that says, "Welcome to Willowbrook". Right under it shows another sign that points out that this building is the reception center.

I move my feet simultaneously, only taking off my hood once I make it to the sliding doors that open instantly. I clutch onto the cherry blossom that dangles around my neck, careful not to tangle it, as my feet move forward.

Once inside, I headed to the front desk where a young lady sat. She looks as if she is about late 20s, curly blonde hair, and olive skinned toned. I stand in front of her as she types on the computer with ridiculously long nails. They're cute, pastel colors and all, but still long as fuck. I clear my throat trying to catch her attention, but no luck as she continues to type away. She must get paid well to ignore people in this community center.

"Excuse me," I announced, sternly looking at the side of her head as she faces the computer.

"Sign your name on the paper that is in front of you, and then I can get back to you. Visiting hours close in about an hour," long nails said, only taking her eyes off the computer screen to take a sip of her giant water bottle. Everything in her life must be large in replacing the respect she gives. *Or maybe she can already tell you how annoying you seem. Just like everyone else.*

"I'll sign my name, but you can take your eyes off the screen for two seconds and guide me to Ms. Wilma's room," I paused as she held my stare, "Please, an extra cherry just for you," I said bluntly, not stuttering a word.

She finally takes her eyes off only to try to burn through mine from my remark. I broke away from the gaze to sign my name only to return to eye contact.

"Save your hateful glares for someone else who is affected by it," I said, forcing a smile to the *delightful* woman that sits across from me. She's lucky this desk is separating us. Long nails grunt, returning the hateful smile, before writing a post it notes.

"Give this to the security guards on your right and they will let you through the doors. Once you're through the doors, you're going to turn left and go up the flight of stairs that leads to the room. Ms. Wilma's room is in 861; I'm going to call her to let her know she has a visitor," long nails pause, looking at me up and down before she continues.

"I'm sure she won't mind an unexpected visitor." She says while handing me the post it. I drop the smirk and mumble a thank you as I head to the security guards. They open the door for me reluctantly and then I enter a long corridor.

The floors are brown and green marble, stretching like a field. The walls hold posters and pictures of various people, doctors helping others and group activities where woman and men are smiling with each other. It looks like the typical dentist set up as you wait for hours in the waiting room.

I managed to make it to the staircase and reach the next level in no time. As I enter the other wing, doors are spread throughout the hallway. I look at the first one on my left to see number 857 on the door. I walk further down the hall, and it takes 17 steps until I reach room 861.

I knock three times and wait for a moment. My hands are getting sweaty again and I can feel my heart ready to jump out. *Why are you nervous? Scared for another person to dread you?* I shake my head, fist clenching, as I get ready to knock again.

Just as I was about to knock again, the doors opened to reveal a short, aged lady. Her grey hair is slicked back into a neat medium bun. She wears glasses that look almost too big on her, with a smile that seems welcoming. She wears a brown blouse with white trimming and dark green pants to match her eyes.

"Hello, come in, come on don't be shy," the lady says, holding the door for me to enter.

"Would you like anything to drink, dear? I fear I only have water and apple juice; the nurses here think I can't have too much sugar." She laughs effortlessly.

"What they don't know is that my nephew sneaks me iced tea from time to time." Wilma asks, her youthful tone flooding the room as I sit on the couch nearby in the living room, one that is olive green but has plastic over it, making a crunchy sound as I sit.

I look around to see mountains of pictures that cover almost every inch of the walls. The light pours in from the balcony through the white, sheer curtains.

"I'm okay, thank you though," I announced, taking off my jacket only to place it on my lap.

Wilma heads over to where I'm sitting and sits on the rocking chair across from the couch. The only thing that divides us is the round, glass coffee table; it has a few books that look like it could be for travelling along with some figurines. One of which is two doves that circle each other as they hold a candle between them.

"To what do I owe for this surprised visit Charli?" Wilma announces, catching my attention from the coffee table.

"You remember me? I only came here once." I said with a small smile. A feeling of relief spreads through my complete system.

"Of course. I remember anyone that comes with my nephew, especially since I'm not able to see him as often."

"D.J. is your nephew?"

"D.J., pfft," Wilma says, laughing into her mug as she drinks her tea. "Dario comes at least once a week but sees me the least. I can't say I can blame the young boy. I'm his father's aunt, the one who is God knows where now."

"I'm sorry to hear that, Wilma. Would it help if I were to talk to him?"

"No dear, your presence alone is enough. Besides, I want my nephew to talk to me on his own terms, not for his girlfriend to force him," Wilma says with a questioning smile written on her face as she places the mug back down on the coaster that is shaped like a rose.

I laugh, a genuine one. It takes a few seconds for me to collect myself before speaking.

"Sorry to disappoint, but I am not D.J.'s girlfriend. I don't think I ever can be."

"No? So, then what are you guys? Friends?"

"I guess. We've known each other since childhood, though we haven't spoken to each other for years until that last month or so when junior year came around," I responded, grabbing the water bottle out of my bag before taking a sip.

I can feel the heat come up from my neck to reach my temples. Clenching the water bottle in my hand as I think of D.J., the friend I lost contact with only to pop into my life once again. Back then, things were simpler, not complicated as they are now. I absently rubbed my wrists, fingertips grazing the stacks of bracelets that conceal my skin.

*~~~~Dario's 12th birthday party~~~~*

*I can feel the cold breeze on my bare legs as I walk to Dario's house. His parents decided to throw a huge party at his house, inviting the whole seventh grade class. Of course I am automatically invited; I have never missed any of my friends' birthday parties ever, unless I was sick, but even then, I would call them to make sure my presence was there.*

*I'm holding the small gift box close to my yellow dress; the print is filled with white daisies and has white daisies straps to tie it together. I paired it with my light denim jacket and white converse, my go to sneakers if I wasn't wearing anything basketball attire. I smile as I feel the sharp edge of the gift box, picturing Dario's face when he sees my gift.*

*It's not much, but I would love it if it were a gift to me. It is a bracelet, with white and black beads to stand for everything that has happened between us: the light and dark phases throughout our life. In the middle of the bracelet holds a compass charm, remembering the time we would go on adventures together, just us two, two peas in a pod. It helped that our best friends, Shaya and Lio, ditch us to hang out with each one another but we didn't mind, it was nice to hang out with someone who shares the same pain.*

*It has been four years since my mother, Dario, was without his father, but despite it all we stayed friends, having him rely on when things got bad with my dad. Dario doesn't know, nobody does, about how angry my dad gets. At first, he was sad, then about a year ago, when I turned 11, he got really mad about things that were too simple. I try not to take offense to it, but it's hard not to when he blames you for everything; I wonder what happened to my loving dad. Did he die with my mother?*

*I shake my thoughts out of my head once I make it to the porch of Dario's house. I flatten my dress as I reach for the gold doorbell. I stare at the brown door ahead of me, waiting a few minutes before I hear rummage through the other side.*

*I smiled, ready to bombard Dario and give him his yearly birthday punches, but my smile left as fast as it came. Quinn opens the door and gives me a hasty look.*

*"What are you doing here?" Quinn says, looking at me up and down. "And what are you wearing? You look like a fifth grader," she continues, laughing with her whole chest.*

*I look down at my dress, knowing this was one of my mother's favorite dresses for me, I feel the heat rise from my neck.*

*"What do you want Quinn? I'm friends with Dario, where is he?" I said, rolling my eyes, trying to pass by only for the doorway to be blocked by her. I stared hard at her in the face, wanting her to move but she doesn't budge.*

*"Why? Why are you friends with Dario?"*

*"We always been friends, what are you talking about?"*

*"I know that, but why now? It's not like… you know what never mind, just leave," Quinn said, starting to close the door. The door stops on my foot, leaving merely a few inches.*

*"No Quinn, tell me what you were about to say, unless you're just as scared as you are a bitch."*

*She laughs and then opens the door fully before stepping out onto the porch and closing the door behind her.*

*"Why would you be friends with Dario if you were only going to drag him down?"*

*"Oh, come on Quinn, everyone knows you had a crush on him since first grade, and yet that still didn't stop you from being in my way of being friends with your epic crush," I exaggerated, now clutching onto the present in my*

*hand. I hate getting mad, angry even; it only reminds me of my dad, a version that I don't even recognize anymore.*

*Quinn's face instantly changes from bitchy to sincere, a look I never saw before, not knowing if it is real or a facade.*

*"It's not about my crush Charli, it's about you. If you genuinely cared about Dario, then you would just leave him alone. I mean really, do you, the girl whose mother killed herself, will help Dario?" Quinn said, not holding back any emotion in her voice.*

*"Do you really think having you as a friend will help him? A girl with enough damage that can only be passed on? You will break him Charli and you know it," she finished before entering the house again. I can hear the music vaguely as I stand there on the porch, the wind hitting harder than before.*

*Quinn turns around before closing the door behind, "Think about it Charli, I know you care about him like I do." And with that she closes the door that holds my dearest friend, never entering his birthday party.*

*I leave the porch after ages of just staring, contemplating knocking again to hopefully see Dario instead of Quinn. But what she said is right, I must leave a friendship that has been by my side for as long as I can remember. I open the gift box revealing the bracelet, a tear coming down my cheek as I quickly wipe it away. I put the bracelet on, never wanting to take it off, having the only reminder left of another person I would lose.*

*I never look back, if I did, I would want to change my mind, but for Dario, I gave him a life without my messed-up problems. For him I stepped away before I could break him. My fists are clenching only to release a moment later.*

"Hello? Charli? Are you okay? Should I call someone, dear?" Wilma asks, concern etched on her face.

I shake my head and wipe my face. "No, sorry, Wilma. I didn't mean to zone out. My apologies," I say, still seated across from her. She stands briefly before settling beside me, taking my hands in hers. The warmth is reassuring.

"Let me tell you something, dear. I used to babysit a little girl—an angel. She was about four, but what caught my attention was her older sister," Wilma begins. I straighten, giving her my full attention.

"She was around fifteen, a light in the room. Just her presence alone announced her. But she always made sure I had everything I needed for her sister. Her parents let her roam the neighborhood—typical teenager stuff," Wilma smiles, glancing at our joined hands before meeting my gaze again.

"I forgot her name, but I called her Comet. A person like that is rare but leaves a lifetime of memories. She and her two rowdy friends would make sandwiches before bike rides." Wilma stops to take a breath.

"Comet hated mayonnaise, so I'd draw a comet on her bag to tell them apart. She never complained, always making sure her friends had enough to eat—even splitting her own sandwich if needed. That's when I started making extra, so my Comet wouldn't go hungry," Wilma chuckles, sinking into the couch.

I watch her, captivated, as if she's reliving it.

"One night, Comet and her friends had a movie night in the living room. She made sure I had everything for her baby sister, as always. I remember coming down the stairs and seeing her fast asleep on one of her friend's laps. He played with her hair, looking at her like she was in the universe. The other friend lay across her lap; all tangled together in sleep. The movie volume turned low. It was... a picture."

I hesitate before asking, "What were her friends like?"-

Wilma hums. "Similar, but different. The one whose lap she slept in—steady, predictable, always watching out for her. The other? A firecracker. He made her laugh like no one else. But he had a temper. One day, Comet came home asking for bandages. I worried it was for her, but she said it was for her friend—got into a fight at the basketball court." Wilma shakes her head, reminiscing on the memories.

"I warned her about the company she kept, but she just smiled and said, 'Sometimes good people do terrible things because they don't know any better. It's not their fault, Miss Wilma."

Wilma sighs, squeezing my hands before letting go to reach for her tea. I passed her the mug.

"Wilma?" I ask as I fidget with my fingers.

"Yes, dear?"

"Why did you tell me about Comet?"

Wilma studies me before answering. "I thought you might ask why I recognized you. The truth is... you remind me of her. You look like her, but you carry yourself so differently."

Before I can respond, a knock interrupts us. A nurse steps in. "Visiting hours are ending in five minutes, but you're welcome to return tomorrow."

"Of course, no problem," I say, gathering my things. I glance at Wilma, who sips her tea, unbothered.

"Thank you, Wilma. For everything," I tell her, turning to leave.

As I reach the door, a hand touches my shoulder. "Charli, please visit again. My door is always open. Just call first," She presses a note with her contact information into my hand.

I smile. She pulls me into a hug, and for a moment, my eyes sting, but I blink the feeling away. To hold a woman that felt safe, any adult at that. As we parted, her gaze fell on my necklace.

"I love that necklace. Comet had one just like it... or at least, I think so," she murmurs, then smiles, holding the door open.

I step out, brush my fingers with my pendant, a knot forming in my chest.

"Don't be a stranger, Charli," Wilma calls as the door clicks shut.

I stared at the closed door. I came here for answers— yet I leave with more questions. And all of them lead back to my mother, a mystery even in death.

I retrace my steps back down to Wilma's apartment, my mind juggling questions like a circus act, each one more desperate for an answer than the earlier one. My breathing gets heavier with every step I take; every moment I blink my eyes I can feel the blood rushing to my head.

My vision is spiraling, feeling myself blinking the tears away as fast as they come. Footsteps echo off the tile as I push past the reception desk. The sharp click of Long Nails' fake nails against her phone barely registering in my head. I pass by the security guards, and their questioning looks as I head for the exit, desperately wanting to get air.

The moment I step outside, I collide into something solid—too warm, too alive to be a wall. The faint scent of cologne lingers in the air, confirming what my dazed mind can't process fast enough.

I look up through the blur of tears to see D.J. standing before me. His grip on my arm is firm—steadying, but not forceful. Of course he would be here right now, in this moment, a moment where I can barely keep myself together.

"Hey, are you okay?" D.J. asks concerningly, his eyes begging for an answer.

"Yeah," I replied, wiping my face and sniffling, "Just allergies."

"River you were just inside. What God damn allergies are you talking about?"

"It doesn't matter. I'm fine," I say, my voice thin, unconvincing. I keep my gaze anywhere but on D.J.—the ground, the plants, the tiny ant making its way across the pavement. My breathing refuses to steady, my hands find each other as my fingers pick at the skin with my nails, a habit I can't shake.

A pair of hands land gently on my shoulders. I look up, and there they are—D.J.'s forest eyes, deep, wandering, open.

"River, come on. Just come," he says, prying one of my hands from the other and pulling me toward him. Before I can stop it, I'm in his arms, my chest pressed against his, his heartbeat steady while my stumbled. One of his hands finds my hair, stroking gently, the other rubs slow circles into my upper back.

I pushed him against it. Punch on his chest. Fight. I need to get away from this—this warmth, this comfort I crave but don't deserve. My fists press harder, my knuckles stinging from the impact. If my hands hurt, I can only imagine his pain. *No more pain than you being in his life.*

"Stop River, I am right here, it is okay. Breathe River, breathe." Dario sympathizes.

"No, stop let me go D.J." I spit out, tears falling and my words getting stuck in my throat. I still try to fight him off as if his touch is lava and I am getting burnt. *You shouldn't be by him, let alone in this world either.*

"I am never letting you go River, just please, talk to me."

"I can't D.J., please leave me alone, just leave me alone. I'm begging you." I beg, now looking up at D.J. as he holds me shoulder length. D.J. shakes his head and grabs my hand once again before looking at me again. *I can ruin him; he can't be here; he shouldn't be here.*

"Just come with me River. I will not hug you again, just trust me again. For your sake River."

"I don't care about myself," I feel D.J.'s grip gets tighter in my hand.

"I do not believe that, if you would not do it for yourself then please do it for me." D.J. pleads, his eyes matching his tone, waiting for my answer. I nod reluctantly and not a moment to waste he starts pulling me towards the driveway. It takes 13 steps for us to reach his car; he opens the passenger door for me to get in, and only then do I hesitate. I look up at him, feeling the puffiness around my eyes start to form.

"Where are we going?" I ask, my body and mind are both drained.

"I do not want you to worry about that. Do you trust me?"

"Well considering you won't tell me shit about where we're-"

"Charli," D.J. interrupts, coming closer to me as he closes the car door merely. "Do you trust me?" His voice is tense, but soft.

I nodded my head and duck under his arm to get in. It was as if my body is speaking for itself before my mind can. *If you listen to your mind, you wouldn't even be in this moment right now. It's a shame D.J. is stuck with you.* D.J. closed the door as I put my seatbelt on; a few seconds later he joins me on the other side, the center console separating the two of us.

I can feel the heavy boulder of tiredness hitting me, washing over my body like a wave to take me whole. I blink heavily, focusing on the view in front of me as D.J. pulls out of the community. The community where I got constant information about a person I knew for less than my actual age.

I hear D.J. clearing his throat, making me turn towards him, ripping my gaze from the front into the sea of his presence.

"It is okay to sleep Charli; I will wake you up once we are there." D.J. says as he gazes hard, compelling me not to look away.

"It's okay, I'm not tired D.J." I say as I push off his gaze. I turned towards my window, looking at the view as we waited for the stoplight. I feel a hand on the side of my face, pulling me away from the window, from the view that seems so uncanny that it is serene.

"You do not have to be like that with me Charli, sleep, rest, be yourself. You forget that I know you River," D.J. declared, holding my chin in the palms of his hand, the other on the steering wheel.

He asserts his dominance in his eye, making sure I got what he was saying. A whole conversation with the eyes and touch of D.J. Black, no words said.

He only let go when the light turned green six seconds later. I lay back in the headrest, holding eye contact with D.J.

until he turned towards the road. I still look at him, looking at the person I let go of many years ago. A deed I will never regret but will despise. I stared at him, the only person that truly noticed everything as slumber takes over.

The darkness overwhelms me enough for suffocation to take place, the ideal denouement that I am bound to.

# *Bellyache* Billie Eilish

October 20, 2023

No one likes to admit the feeling of stepping backwards. The idea that you poured so much work into building a habit you forced yourself to keep — only for it to crumble the moment an open chance presents itself. To destroy seconds, minutes, hours, days, months, even years of torture through the mind and body because of a slip up, a mistake.

Some people try to go 100% every day, carefully repairing their mental and physical health as if it were part of a daily routine. While others don't pause to replenish, discipline themselves until there's nothing left.

Should we work until there's nothing left but exhaustion? Or should we rest first, to have something to give? What's the right way to live: pouring out everything each day, or rationing energy until the meter finally hits zero?

I sit in class, dissociating from the lesson in front of me. I shouldn't consider it the fundamental course of a student's high school career. Nevertheless, here I am, ignoring my history teacher's lesson, the constant talk of how white people conquer the world and everyone else is just collateral damage.

I write in my notebook, scribbling furiously, nearly tearing through the page with my thoughts that have been clouding my mind since I met Wilma on Tuesday. It is now Friday. Every time I try to gather my thoughts together, trying to pick the answers that Wilma spit out for me to piece together, my mind just lingers on D.J. and the weird friendship between us. Two souls lingering around each other, waiting for the other to grasp on.

*I woke up in the car, hearing the engine turn off. I look to the side to see D.J. typing away on his phone. As if he can feel my eyes on him, he looks up and locks his gaze on me at once. I sit up from the resting position, wiping my face away from sleep.*

*"Yeah, you can wipe your drool while you are at it," D.J. says.*

*I roll my eyes and send him the meanest side eye that one can conquer; nevertheless D.J. still holds his smirk, never faltering.*

*"Where are we?" I ask, now sitting up facing D.J. with my whole body.*

*"The diner, the one you used to make everyone go to after your games," D.J. replies, stepping out of the car and closing the door behind him.*

*I step out as well, following D.J. before he decides to leave. The car locks behind me, and I am now standing alongside D.J., our footsteps aligning with one another. A strange mix of warmth and ache spreads through me as I look at the familiar building in front of me.*

*The Diner; a place full of memories. Many kids liked going to Chuck E. Cheese, but my special place was this. It didn't have games, or flashing lights, or a creepy ass mouse giving you tickets. No, instead this place holds the memories of family dinners. Family, including my parents of course, but it was also where my childhood felt regular.*

*Having friends join me, specifically my teammates at times. The moments I cherished the most were when I had a table with my closest friends: Shaya, Emilio, and D.J.; this is where we gossiped, played video games as we waited for our food, racing to see who could finish their milkshake first. Where I would write freely, about stories with successful conclusions because I used to be so scared about depicting my characters and torturing them. I wanted them to be happy, so I made them to be, despite the false reality of life.*

*We entered the building, instantly greeted by the host. D.J. responds by saying a table for two and not even a minute later we were following our guide to a table next to a window. I choose the seat in the corner against the window while D.J. sits opposite.  If I sit in the corner, it means I can see everything and not have to worry about what is behind me. Especially when it's just a damn brick wall.*

*"What are you thinking about?" D.J. asks, his elbows rest on the table as he massages his hands in front of him.*

*"About whom would finish their milkshake first," I remarked as I smirk, D.J. returning it swiftly.*

*"I think I would win, as always."*

*"You never won fairly; you would always cheat when we were younger."*

*"How would I cheat? I would simply drink the milkshake fast. It is not my fault you are slow at it," D.J. chuckles out, resulting in a glare from me for a moment.*

*"Just admit it, I won fair and square. You are just lucky I did not quit like Shaya and Lio would," D.J. continues, reminiscing as well on the childhood memories shared between us.*

*"Do you remember Emilio threw up that one time and my parents yelled at all of us. My mom couldn't hold in her laughter but still managed to help Lio's dumbass," I laughed out, smiling at the memory of my mother. Looking down at my lap as my hands fiddle with each other, I hear D.J. cough out.*

*"Yeah, I do," D.J. says, his voice changing its demeanor, making me look up at him. His hands are now laying in his lap as he gazes at me, almost as if he is trying to figure out the puzzle in front of him.*

*"Charli." D.J. says my name without hesitation; his voice laced with concern—but there's something else there too. Curiosity. His body tenses, just slightly, as he waits for me to meet his gaze.*

*"Yes?"*

*"Why did you go see Wilma?" His eyes searched for mine, waiting, pulling.*

*"Who says I did?"*

*"Who else do you know? Before I took you there, you did not even know the place." He turns his head slightly, mirroring his concern.*

*I sit back in my seat, feeling the cold metal against my back and the soft cushion underneath me. My hands find their way to the bracelet, gliding over the small compass charm.*

*"Does it have to do with your mother?" D.J. asks hesitantly.*

*I look up at him, my eyes betraying me before I can answer. I nod slowly, then look down at my hands once again. Eventually I bring my gaze to meet D.J.'s, showing patience pouring out of his body.*

*"I think," I clamp my hands together before continuing, "I think Wilma knew my mom," I still hold D.J.'s eye contact, waiting for an answer. Before he can continue, a waiter pops up to our table.*

*"Hello, my name is Christian, I will be your waiter for today. Is there anything I can get you to drink to start with?" Christian asks, notebook and pen ready in hand.*

*D.J. and I both side-eyed each other at the same time, then smirked, knowing what our answers were momentarily.*

*"Two vanilla shakes, please," we say in unison, in which the waiter smiles as he nods before leaving the table: leaving us alone with the weight of unspoken words pressing between us.*

"Charlotte, hello? Charlotte Riverson!" My teacher calls out, pulling me out of my thoughts at once. I look up to see a heated teacher right in front of me, waiting for my response.

"Can I help you?" I replied, taking off my headphones and giving him my full attention.

"Yes, in fact you can. What is the answer to question seven? Surely you did the homework from last night," my teacher says cheekily.

"I did in fact, but you can just check the work itself instead of me saying it out loud," I say as I scrum around my bag, pulling out the single piece of paper with useless homework answers.

"If you don't take part in my class, I'm afraid I would have to dock a grade from your existing one. Is that what you want?"

"It doesn't matter what I want if your students show progression from the first grade of the school year, right? That way you can be uplifted as a high school teacher who lectures about one-sided history." I say, sitting back in my chair, looking straight at my teacher as he looks like he is about to explode.

"Principal office, now, Ms. Riverson."

"By all means, it beats sitting in this useless class," I say as I gather my things. I look around, seeing my peers' heads down and writing in their notebooks, all of them trying to avoid eye contact with me, avoiding making any contact with me truly.

I get up from my desk, face to face with my teacher before stepping around him, heading for the door. I open it harshly and before I exit, I turn around. I can hear my teacher continuing his lecture before I disrupt him once again for the hell of a reason.

"Oh, and asshole, never call me Charlotte again," I demand, before slamming the door behind me. I can hear his frustration from the other side of the door before walking down the hall.

I turn the corner of the corridor and immediately regret it.

I see Quinn, Thea, Cameron, and D.J. all gathered around by the lockers. I roll my eyes as Quinn is the first one to notice me and instantly grabs D.J. by his waist, pulling him closer. I put my headphones on instantly, ready to ignore the girl in front of me.

As I walk down the hall, each step getting closer to the wannabe queen bee, my music grows louder. It took 8 steps before I could even manage to pass the group. Quinn stands in front of me, altering my steps to a stop. I try to go around her, only for her to block the path again.

I take my headphones off, letting them rest around my neck. *Something else can go around your neck if you just let everything go, including your mother.*

"Are you going to move?" I ask, grinding my teeth together. My hands grip onto the strap of my satchel, so hard to stop me from punching the bitch in front of me.

"Why should I? What good does that to me?" Quinn remarks, trying to make her voice sound as "cutesy" as it can be. If only she knew it would make her sound like a washed-up singer who begs for change on the side of the street.

I look at Quinn's friends, Thea and Cameron, and then turn my gaze to D.J., only to return it to Quinn's hating ass the moment my eyes laid on him.

"So, you're telling me you have nothing better to do with your life other than bothering me and thinking that you're the shit?" I say as I roll my eyes. With the number of times, I'm surprised they don't get stuck, especially with sharing the same air as Quinn.

"Oh, trust me, I couldn't be bothered by you. I would just like to remind you how desperate and destructive you can be, instead of this sad little girl you put as a front," Quinn says, looking down at me as she comes closer.

She is two inches above me and does less than she notices. Her trying to be alpha female is really embarrassing on her part, especially if she wastes her time to be so obsessed with me. *I'm genuinely surprised to have a fan.*

"It's a shame your mother couldn't be here, you know, to see the disaster of a daughter chasing around dreams like they can ever occur to her." Quinn says, laughing, looking back at her friends. No one returns the chuckle she desperately looks for; it's sad to see this. I just got secondhand embarrassment, but not enough as the anger that boils in my blood.

I look around, seeing the pitiful stares from Thea and Cameron and then I avoid them before looking at D.J., who is watching my every move from leaning against the locker. He holds eye contact with me, to which I return only a few seconds before looking back at Quinn, who is playing with her ponytail, everyone waiting for my response.

I breathe in and then out, before putting my headphones back on and turning around. No music playing and I managed to take two steps before wannabe barbie opens her mouth again.

"I knew you would run away. You would always be your mother's daughter; scared to do anything."

Frozen, stuck. My fists clenching and my nails digging into my palms.

*Nope. Not worth it.*

*Don't be like him*

*Like your dad.*

I turn around, Quinn still playing with her hair and everyone else with their heads shaking, as she manages to spit out a laugh. I retake the steps, facing Quinn once again.

*Breathe Charls.*

*One...three...five...*

Before she can even prepare herself, I grab her hair and arm and slam her head into the wall near the window. I kick her legs down, making her on her knees and her arm I'm holding bend behind her back. I took her head away from the wall, only to bang it against the pillar once more, this time harder. My grip on her arm is getting increasingly tighter, only to stop once I hear Quinn whimper beside me.

I turned her face to the side and let go of her arm, only to place my hands on her chin, squeezing it harshly as I made her look up at me. *Those two inches don't mean shit now, huh?*

"Please say something else." I waited for her answer, but I was only met with silent breathing.

"Please do, so I can have an excuse to beat the living shit out of you and leave your blood as the new and improved color for the school's floors." I said, not missing any word hastily and not once stuttering. I lace my voice with hatred, and I can feel a hand on my shoulder. I don't look back as I only focus on the little ass girl in front of me.

"Well? No words left to say. Huh Quinn? Nothing?" Quinn shakes her head, biting down her lips and trying to hold back another whimper. Pathetic.

I let go of her and took a step back. I allow her to get up as her hands wipe her face. Her chin never faltered, and she never broke eye contact with me, like two predators circling each other.

"Watch yourself," Quinn said before she grabs her bookbag from her friends and all three of them pass by me, leaving the corridor.

Thea and Cameron look back, surprised written all over their faces as I just stare with my arms crossed. I turn behind me to see Lio and D.J. standing behind. Lio's hands resting on my shoulders are still waiting for me to calm down.

I breathe in harshly, looking at my hands like they committed murder. I open and close them, shutting my eyes in the process. *Well, you're just like your parents, aren't you? They said if you can't beat them, join them.*

I bring my hands to my face, massaging my temples as I try to push out what just happened. *I don't get mad, I don't get angry, I don't use force, I am not my father's daughter. I cannot. I cannot, I cannot, I cannot, I cannot.* I can feel my hands grabbing my hair before Emilio speaks up, pulling me out of my thoughts.

"Are you okay? Do you want a kiss?" Lio asks, massaging my shoulders up and down. I look at him weirdly and then look at D.J. to see he is sharing the same expression.

We both look at Lio to see him rummage through his bag. A few seconds later he fetches something and, in his hands, lays a Hershey kiss nudging it towards me.

"Emilio, what the fuck?" I asked, confused yet amusingly in my eyes.

"What?

"What would I have gotten if I beat Quinn up? Do I get a chocolate fountain?" I ask, earning a low chuckle from D.J., who is still against the lockers. His eyes met mine and then he looked at Lio.

"I'm sure he would've brought you Willy Wonka himself," D.J. remarks, laughter dancing in his eyes.

"Okay, I was just helping a friend. Better than you though, Mr. I'm too cool for this shit, so I'll just lean on the lockers. I mean seriously, what if Charli did punch the shit out of Quinn?" Lio says, walking towards D.J. and nudges him in a mocking tone.

"Then she would have punched Quinn. She deserves a punch here and there," D.J. shrugs off.

I stared at the two friends ahead of me, D.J. crossing his arms showing boundaries and leaning against the lockers. Emilio stands straight up, constantly fixing his hair every moment he gets. They fall into conversation as I just observe; they have the type of relationship I have with Shaya, brotherhood. You can tell how they mock and tease each other, like nothing else matters if the other is okay.

I leaned against the pillar where I pushed Quinn's face onto, glancing from my friends to the window that overlooks the front of the school. Emilio was always a close friend to me, since diapers, but growing up we stayed close. I don't think I have the same bond with him as I do with Shaya, as he does with D.J., but nonetheless Lio is the brother I never had.

D.J is complicated; our story is complicated. As much as I try to push him away, it is no use. It is almost like we are two ends on a string, pull each other to meet but never do so; the only outcome is to be tangled up in each other's lives, mine specifically.

"Charli, are you coming?" D.J. turns and asks.

"Huh?" I said," wiping my thoughts away. D.J. chuckles and just stares as he puts his hands in his denim pockets.

"Are you coming? We are going to meet Shaya by the bleachers and smoke trying to ignore her," D.J. announces, earning a push off from Lio, which makes him smirk.

"Don't say that about my girl, she can talk as much as she wants, and you guys' better listen to her, especially you Charli," Emilio says as he points a finger at me.

He comes to my side of the hall, wiggling his eyebrows at me jokingly. I give him a weird look that breaks into laughter as he holds out his hand for me to take. He pulls me into a step and places his arm around my shoulders. D.J. joins us and now places me in the middle of both, making me feel short when I'm not. *Fucking giants.*

We all step in unison towards the back of the school, moving through hallways and making twists and turns. Lio released his arms moments ago to text on his phone, most likely letting Shaya know we were on the way. Eventually he leaves us for the rest of the walk, complaining that we walk too slow and how he wants to see his girl. Some friends he is, but a great boyfriend he is as well.

As it was just me and D.J., we entered the field that had bleachers. It is a cloudy Friday; the boys' game is getting cancelled due to the weather. As we quietly walk side by side, I look up to the clouds, but I feel a stare on the side. Not looking his way, I broke the silence.

"Is there something you want to ask me D.J.?"

He chuckles, grabbing my attention and now facing him as we both stop.

"Why do you only play with that bracelet and not the other ones?" D.J. asks, pointing to the bracelet with the compass. *His bracelet.*

"Very observant, are we?"

"Yes, indeed. Are you trying to avoid the question?"

Yes. "No," I spit out, still holding eye contact with D.J.; his expression holds contempt and sincerity. He never falters with the emotions behind his eyes, always showing them before his body does.          "So, answer the question River, why?"

I ignored him as I took the bracelet off. I stare at it, the memories it holds. Holding onto it tight, I look up at D.J, who holds a questionable gaze. Grabbing his hands and placing the bracelet in the middle of his palm, he looks down at it and then looks back at me.

"You answer nothing," D.J. remarks, begging for an answer.

"Just keep the bracelet, consider it a gift," I said to D.J. before starting to walk again towards the couple that is making out on the bleachers. I smile at my friends, admiring the love that they pour out. D.J. never left my side, even with my head start, only moved three steps before he was by me again.

I did this walk many times, knowing it takes approximately 19 steps for us to reach Shaya and Lio. I look at the grass below me, staying in place with the dirt that surrounds it. The flowers and weeds poking out here and there as D.J. and I continue to walk. I look up to the clouds, seeing the blue poking out of the grey, the sun trying to poke out through the clouds, but not doing so. I turn my head towards the left, seeing D.J. staring with what looks like admiration. I raise one eyebrow at him, in which he returns hastily.

"You know, I am always mesmerized at how you look at things," D.J. says, breaking the silence.

"Are you now?" I replied, still looking around at the world that I step and breathe in.

"You look at it like you've never seen it before, but also very calculating like you are measuring the number of times you see the same things. Why?"

"Why are you trying to figure me out D.J.?"

"Who said I am?"

"Your questions. Stop dodging mine while you're at it," I say as D.J. smiles and shakes his head, breaking eye contact with me momentarily.

"Only if you stop dodging mine," D.J. responds, squinting his eyes as if he is analyzing me. I roll my eyes and take a breath.

"I look at the world and count, that's all. Just count. I started doing it when everything happened," I say, I look away from D.J. and stare at the ground below me. A dandelion lays below me before I pick it up from the ground. I stare at it, not making a wish at all. I held it out in front of me, waiting for the wind to blow the flower away, but it never came.

"At first, I just started counting down the seconds until I see my mom again, but overtime it just started to be a way to cloud my thoughts, to ignore or distract me from other things," finishing my sentence, the dandelion started to blow in the wind, releasing from the stem I am still holding. I look up in the sky to see the dandelion soar freely.

"You do not have to count with me, River, just talk to me and I will listen. Write a book and I will read it," D.J. breathes harshly. "Just do not shut me out Charli, not again," He continues, before walking again, catching up to Shaya and Emilio.

They broke into a conversation with D.J., the only thing I can hear is the spark from the lighter and the smell of the burnt joint that is going around in a rotation. Surrounded by all my friends, I let my thoughts go and the smoke comes out of my mouth.

# *Where's My Love*

*SYML*

October 28, 2023

What happens to the things we once loved? To the hobbies turned into chores, to the people that turned into enemies. Children at a youthful age are creative, optimistic, challenging even; but what happens when those children who love themselves turn into their own enemies and become human beings?

An entity that only shows the shell of the young mind they once were. When all the hobbies they once yearned for turn into antagonizing chores they get bored of? To what extent do human beings turn into robots that only feel in demand?

I'm sitting at the edge of my bed, folding thin slices of wrinkled wrapping paper—reused wrapping paper from last year. Each corner that I fold I carefully taped, the tape not sticking as much to the thin cardboard box that holds the mesmerizing gift.

My gift. A gift for Shaya that I stayed up all night making, reliving the moment it was made. A pencil portrait of her and I as we sit courtside in our middle-school game. Our cotton candy toothy grins etched onto our young faces, a picture I hold in the deepest part of my mind, a memory drawn into reality. I didn't think anything of the memory as I was drawing; it was just that. Drawing, releasing, breathing.

Taking my mind away from wrapping the gift, I hear heavy and slow footsteps hauling up the stairs. I did not move an inch, staying in my place as my door burst open, knocking into the drawers next to it. I see my dad with his heavy eyes and his swaying stance. I look over my clock and see it is 11:34 am, not even 12 p.m. yet. Shaya's birthday party she talked about all day at the bleachers yesterday started at 12:30 p.m. So, I have an hour to get ready, get there, and be present.

"Aye, you got twenty bucks?" My dad slurs out the question. His beer in his hand as he takes a sip, leaning against my doorframe to keep himself upright.

I didn't look up to my dad as I continued wrapping the gift. "It's all I got," I mumbled.

"So?" He shrugged, drunk and heavy eyed, "I asked if you had it."

"If I give it to you, will you leave me alone for the rest of the day?" I clenched my jaw and spit out.

My dad scuffs, "Where are you even going?"

"Shaya's birthday."

My dad lets out a laugh, one that doesn't sound like one. "Don't go and ruin her birthday now," he chuckles out, his version of being happy. "Not like how you already ruined my life," he continues and then snatches the bill from the dresser, then left. I don't even think he said it to hurt me, no he just meant it, and that's worse. *It's not like it's a surprise.*

Leaving me with absolutely nothing except the gift in my hand, I just stare at it. The wrapped gift with wrinkled paper and tape almost every fold mocks me. I sit there, frozen, as I stare at the empty space my father left. I look down at the gift once more, realizing this is all I have left. My gift, my talent, my torture.

It is the only thing that allows me to breathe the moment I put the pen to my journal, or in this case, the pencil to my sketch paper. I create the words I have not said, the actions that I have not allowed. I have created it. The only thing I have left is the ability to create in the disastrous world around me.

I get up from my bed, stretching my arms above my head, cracks from my back announce themself. My mind is already running, moving faster than my limbs can catch up. I head towards my desk and open the top drawer, rummaging around as my finger brushes over the old, new pens along with a few paint brushes. My hand goes further into the drawer, just behind the loose paper, to find the hidden compartment. I pull it open, revealing my stash—just enough for a few blunts.

I grab the bag and then head over to the chair aligned with my desk. The cushion welcomes me with open arms as I set everything in front of me: weed, tray, and rolling paper. I put my headphones on, playing songs with a familiar intro to XXXTentacion filling my ears. My hands find their way to the weed, and I break it harshly over the tray.

Grinding with my hands, I can feel the grains stick to my fingers like another layer of skin. My hands continue to move automatically from one step to another, and for a moment, just a moment, the rhythmic pulse of the music helps steady my breathing.

Once I was done, I moved my way to the window and opened it enough for me to climb out. I step out, blunt and lighter in hand, and land onto the platform that stretches over my porch. Sitting down, my legs to my chest, and my back against the wall that shares my window. The blunt between my fingers as I start to light it, the smoke curls in the air. The scent mixes with the smell of weed and wet grass below.

I inhale deeply, letting the thoughts that have been rattling my brain slip away with the exhale. Only they didn't, I tried, but it never slipped away.

Like a dam breaking, thoughts flood my mind and my dad's voice echoes in the back. *You ruined my life.* Different words but a familiar feeling. Almost like what Quinn had said to me so many years ago. I took another hit, this time long enough for me to feel the burn in my chest. I exhale, but the burn still lingers; it always has. Settling deep in my gut, a tenderness that won't go away.

*Am I the problem? Yes. Am I the one that destroys people's lives? Yes. No. Yes.*

My music stops abruptly in my ears, followed by a ping of my phone vibrating in my pocket. I pulled it out, scanning the message from Emilio.

```
Lio: I'll pick you up at 12:15. Be ready.

Charli: Do I have a choice:/?

Lio: If I give you another kiss, will you be
ready?

Charli: No, never again.
```

I hit send as I let out a small chuckle. Finishing the blunt, I toss it away towards the edge of the roof. I take a deep breath, trying to push all the chaotic thoughts out of my head. I'm not sure if it's in my ability to do so, I do it anyways, for my friends. I climb back into my room and start getting ready.

~~~~~~~~~~~~~~~

I stand in front of the mirror by the door, adjusting the strap of my brown leather purse. My outfit feels like armor—something to help me stand taller, feel more secure. The black fitted turtleneck hugs my body in a way that's both comforting and confining. Two sides of a coin.

The flowy black skirt brushes against my ankles as I shift around, trying to feel ~~less trapped~~ enjoyable. I glance over to the table next to the mirror, the one that lays on the opposite side of the door, where I spent hours on the gift for Shaya, rests on my sneakers—brown Adidas, classic but still me.

I glance down at my wrist and adjust the gold jewelry that is layered loosely, usually my wrists are filled with string bracelets and rubber ones, but I tell myself it's because the difference will make me feel better. *If I look good, I'll feel better*. A lie.

The brown leather sailor hat on my head feels more like an accessory in my mind than an outfit. My mascara hid the constant puffiness in my face, the only make-up I etched on my face. Just as I finished my lip combo—brown lipliner and a faint red lip gloss—the honk from outside breaks through the stillness in the room.

I glanced in the mirror again and nodded at myself, more for reassurance than anything. *Anything to convince myself*. I sling my bag over my one shoulder and grab the wrapped gift, holding it securely in my hand.

I head out the front door, feeling the cool October air hit my face once again. My steps are quick as I make my way
~~~~~~~~~~~~~~~

down the rocky path that leads to the car. I see Lio's parents sitting in the front, Emilio leaning back in the back seat.

"Hey Charli," Mykel calls from the front, "You look great!"

I have him a small smile, now conscious of how I look and ruffling my skirt a little before sliding into the car next to Lio.

"Hey, Mr. and Mrs. Cardiner," I greet them.

"Good to see you, Charli," Persephone says, her smile warm and inviting. She has softness in her eyes as she takes me in.

Lio interrupts, his usual teasing grin on full display. "Of course it's *good* to see her. I'm the one who had to put up with the silence all week, not telling me about Shaya's gift and all."

I roll my eyes, my chest filling up with warmth from the amusement. "You'll find out once Shaya sees the gift. Besides, I know you want to tell me about your gift," I say, turning towards Emilio as he holds his gift bag in his lap.

"Yes, finally. I thought you would never ask," he exclaimed, his parents laughing from the front as a smile creeped across my face.

"So, I bought this nice scrapbook, one with brown, green patterns all over it from Michaels, and printed out all the photos I took of us, and I mean everything." Lio said as he took out the gift carefully.

He shows me the cover, with brown and green swirls all over. In the middle of the book lays Lio's writing that says, "Core Memories". He opens it up and the first page flashes two young kids with silly smiles and sticking their tongues out. Underneath are stickers and little paragraphs in Emilio's handwriting once again.

109

"I made a scrapbook of all the photos we took with each other, even the ones from Chuck E. Cheese that I had to scavenge through all the drawers in my house for," Lio flips through the pages, each one having a paragraph underneath each one.

The scrapbook shows them throughout the years, growing up with one another. The love from my best friends is pouring off each page. I look at the last page and see that Emilio had taken a picture of them on top of a Ferris wheel. He is kissing Shaya's cheek as she is smiling with her dimples popping out. In love. That's what they are, always will be.

"You think she would like it?" Lio asks, closing the scrapbook and placing it in the gift bag.

"Like it? She would bring it on your wedding day and make every single one of her guests see it. She'll love it," I say smiling at Lio. He returns the smile and then the smile drops.

"Okay, so now tell me yours," he said, glaring at me playfully.

"Nope," I said, enunciating the "p" in my words, which earns another chuckle from Mykel.

For the rest of the ride, I lean into the comfortable silence that is accompanied by the radio music. To my left, Lio is typing on his phone; most likely texting Shaya. I look over to the front momentarily, seeing Emilio's parents hold hands over the center console.

I sit back into the seat, the gift in my lap as I think. Back when my parents would drive me home after my games, their hands held over the center console. I remember singing myself to sleep from the radio songs after the away games. The picnics we would have almost every Sunday since it was the only free day where I did not have school or basketball, and my parents didn't have work. I remember the love that I once felt in a different lifetime.

Now sitting here, I can only see it in other people, from the people in my life that try to love me, but I only push them away. *That's because everyone you love you kill, or worse, turn them into something they're not.*

The familiar sights of the neighborhood fade into the background as I watch the street blur in my vision. The feeling of Lio's parents' hands touching over the center console sticks with me longer than I thought it would be. Their love, the warmth of it, something I haven't felt in so long.

I try to shake off the thoughts, but they linger, weaving in and out of the silence of the car. The music fades for a moment, and I hear the faint tapping of Lio's fingers on the phone screen. I shift in my seat, staring at the gift once more in my lap, hoping it'll distract me, but it doesn't. Not today.

Just as my thoughts start to settle into the quiet chaos I have endured, the car slows down and pulls to the curb in front of Shaya's house. Emilio's parents glance back at us.

"We'll find parking," Mykel said, with a nod to the front.

Lio and I are already halfway out the door before they finish the sentence, our feet hitting the ground as we head towards the house. The frigid air rushes at me, pulling me out of any lingering thoughts.

We burst through the front door, almost knocking it down off its hinges. Shaya is standing by the kitchen island, a tray of cupcakes in her hands that she put down, her face lighting up in surprise as we come into view. Lio takes his camera off from around his neck and places it on the table nearby.

"Happy birthday!" We shout in unison.

Before she can even react, we're both on her, knocking her to the ground in the best kind of birthday tackle. On the one hand Emilio is giving her pecks and I'm giving her birthday punches. Laughter fills the room as we pile on top of her, trying to hug and smother in one combo.

Shaya laughs, trying to push us off her, "Get off me, you two! You're going to ruin my hair!"

"Not possible," Emilio grins, his voice full of teasing affection. "Happy birthday, princess."

Just as the moment settles, a flash of light catches our attention, and we all turn to see D.J. with Lio's camera standing in the doorway, a smirk on his face. "What? Somebody must capture the memories."

We all stare at him for a beat, and then I roll my eyes, unable to stop the small smile tugging at my lips. "Really, D.J.?"

He shrugs with a grin. "Maybe I should be the photographer instead of Lio."

With a chuckle, D.J. reaches out to help me up, his hand warm against mine. Emilio offers Shaya a hand, pulling her to her feet as well.

"Did you miss me princess?" He asks, his hands around Shaya's waist.

"Dude really?" D.J. says as he cringes. I nudge him to the side, in which he takes my face in as I glare at him.

He takes my appearance as he looks up and down at me and then smiles. I can feel the heat from my chest rise, taking the opportunity to bring my attention to my best friends once more. They laugh at the encounter between me and D.J. before Shaya turns to Lio.

"Of course I miss you, especially with you texting me non-stop about Charli not being nice," Shaya said, side eyeing me playfully, in which I roll my eyes.

"She wasn't! I was telling her all about my gift to you, which by the way you should open now since I'm special and everything." Lio says as he hands Shaya his gift. But that didn't stop his tangent. Not one bit.

"I asked about her gift, and you know what she said? She said I couldn't know until you found out, so please, open mine first and then hers. In this moment," we all stared at Emilio before breaking out into laughter as he exclaimed.

"I'm serious! She would rather talk to my boring parents than talk about her gift to you. I've been waiting all week to see what she got you."

"Wow, I would say you're more excited than Shaya about *her* birthday gift. And maybe Charli doesn't want to talk to you because you're the boring one, son," Mykel announced himself as he and Persephone walked into the house. Persephone holding Mykel's arm as they walk in unison, elegantly.

"Happy birthday dear," Persephone says as she pulls Shaya into her arms. Shaya then returns the hug to Mykel afterward.

"How's your parents?" Mykel asks, his hand on Shaya's shoulder when they pull apart.

"You know, my dad is trying to grill again—God help us all—and mom is ordering food behind his back," Shaya laughs off. A smile creeps across my face as I look around at the people beside me. A family, one that I am apart from but from a distance.

"Well, what do you say we help out our friends before he starts a fire in the backyard?" Mykel said, grinning towards Persephone, while holding out his hand.

"I'll convince Calista to order more wings, since you boys want to eat it all up," Persephone says, pointing at D.J. and Emilio before taking Mykel's hand. Lio and D.J. hold their hands up as his parents walk out towards the backyard, leaving us reckless teens in the kitchen with an open flame.

Before anyone can say another word, the front door busts open once again, surprised that it's still attached to the frame. As we all stand in the kitchen, we hear what sounds like a circus coming through the house, only revealing Shaya's family.

Countless "happy birthdays", pictures, and hugs passed by. Many of Shaya's aunts hugged me as well, asking the same tiring questions. "How are you, dear? How's your dad? Is he still working a lot? You should come over more often; you're never a stranger. Your mom would be so proud." I don't like going anywhere, but I will go for my best friend. Any of my friends really; they are the only thing I have left in this world.

My distant relatives--really my mom's baby sister doesn't live in the same country. Good for her really, travelling in her twenties. She always says she is a phone call away, but she's away for a reason. I'm not the one who should bother her.

Eventually I make my way to the living room, Shaya and Lio are taking pictures and engaging with their family. I tried to gather my thoughts together, trying to put on a bright face but I couldn't, hence why I had to remove myself from the situation. This is Shaya's day, not mine. My hands absentmindedly find my mother's necklace. I am so sure this is hers. The moment I found it I was instantly connected to it. It's a hard feeling to describe, to feel it in your gut that a piece of metal and plastic holds a love from someone that isn't even there anymore.

I question every day, write simultaneously, about this necklace. Why wasn't it found on my mother? She used to wear it every day, only taking it off when she showered. I sit back further onto the couch, looking at the room around me. The couches are a bronze brown, no plastic like Wilma's. The T.V. is mounted on the wall, leaving almost no space except for the little shelves that hang below. Pictures of Shaya and D.J. throughout the years, pictures of me and Lio with them during our camping weekends, wedding photos of Calista and Amir—D.J.'s mom and Shaya's dad. So many memories, so many moments captured and on full display; always to be remembered but never to relive.

"Hey champ, you're not hungry?" Mykel said, holding plates full of food; pizza and wings. He sits beside me, handing the plate over my lap.

I smiled at him, picking up the pizza and taking a bite. "I'm guessing you couldn't help Amir with the grill?"

Mykle chuckles out, wiping his mouth with a napkin, "I don't think anyone can help him out, Calista really came through with the food though."

"She always does," I say as I take another bite. Crunchy pizza, the best kind.

A moment of silence passed, hearing the music pour in from the background as we both took in each other's presence.

"How come you're not with your friends? I'm sure my annoying ass son and Shaya never mind you," Mykle asks, still staring ahead. I can hear him biting on the pizza like his life depends on it.

We always had a close relationship, even when my parents were still parents. Every time I played on the court, he was right there with Lio cheering me and Shaya on; if I was scared to tell something to my parents, he was there to sometimes hear it first. Like an undeniable bond that we share. He calls me the daughter he never thought to have, calling me family when I felt like I had none left.

"I don't know," I said, swallowing the pizza along with my response. *Maybe because I don't belong here, maybe because I don't deserve their friendship, maybe because I'm such a disappointment where my friends feel obligated to invite me everywhere.*

"You know Emilio talks about you with Shaya all the time; they'll always include you Charli," Mykel says, putting his paper plate onto the table in front of us. He turns to me, in which I return the favor.

"Never once in my life I seen a group of friends so close together before you all. Maybe once, but that was a long time ago," Mykle looks down, his hands gripping onto each other, a feeling I was remarkably familiar with.

"Mykel?"

"Yes Charls?"

"What's the point of all of this? Growing up?" I asked, lingering onto the response waiting to happen. My hands rub each other hard, trying to smooth out the anxiety that is creeping into my body.

Mykel looks up at me; he looks down at my hands before taking one into his hand. He holds onto it, squeezing it for reassurance. "Love. The answer is love." I shake my head before responding.

"That wouldn't be true, and you know it. My mother would still be here if that were the answer. I *love* her." I said, gritting my teeth in the last sentence. I can feel a fist forming in Mykel's hands, my other one gripping onto the leather couch, yet Mykel doesn't budge. Not once.

"I know you do Charls; no one is denying that. But you asked me what the point is. It's love. Of all kinds."

I take my hands out of Mykel's, crossing my hands and looking up at the ceiling before closing my eyes. My head is starting to pound; my breathing is starting to get heavier.

"Look Charli, you may not like my answer, but it is how I see it. Love comes from relationships, from friendships, from neighbors, even teachers," Mykel announced. I can feel his stare on my face as he continues to lecture me.

"Love is all around, you have love in your life, but you are focused on the negative, too much on the negative. What happened to you is a lot, more than many people in this town have dealt with. Astrid..." The moment I hear my mother's name my eyes shot open. I look over and see Mykel's face in his hands, rubbing his temples back and forth.

His foot is tapping onto the hard floor, creating a creaking sound every second. The music fades as I witness my habits, the habits of keeping everything inside, from another person.

"Astrid was love, will always be love. Her life, her youthfulness will always be constant," Mykel says, taking a deep breath as he faces me. "Life is worth living because your mother has lived, had you, and loved everyone around her," I can see the tears brim in Mykel's eyes, his comforting eyes now being tortured by the same pain I endure every day.

I shake my head, trying to think of his words and my mom. She loved everyone, everything, so why did she leave? Why did she take a gun to her head and shoot herself? Why did she leave me? Why did she leave me with a monster who abuses me every day? Why? Why? Why? Why? I never asked those questions aloud. Not once.

"What love did you experience in your lifetime? You and Persephone always show it—it's no wonder Emilio does the same," I said, swallowing the pit in my throat. My fingers curled around my necklace, and Mykel noticed. His expression shifted—subtle, almost startled. I caught it but didn't say anything.

*Recognize something?* I wanted to ask him; I wanted to ask him a million questions about my mother, but I didn't. Why put him in pain of a loss he also endured? *Why was the necklace in his house?*

Mykel looks down momentarily before looking back up. "Yeah," he clears his throat before continuing, "Persephone and I are quite the pair. I love that woman to death," Mykel said before getting up from the couch, his face holding distraught and pain. I can feel the pit now in my stomach, knowing I am the one who caused it.

"I'm sorry, I shouldn't have asked anything." I said, making Mykel turn towards me. I stand up, a few feet away from him, avoiding his gaze shamefully.

"Charli, you can ask me anything about your mother. I'm not sure I can tell anything your father hasn't said already, but I'll answer anything you have to ask." Mykel said as I looked up at him. He gives me a reassuring smile and then heads out of the living room.

As he heads out the doorway, Shaya and Lio pass by him. He steals a wing from his father's plate before he is pushed away. My friends approached me, smiles and laughter written all over their faces.

"What are you doing Charls? Come on, we brought out the karaoke machine into the backyard." Shaya said enthusiastically. I look over at Emilio, who is eating his wings like he hasn't eaten before. I roll my eyes before laughing. Shaya loops her arm around mine, as we just look at Lio in disgust.

"Jeez, I wonder sometimes why I am a girlfriend of a dog," Shaya says with laughter in her eyes, "Come on, what do you say Charls?"

"I'll come but I'm not doing karaoke, even if my life depends on it. I'll support you from a distance," I respond, returning the same look at my beautiful best friend who just turned 18.

She's wearing a white crocheted top with bright sun stitched in the middle. Her waist beads shimmer under a long brown skirt that brushes her feet, paired with tan sandals. Her beautiful locks are tied into two ponytails, with charms dangling, framing her glowing face. Sometimes I wish I was into girls so I would just steal Shaya for myself.

"Well of course not, that's why we're making D.J. and Lio sing the first song," Shaya said brightly.

"The hell I am," a voice calls out. D.J. appears around the corner, standing by Emilio as he wipes his saucy face with a napkin. D.J. looks between me and Shaya, lingering his captivating eyes on mine.

"And why not?" Shaya remarked, letting go of my arm only to cross hers. She looks at Lio, who was already staring at her and tilts her head. I can literally see his eyes soften before he straightens up and, in a moment, does he grab the fist of D.J.'s shirt and pull him close, all without taking his eyes off Shaya.

"Dude, suck it up and sing with me. Be the Aladdin to my Jasmin," Lio said, taking his eyes off Shaya to look at D.J. with pleading eyes. D.J. turns his head, glancing his gaze towards me to return to Emilio a second later.

He scrunches his face at Emilio, "You are so down bad," D.J. says as he makes a disgusted look. I chuckle softly as Shaya is beaming at the boys in front of us.

D.J. pushes Lio off and smooths down his shirt. "Fine, just never say that again." And in that instant, he was cheering along with Shaya. They leave the living room, shout and cheer songs, and go to the karaoke machine. D.J. and I alone in the living room, tension fills the air.

"Coming River? Don't leave me alone with those two morons again," D.J. says, his hand holding out. I grab it loosely and we both head towards the backyard. His hands feel warm, safe, compared to my cold ones.

"River, why did you not tell me you were freezing? Your hands are icicles," D.J. says as we stand in the kitchen, the sliding door to the backyard across on the other side.

"I'm not, my hands are just always cold," I say, looking at the door behind D.J., my back is leaning against the kitchen island, where it is filled with cookies, gifts, and cupcakes.

Before I can stop him, D.J. brings my hands into both of his and brings it to his mouth. His warm breath instantly warms my hands, bringing it back to life. He rubs against it, never taking his eyes off me. I look down at our hands together, breaking away from his trapping gaze. A gaze that leaves me questioning everything, questions I have never asked before.

"Come on River, before Shaya drags us introverts outside," D.J. smirks as he leads us outside.

The moment we went outside, the light from the sunset was placed onto the entire backyard. The tables and chairs were all decorated with gold and green colors. I look around the sea of people, cousins of D.J. and Shaya, which I recognize over the year. I carefully look all over, not sparing a second glance at anyone to give them room to converse with me.

I see Shaya in front of the karaoke machine, sitting at the table as Lio sets up the machine. I nudge D.J. and signal towards Shaya as we start walking together. I tried to let go of his hand, which only resulted in him looking back with a confused look. He grips tighter as we move through the crowd, eyes glancing my way specifically so that I don't return.

It takes us 16 steps, or us hopping around really, until we meet Shaya at the table. D.J. only let go of my hand to help Lio choose the song he is forced to sing. I sit down beside Shaya, who is just staring at me with an interesting look.

"Nope, don't even start," I said.

"I didn't even say anything," Shaya said, holding her hands up in defense.

"You didn't have to, your eyes said it all."

"So, you know what I'm questioning then, might as well answer it if you know," Shaya said, smirking as she takes a sip of her drink. I look at her drink and look up, tilting my head in the process.

"Nope, no alcohol. I think my parents would kill me even on my birthday," she says. I smile lowly and shake my head. "But don't change the subject Charls, I want my answer." She says as she looks over to D.J. and back to me. She holds up one finger on each of her hands and brings them together, which earns me a laugh.

"Shaya, no."

"Charli, yes."

"No."

"Yes."

"No-"

"Charli, come on. I'm not blind, neither is Lio. We've *been* saw the sparks between you two since kids."

"Sparks? Are we computer wires now?" I chuckled out, grabbing Shaya's cup before taking a sip before setting it back down.

"Might as well be, shit. I mean you all have been getting closer, especially after years of not talking to each other,"

I look down at my hands, wanting the earth to swallow me up in this moment. "Yeah, we have been. But I don't know Shaya. Our friendship is never going to be the same, not how it was. That ship has sailed."

"Who said anything about a friendship?" Shaya questioned, holding her eyes on me, locked. I look at her as if she has two heads. Okay, maybe four.

"What *the fuck* are you talking about?" I asked, feeling the heat rise.

"You just admitted there was a ship to begin with." I nudged her, resulting in her smiling at me. She grabs my hands and the laughter between us dies down, only room for calmness and sincerity.

"Our lives are too complicated; it couldn't even hold a friendship." I say as I hold Shaya's comforting eyes.

"Look Charls, a ship can always sail back, especially through a giant ass storm. Just wait until the clouds clear to be ready to sail again." Shaya says as she smiles.

I return the smile, chuckling at her words, "Very Toni Morrison of you," I say as Shaya pushes me off. We both laugh in each other's presence, lightness filling my chest.

Before another conversation can start, the karaoke machine blares to life, blasting music from the speakers. D.J. and Emilio stand in front of us, each holding a microphone. They begin singing—or at least Lio does, completely off-key.

I catch D.J. rolling his eyes as Lio wails his way through the lyrics of "Baby" by Justin Bieber. His usual smirk creeps onto his face as he shakes his head at the absolute clown he calls his best friend—our best friend. D.J. throws in a line or two, mostly just to back him up, but the performance is all Lio, pouring his heart out to Shaya with zero shame and even less pitch.

I look at D.J. ahead of me. Thinking of Shaya's words just a moment ago. I think about our childhood, our friendship, and our innocence. I think about the time when he held me as we cried in each other's arms the night we lost our parents. D.J. has been there for every moment of my life, the parts where it was important. The moments when it mattered. *You didn't return the favor; you never will.*

*All you do is destroy others. Destroy their lives and their future. What are you even doing at this party? It's a pity that you're still here. Shame really.*

D.J. was there when it mattered. *He felt sorry for you.* He held my cuts as he was bleeding himself. *How careless can you be?* I made a promise not to shut him out. Not anymore.

How can I if our wounds bleed the same?

# *Nothing's New* Rio

## *Romeo*

November 1, 2023

Sometimes people want to believe that they have the answers. They want to believe that they have a plan that everything works out okay. They don't want to put their faith in the negative, into something that can turn their life upside down.

Sometimes, if not all the time, individuals like to think they are right; that's all it takes for someone to go overboard. The final confirmation to end the story.

I don't want to go to school. I don't want to do anything in this life, but here I am, lying in my bed. I have my maroon covers up to my neck, covering every inch of my body as I stare at the ceiling. The weight pushes me down as I sink into the abyss that surrounds me. I look over my clock and see that it is 7:15 am, meaning school starts in 30 minutes. My commute to school is about 20 minutes long by walking. I'm not going to school today.

I close my eyes, wanting this day to drag by as the world moves around me, without me. I drift back to sleep, the familiar cloud that comforts my mind.

*The sky is grey—not the soft kind like in a nursery, the haunting hue. The kind that presses against your chest as you try to grasp for air.*

*I stand by the edge of the river, the one that has haunted me ever since I was eight years old. The river that holds silence that speaks too loud as mist rolls over the water like it is breathing, slowly but surely. The river that I turned into a motherless child.*

*I look around, through the fog that clouds my vision. I reach out but no one is there to take my hand. I am truly alone; no Shaya, no Lio, and no D.J., nobody that is left to care for.*

*Just me, the water, and the wind that howls every chance it gets. I look down at my sneakers; the color is not depicted as I just feel the wet socks and soles from a fluid, I don't remember stepping in.*

*I crouch down to the water, seeing my reflection through the mist. It ripples along with the movement of the water. Then—a hand breaks through the water. Wrinkled. Pale. Familiarity.*

*I stumble backwards on the hard ground, my heart slamming through my chest as I try to catch my breath. I need to go, but everything inside of me is saying to stay. I am grounded by my own body, like stone embedded into the ground.*

*I can see my mother's face come into focus as her hand still reaches out for me. The moment she connects her hand in mine it doesn't stop; it goes from hand to my arm and finally rests on my face.*

*Soaked curls hung over her eyes, blood trickling down from the side of her temple. Her lips are bluish, slightly parted, and chapped. Her eyes reach mine as she pulls me into focus—holding knowledge in the soul that left too soon.*

*She doesn't scream. She doesn't yell at me. No, instead her voice cracks, like dry leaves underfoot.*

*"Why are you digging Charlotte baby?*

*I shake my head, tears brimming in my eyes but not falling. "I--I didn't mean to." I say, stuttering as coldness overtakes my body.*

*"You were never meant to know," My mother said, her haunting eyes with soothing voice echoing through me.*

*My mom then takes my hand which I hold onto. She grips harder and her hands start to feel like piercing icicles. Before I realized it, she pulled me into the river.*

*I gasped as I hit the water instantly. I entered gracefully, no splash, no commotion. No resistance as I fall into the black void that surrounds me. The river surrounds me like smoke, dragging me further down every chance it gets.*

*My lungs scream, as if they are on fire, and I fight to escape. I tried to bring my mother as well only to realize her hand was no longer with mine. I search all around, clawing at nothing in sight. I desperately search for something that isn't there anymore.*

*Only then do I look up at the surface. As I drown slowly, I see a figure on top of the bridge ahead. A figure I can't depict. The black and shadowy figure doesn't move, he just stares. I tried to call out to him, but no luck. The air bubbles choke me and the fire in my lungs escalates.*

*As I feel darkness creep in, the figure turns away and walks away. My vision starts to blur, and I can feel my heart slow down.*

*Just before everything fades, I hear my mother's voice again soft, like the wind carrying a lullaby:*

*"He knows Charlotte baby. He always knew."*

I jolted upright, gasping and my hand grabbing my throat for support. I can feel my chest rise and fall in uneven waves and uneven patterns. The sweat on my skin sticks to me like static as the dream is still clutching to me like a fist. I can feel pieces of my hair stick to my cheek as I try to wipe the sweat away from my face. I look at my bed, my sheets tangled all around my legs like vines in a forest. I blink one...two...three times, feeling disoriented from reality.

I look over my phone as it lights up from my nightstand. 1:30 p.m. I groan loudly, as I stretch over with trembling hands. Notifications fill my phone—messages from Shaya and Emilio, none from...it doesn't matter.

I don't answer any of the messages as I lay back down in my bed with my phone on my chest. I try to breathe as my chest feels like armor suffocating me. My mother's voice echoed in my mind, haunting the thoughts that ring in my ears.

*He knows Charlotte baby. He always knew.*

A buzz vibrated against my sternum. I lift my phone and see the bubble notification that lights up Philo's name. I roll my eyes before opening the message.

```
Philo: yo you home? Wanna talk about that
tattoo we agreed I could get you around?

Charli: yeah. Doors open.
```

I let the phone slide from my hands and climbed out of bed. My limbs still feel heavy, regardless of the hours of sleep I have gained. I still feel the dream grip onto my skin, like another organ, a part of me. The river, my mother's voice, the man. I want to peel my brain apart and scrub it until there is nothing left.

I step into the bathroom and turn the water to the hottest setting. I let the mirror fog up the mirror—like the fog that clouded my vision in the dream. I stepped into the shower as the heat hugged me—welcomed. I rub my arms, my shoulders, my face—trying to mimic my mother's touch. Nothing worked; it never worked.

I stayed in the shower for a good twenty minutes before I stepped out. I didn't bother drying my hair as I threw on a pair of black sweats and a shirt, my movements quick as I was distracted. The towel that was wrapped around my body dropped from the hanger, not bothering to fix it.

I walk back into my room, grabbing the half blunt on my desk along with the lighter. I make my way across from the room to my window, climbing out effortlessly. I sit down in my usual spot and light the blunt. I can hear the birds chirping and the wind singing. I inhale and exhale smoothly, letting the smoke coat my lungs like a shield.

Just as everything gets quiet, I see Philo's headlight pulling at the end of my street. I see him walking over from his car, strutting confidently as he opens my door. I can't hear him anymore until a few minutes pass by and I hear him in my room.

He says my name twice before realizing my window is open. He hops out, not as smoothly as me, and he nodded at me as he took the seat beside me. No questions were asked between us as I passed the weed. We sat in silence, smoking half blunt, smoke surrounding us and the smell hitting my nostrils.

"You still want to do the ink?" I asked, my voice rough and hard.

Philo took another hit before tossing the blunt away. He exhales through his nose smoothly. "Nah," he said eventually, "Wasn't really about that."

"I know." I spoke. I climbed over him back into my room. I sit on my bed, waiting for Philo as he climbs in after me. He takes his jacket off and throws it on my floor, one that is littered with my bed sheets. Philo meets me at the edge of the bed, hovering over me. He leans in, each of his arms on the side of me. He grabs my chin, making me look up to him. His eyes are full of lust.

He leans in more; I don't turn away. I didn't move an inch at all unless Philo was guiding me. His touch was warm but distant. I feel it all over my body but just out of reach. I can feel the high take over and cradle me in a thick fog, I reel into it.

Philo is over me, planting kisses on my hot skin, but I still feel cold. Everything was static. Muffled even. My body moved but my mind didn't follow, I didn't allow it. It was like I was witnessing myself outside of my skin. From above I see the girl that holds onto reality desperately but does not do so.

I blinked, one...two...three times as my mind is pulled away from the weight, from the warmth, from the now. I see the blur of the ceiling in front of me. The same ceiling I stared at this morning, when everything felt so unbearable, but it was a feeling. It was real, unlike now.

I keep waiting for something to happen, something to feel. But all I could hear was my mother's voice.

*He always knew.*

# *The Scientist* Coldplay

November 1, 2023

Like love and hate, fear and desire go hand in hand. Most people are driven by one of them, letting it take control rather than simply guide them.

Fear strips the soul, pushing people to act—or freeze. Desire makes us yearn for something that isn't always there. But when do both coexist? When does one overcome the other? The truth is, neither can survive without relying on the other.

Right now, I have no idea which one is leading me. If I ever had a choice to begin with.

I can feel the wind blow against my neck, goose bumps rising as it causes me to shiver. A sign that I am alive, a sign that I can feel. I look down as I count my steps.

The hard concrete separated from each pavement that is laid down smoothly.

One...two...three steps, followed by many more, as I walk back from the river. My bag is slung over my shoulder, bringing it down from its constant weight. My shoes are tracking mud, hearing the constant squish noise from the moisture.

The sky dims as I take my eyes off the ground, my neck instantly cracking. The sun slips into soft half-light, one that makes everything look like a dream.

Philo left my house hours ago, and the moment he did I left for the river. I needed to feel close to my mother again, anything to feel again. Whether it was sorrow, anger, pain, or just doubt, I just needed to feel it. *The only thing worth feeling is the blade across my--*

I shake my head, rubbing my tired eyes as I turn the corner of the street and enter my front yard. I could feel a presence the moment I entered, and there he was on my front porch.

D.J., sitting on the steps with his arms resting on his knees. He didn't notice me at first, regardless of my loud steps. His head is lowered, strained, as if he is deep in thought, a feeling I am familiar with. Eventually he looked up, feeling my presence as I did his, and stood up slowly. His eyes scan over mine as they hold the familiar concern that both torments and comforts me. I stand across from him as I reached my stairs, him towering over me with just steps above.

"What are you doing here?" I asked flatly. *He shouldn't be here; I shouldn't have him in my life. I don't deserve him.*

"I did not see you at school," D.J. responded, his eyes trying to find mine as I looked anywhere but his face.

"So?" I play with my hands, instinctively reaching for the only bracelet that brings me comfort, only to see him wearing it.

"Do not be like that River, something is off. I wanted to check on you," D.J. says, coming down the few steps as he lands on the same level as me. I am leaning against the railing as he is still in his spot across from me.

I stared at him. Just that. Something he said, no, the *way* he said it—how simple it came out—broke through the numbness. No matter what, no matter how, I can't shut D.J. out if he shows up. *You mean again?*

D.J. steps closer, just a step, but the tension grew instantly with that little step.

"Are you okay?" He asks. I twisted my head up to finally meet his gaze.

"Why would you ask that stupid question?"

"To see if you would tell me the truth or not," D.J. says, ignoring my attitude. He did not hesitate whatsoever. "What is in your mind River?"

I look away, breaking our gaze as I look down the street. If I don't look at him, he can't read me as easily. *He can't break the dam I tried so hard to build.*

I take a deep breath before spitting out an answer.

"I just wanted to go through the attic. My mom's stuff. Never really got around to it." I say, my fingers unconsciously find my mother's necklace.

"How come?" D.J. asks; he tilts his head to the side, gaining a closer look at my face as he scans it.

"It's just hard to do alone."

"Is your father not there to do so? Even after the years?" D.J. asks innocently.

Despite his concern, my blood boils at the questions. He means well, I know he does, but my father being brought up just brings anger and sorrow towards our relationship, if you can even call it that.

I can feel my jaw clenching, my fingers rubbing against my wrist hard. I coughed a few times, clearing my throat of the ache that appeared within seconds.

"He's just...occupied." It was the safest truth I could spit out; it leaves the details of the reality of things, of a situation that I do not need pity from. I have had enough of that for a lifetime. *A short one at that.* Moments of silence passed, just seconds really. I look down at my wrist, my fingers traveling over each bead as I feel D.J.'s eyes directly on me.

"Come on," D.J. says, instantly grabbing my cold hand into his warm ones.

We walked up the porch and headed to my house. Only seven steps are taken before we make it to my rustic door. D.J. turns to me as he waits for me to open it. I look at him sideways, waiting for him to let go of my hand and walk away. He never did; I don't think he ever will.

I open the door with ease, no keys needed. D.J. holds a confused look as we enter my house. Our footsteps enter the hall that leads into the living room and the staircase to my bedroom, along with the attic. I headed up the stairs, each one feeling heavier than the other. I feel D.J's body heat following mine as we climb the stairs.

I enter my room first, expecting D.J. to follow as I place my bag onto the desk. I turn to see D.J. by the doorframe, leaning against it as he only looks at me, nothing else.

"You know you don't have to-"

"I know River. I want to," D.J. cuts me off.

He walks away from the doorframe and heads towards the other side of the hall, by the only other door that exists on this floor: the attic.

I walk out of my room, my breath catching as I see D.J. leaning against the windowsill, his arms crossed and his face contents. Nothing is showing, no emotion, no pity.

"Ready?" He asks, patiently waiting for my answer, except it never came. I nodded, resulting in D.J. coming towards me. My head goes down, looking at the bare wood floors as my hands get sweaty and my chest feels like it will rip out.

I don't think I am ready, I don't think I ever will be. I accepted my mother is dead, but I don't think I can accept seeing the things she touched last have collected dust. I can feel myself getting lightheaded as grief washes over me. My mind is starting to spiral, in and out, all around me. Like lightning, not knowing the place it will strike next.

I can feel a hand under my chin, lifting it with ease as it pulls my thoughts together. I look up to see D.J. and his stern eyes. A forest that is filled with comforting air and trees that bring serenity.

"Let me be here Charli, trust me to be here," D.J. says, comforting me before the internal battle I am about to face.

I nod my head, and D.J. lets go of my chin, turning to open the door. The same familiar creak echoes as it slowly gives way. The tension kicks in instantly. I can feel her—my mother—even from a distance. I can feel the love pouring out of the attic, like it had been trapped, waiting all these years to be released.

Something about it pulls me in. I move before I can think, drawn like a moth to a flame. I'm in front of D.J., climbing the stairs so fast, he must catch my hip to keep me from falling. His hands—soft and steady—wrap around me like a shield. I mutter a quiet thank you before continuing upward.

It takes 14 steps before we enter. The scent is filled with dust and time, memories all frozen. D.J. guides us as we move around, heads low to not hit the ceiling. The small space evokes a whole old world, one filled with boxes of Halloween decorations; fake cobwebs, tangled string lights, and costume bins.

My mother and I were always obsessed with Halloween, truly it was our favorite holiday. *No wonder you pretend something you're not.*

D.J. laugh pulls me out of my trance. I look behind me and see he is holding up a purple fairy costume. I smiled at the image in front of me, the boy that shared the memory with me and the friend that gave me the strength to do this.

"Remember this? Your mom made me wear wings one year with you since you complained Shaya and Lio had matching costumes," D.J. said as he placed the costume back down. "She even called me "forest guardian" or something like that," D.J. chuckles out.

I crack a smile at the thought. Barely, softly. But it was real.

"You literally cried because it had glitter on it," I say as I smirk towards him.

"You cried because I stole your candy," D.J. responds sharing the same smirk, which makes me drop mine and side eye him.

D.J. grins as he tosses me a witch hat, "Here, it matches with your attitude you throw around." I catch it instinctively and dust it off before placing it on my head. For a moment, everything felt simple. Light. The heaviness lifted just enough for us to laugh like we were eight again, just moments before tragedy shattered our world. *Not ours, just yours.*

I dug deeper into one of the boxes, rummaging through the endless decorations that piled up. I pulled out a small, dusty scrapbook. Or at least it looked like it at first glance. I can feel the soft cover as its soft cover cushioned slightly against the hardwood binder.  I blow off the dust and wipe it repeatedly until a familiar object comes into view.

My baby book.

I can feel the air shift around me. I sit crossed-legged onto the dense wood. The book lays on my lap, my fingers brushing over the faded pink cover. D.J. grew quiet and stopped rummaging through the boxes. I can tell he felt my energy; anyone can in this moment.

I can feel him on my side as he copies my movements and sits alongside. He leans closer, watching my fingers tremble as I flip the pages. A soft smile appears on my face as I see photos of a chubby baby with tufts of dark hair, birthday cards, and little notes in my mom's handwriting.

I can feel my eyes starting to brim with tears as my fingers brush over my mother's handwriting—elegant cursive that danced across the page, full of warmth and care.

"You were a cute baby," D.J. breaks the silence.

I chuckled, looking at him to see him already staring at me.

"Don't lie, it doesn't suit you."

He doesn't respond. He can only focus on me—the book was no longer the center of attention in his eyes. I can feel the tension build up, captivating me in mere seconds. The cool breath that brushes against my cheek, realizing now how close he truly is.

My back was to the wall, the one that shared a tiny window, the only source of light other than the light switch. D.J. was only in front of me; his knees brought to his chest as his arms held it lazily. I dare to bring my gaze to his, our eyes instantly locked. I can see his pupils dilate.

"I would never lie to you River."

Something shifted. The air, the vibe. *Tenderness.* Something is left unspoken between us. Neither of us knew what to say next, what to do. Though I can speak for myself, I knew I did not want to move an inch, to live in this moment that brings me clarity.

Only then does the universe speak for both of us. I can feel something fall out of the book from my lap, hitting the floor simultaneously.

A letter.

I reach for it, breaking away from D.J.'s gaze, as I frown at the unfamiliar envelope. I slowly unfold it, only to tremble. My eyes scanned the page over again, multiple times; it was only the first few sentences. Still, the handwriting was my mother's, but it wasn't comforting or loving; it was urgent, messy, irregular from the rest of the book.

I've been wondering about the river again. About how it used to mean something different—before everything got messy. It was ours once. ~~Wasn't it always?~~

I used to believe I could be safe with either of them. ~~I was, wasn't I?~~ That there was still good in both. Maybe I was just young. Or blind. ~~Or stupid.~~

*One of them loved me. The other needed control. And I let them both in, thinking I could keep them separate I should've known better. They are best friends after all. ~~A pair I destroyed.~~*

*He doesn't forgive me. I see that now. He pretends, save, but I watched it in his eyes—he waits. I feel the silence was enough. That if I just stopped talking, it would all stay buried. But the past isn't buried easily—not when someone is still digging.*

*I don't think he believes I'd stay quiet forever. I haven't told anyone. Not even my Charlotte baby, especially not her.*

*But I know that he knows. That's what terrifies me.*

I can feel my face turn pale. The words I read haunt me, just like a nightmare. The digging, the bury, the mystery.

*Why? What happened?*

She was scared, as was I. I couldn't feel anything, I couldn't breathe. I can feel my chest tighten, begging for air to come through, but I don't let it go. My face is breaking apart, and I blink rapidly.

*Did I just find her suicide note? Was it one? Did she really commit? After all these years of doubting?*

"Charli?" I can hear D.J.'s voice, barely. It sounds so distant, like he is miles away when he is next to me.

I didn't answer as I dropped the letter on my lap. My foot shaking along with my hands; I can feel the coldness spread from my hands to my whole body, instantly and slowly.

I stare straight ahead, looking at D.J. as he fades out. I can feel him shift beside me, trying to get in front of me to read me, to help me. *Not when someone is still digging. Why are you digging Charlotte baby? You never meant to know.*

I feel my hands gripping my hair, a feeling so familiar that it is hurtful. D.J. leans towards me, his warm hands over mine. I squeeze my eyes shut, not wanting to see the concern in his eyes. I cannot do this. I can't, I don't want to. I should never have done this. *I'm too weak.*

*Was someone after her? This can't be a suicide letter. I must dig. Dig. Dig. Dig.*

My breath continues to turn shallow. The words underneath me are blurred as my eyes blink rapidly. Only a moment passed as the letter was taken from my lap, only for D.J. to return it. A strange, drowning feeling claws at my chest.

"Hey, hey. River, look at me." D.J. says, trying to pull my hands away from my grip on my hair. It hurts so badly. I can feel a headache forming.

I shake my head, trying to push him away. I push and push. Like a robot, it is the only mechanism I have built in. D.J. never moved an inch, his goal of removing my hands worked, but only for me to push him against the chest. I can feel my throat tighten up; words try to form only to fall. Tears are blocking my vision, and I just feel torn. *Defeated.*

I pushed D.J. five times, trying six when he takes my shoulders and my hands instantly fall into my lap. The letter crumbled in my hands. I want to rip it, burn it, and erase it but I can't. It's the only piece of truth that I have received in years.

D.J. wraps me in his arms, stroking my hair as he holds me. I can feel his breath on my forehead as he breathes heavily and smoothly.

"Breathe with me Charli, I cannot let you go until you do," D.J. says as he rubs my temples. "Just breathe with me, please."

And I finally did. I clutch onto D.J.'s shirt, a fist full of it as it hurts to breathe. I can feel the sobs threatening to come out, making me squeeze harder.

"Let it out River, you are with me. You are safe, let it go." D.J. whispered softly. His voice fills my ears, breaking my dam instantly. The waves fall over, flooding the entire area.

I finally let go. I cry so intensely that it makes D.J. grip on me harder. I scream as I continue to cry. My chest is burning with emotion. Burning with rage and confusion. With fear and desire.

# *Sailor Song* *Gigi*

## *Perez*

November 3, 2023

    I always wondered about the knowledge that the world has to offer. The power it holds if it's hidden or not. To what extent is it enough, though? Does knowledge matter if there is no emotion to tie into it?

    Would people trade endless knowledge for lack of emotions? To find answers to every problem that exists. Would that be humane if people learned about everything and nothing at the same time? Or would it be predictable to feel raw emotion, even if one were to act on it or not.

The thoughts tangle in my head like thread in a storm. I don't know when they started or where they ended.

A loud scrape of chairs pulls me back. I blink and drop my pen, the ink bleeding across the page as D.J. and Lio make their way to the table. I hear constant conversations all over the lunchroom, trying to focus on my own voice. I blink a few times, massaging the cramps away from my hands. All my thoughts were scattered—like I was trying to grab something that was constantly slipping through my fingers.

Emilio slides into the seat next to Shaya, with D.J. taking the seat next to me. I could feel the weight of their conversation, freely but also constricting. It didn't reach me, just endless thoughts. *Does any of this even matter?* I was listening from a distance. Like watching my friends from a fishbowl as they move around smoothly as I am trapped in water that I am forced to breathe in.

D.J. nudges me, with his sharp ass elbows might I add. His presence is solid, grounded in the distant haze.

"Charli," he says.

"Hm?" I say, looking down at my notebook, with the red ink splattered across the page.

"Shaya just asked you something."

I looked up, blinking a few times to concentrate on Shaya, who was waiting for an answer. I can see her lips moving but hear no words coming out, or at least not catching onto it. A second passed before she managed to repeat the question. *You drive your friends crazy, insane even.*

"Do you want to come to my game after school?" Shaya asked, her voice laced with concern.

I ignore the looks of my friends as I rub my eyes, feeling the world fade away. I glanced at D.J., only for a second, not sure how to respond. He was already looking at me, with a small smile on his lips.

"I am only going if she decides to go," D.J. chimed in, nudging me again. This time his voice is soft but insistent.

Lio leaned across from the table, a smirk written all over his face. "Well, Charls, look like you've got no choice but to go. I'm not going alone—someone's got to cheer for Shaya the loudest."

I bit my lip hard, trying to ignore the guilt that gnaws at me. I wanted to go, I truly did, but for the past two weeks I have been out of touch. I have been ignoring everything around me, trying to just rush out of school to go to the river, repeatedly. It's not fair to my friends, especially to the ones who have been there for ages. I sucked my breath in, releasing it slowly.

"I'll go," I muttered, forcing a shrug to show. I wanted to escape this feeling I have been dragging along. A feeling that engulfed me since I cried in D.J.'s arms. *Embarrassing really.*

The conversation shifted, the sound of laughter and chatter that I tried to follow but, in the end, it remained out of my focus.

A few moments later, like a switch, Quinn shows up at the table, her presence unwelcome as ever. *Just like you?*

I share her a fake smile, squinting my eyes towards her, a gesture I know for sure would irritate her. Quinn rolled her eyes as if I were the one that was bothering her. It's not like I came to her, the delusional girl decided to come over here.

Before Quinn could speak, Shaya jumped in. "No one wants you here," she said, her voice sharp and cold. Quinn's expression darkened, but she didn't argue. Instead, she shot a pointed glare at me, in which I blew her a kiss. A wink would overdo it.

She grabs D.J.'s arm and drags him away. I catch a glimpse of the face he made, only for a moment when he connects his gaze to mine. He looked annoyed but followed without protest. His eyebrows come together, showing confusion. *I should've stopped him. He looked uncomfortable.* I shake my head as I let him go.

In earshot, Shaya continued to talk shit about Quinn; her words spit out hate and spite. I see Lio shaking his head from the corner of my eye, him sharing the same confused look D.J. was wearing just a moment ago.

"I don't get it," Lio muttered, following his gaze behind me towards D.J. sitting at the table with Thea, Cameron, and Queen wannabe. I turn back around to my friends once D.J. catches my eye.

"Why does he hang out with someone like her?" Emilio talks to himself as he bites his apple. Shaya answers his question, saying her brother is just stupid to realize he has a choice.

I didn't answer at all. I couldn't; not when my own mind is at war with me physically, making me chase any type of sanity I can grasp, though every time I try it is just out of reach.

The bell shrieks at 12:30 pm, yanking me from whatever daze I'd drifted to. I shove my half-eaten sandwich aside as everyone gathers their bags. Fifth period stretches before me like a tunnel, one with no ending. A tunnel that drags before me, one I do not want to walk through—physics, history, mathematics, English—four more classes before the tunnel shows the facade of an ending.

I drift through each room on autopilot. Repeating the same actions within each 40 minutes increments. Get in, sit down, write in my notebook, and ignore my teacher. It was only English class that I was dreading. Every. Single. Time. My teacher, Mrs. Cailo, likes to get engaged but it never works. I usually spend my last period in the office, an escape from the stares of my peers and educators.

Nonetheless, all my teachers' voices blended, creating one nuisance of noise. White noise is all I hear as my notebook gets filled one page after another. When I have nothing else to write, I stimulate my mind by tapping with my pen, creating a rhythm that distracts me.

My notebook sits unopened; the letter burned behind my eyelids every time I tried to close it. By the time the final bell rang at 2:40, I can hardly remember what I learned today.

My body moves by itself, like I am a ghost in my own body. Shaya catches my arm in the hallway. Her cheerful but focused energy surrounds us as we head to the gym.

The game doesn't start until another hour, but the coach likes to have that time to warm up. *Stay warm,* she used to say. *Never get cold,* she barked out. If only she knew that is the only feeling that brings me comfort. Familiar pain, familiar frigidness.

As we walk down the hallway, D.J. joins the two of us. I am between the two friends that I had for a lifetime, my third one is God knows where.

"Where's Lio?" I asked smoothly.

"How should I know? Ask his girl." D.J. says teasingly. He holds his smirk which causes me to eyeroll as I look towards Shaya. She shrugs as we enter the gym and leaves to go to the locker room.

If anything, I can remember, Shaya does not play games. Nobody can pull her out when she is concentrating on something. D.J. and I make our way to the bleachers, not stopping until we reach the fifth row. No one was there yet, at least not in the crowd. All around us are buzzing conversations and routines flying around through the air.

As time passes, some people join the crowd: streamers unfurl, cheerleaders practice their cheers, pep-band horns bare their warm-up riffs. The mid-day afternoon sun peers through the window, painting everything gold in the process.

D.J. sits close enough that I can feel the heat radiating off his black bomber jacket, but neither of us speaks as we watch the scene around us. Witnessing people with different lives, a life that I yearn for. *A normal one.*

At some point I can feel a nudge on my side. I take off my headphones and lay them against my shoulders. I look over to D.J. who is looking out onto the court. It takes him about a minute before he glances my way—his eyes automatically stuck.

"You alright?" he asks quietly. I almost missed it with noises echoing in and outside my mind.

I blink, one...two...three...four times. Slowly, I tried to shake the fuzziness in my head.

"I didn't get the chance to sleep," I say, holding my contact with D.J., his eyes piercing through me, trying to search for something.

I can see his jaw tighten; he holds the gaze once more before looking towards the court again. I can see his knuckles being tightened, rubbing hard against one another. It is almost like looking at myself, looking at the same internal battle of thoughts fighting against one another. *I caused that. The torment.*

"You know what I've noticed recently?" I say, trying to level out the tension between us.

D.J. glances over his shoulder as his elbow leans against his one knee—his head resting in his hands.

"What is that, River?"

"You never use contractions," I say, earning furrowed brows to appear on D.J.'s face. Though the rest holds amusement, a glint in his eyes as he holds onto every word I say.

I continue, "You'd never say "I'm" or "can't" --it's always "I am" or "cannot." How come?"

As I finish my point, I see D.J.'s small smile appearing. He lets out a little laugh, turning his gaze towards the crowd that comes through the door. We've noticed together that the opposing team has arrived—Shaya's team made their way to the court for warmups.

"Very observant, are we?" D.J. asks, laughter laces in his words. I shrugged the words off, returning his glint of a smile.

"Are you going to answer my question?" I question.

"Depends on if you are going to answer mine."

I arch my eyebrow at him, "Which question is that?"

He leans over, our faces almost inches apart. Just enough for one another to breathe but close enough to feel it.

"Why do you keep torturing yourself?" he asks bluntly. The words hit me like a brick. I am now turning my whole attention to him. My eyes glued to him, never leaving his figure.

I see his eyes soften; his face relaxes. "You do not have to answer now River. But when you are ready, I will share my answer with you. Promise." D.J. says surely. He looks away from me, looking towards the game as it is about to start. He doesn't move from his position, still as close as ever.

Before I can respond, if I can, the missing Emilio pops up. He is holding a giant poster that is rolled up, arms full of nachos and soda. Lio grins at us as he sits opposite D.J., with me between them. He sets the poster down between his legs before passing us snacks.

"Fuel for the fight, yeah?" he says, beaming, causing both me and D.J. to chuckle as I shake my head.

The whistle blows, announcing the start of the game. At the crack of the tip, Lio shoves his nachos in my lap, catching me by surprise as he opens his poster and stands up. He cheers loudly with the cheerleaders, might as well be one himself.

Just like that, for the next hour or so, there are no rivers, no ghost attic, no crumbled letters—just the roar of the crowd and the thump of the basketball hardwood.

# *Photograph* *Ed*

# *Sheeran*

November 6, 2023

I've learned a lot about the people around me. How their situations or past struggles can influence my own actions. It's the thought behind it that can lead people to regret, uncertainty, and even remorse. Though other actions can shape one to become wise, emotionally intelligent, and human.

That word: human. It is the only word defining people compared to the expectation they brought onto themselves. Many are overachievers that fall short, and others are underachievers who gain it all. Though many people, like me, are stuck in the middle; the grey void that many do not talk about enough.

Those who are forgotten because they were once so fortunate even when life hits them with a brick.

My pen scratched against the lined paper of my notebook as I sit hunched over on the couch. The living room was bathed in a dim, lazy sort of light—one that only came around late Sunday afternoons, slipping through the blinds in thin, golden slants. Outside the world seems so quiet, so serene compared to the ticking clock that hides inside the walls.

The front door creaked open, gaining instant attention. I barely lifted my head up before I heard the familiar drunk mumbling. My father stumbled in, the stale smell of whiskey and cigarettes clinging to him like a second skin. He mumbled something to himself, words blurring together, before he disappeared into the kitchen. Ignoring the world around him along with me.

I return to writing in my notebook, letting the ink guide my mind somewhere else—somewhere safer. The feeling of the same couch beneath me brings out the memory within itself.

*Not old, but softer, newer holding my tiny frame between my parents. My mother's arm wrapped loosely around her shoulders, my father's laughter rumbling from deep within his chest as the movie plays on the television. A laugh so genuine that the smile still lingers on his face as the scene unfolds itself.*

*A movie in which my parents bicker about, my dad saying that it was cheesy as the two spies fall in love with one another between car chases and rooftop battles.*

*My dad groaned at the kissing scenes, covering his face with the throw pillow—the one with a little cherry in the middle.*

*"Love isn't cheesy," my mother teased, elbowing my father from over me. "It's fulfilling. Even you know that."*

*I look up to my parents, their eyes staying on each other, love lingering in the looks they give one another. Even in the middle of them, I can feel the comfort radiating off their bodies and piercing mine.*

*My father grins at my mother, pulling her into a soft headlock, squishing me in the process. "You're lucky you're cute."*

*"Dad, you're squishing me," I call out, feeling my parent's bodies between me.*

*"Oh, I am, aren't I?" My dad says before laying his whole body on me. His body weight instantly crushed mine, just enough that I could breathe.*

*Our laughter fills up the room, thick and wholesome.*

I reel into the memory, like a blanket, the warmth lingering.

Until it was ripped away.

The slap came out of nowhere. A crack of skin against the skin. My head snapped sideways, my cheek stung as it burned instantly. The metallic taste of blood is blooming on my tongue. The room blurs on its edges, and for a moment, I thought I might pass out on the couch, desperately not wanting to wake up.

My father was looming over me, unsteady but full of anger. His hand still hovering over me like he was not finished.

"Who are you to ignore me?" He spat out, low and dangerous.

I stay frozen, one hand hovering over my lap, the other inching towards my fallen notebook. The pages fluttering where it had landed, calling out to me to retrieve it.

Before I can reach it, my dad grabs the notebook first, ripping it from the floor with a violent jerk. He flips through the pages, my life, my words, and my *dignity*. His face contorting as he skimmed my handwriting—the private, desperate words that were never meant for him.

"You're just like her," he slurred, shoving the notebook against my chest but still had it in his hands. The push was so hard that I stumbled back onto the couch. "Always writing. Always thinkin' you're better than me."

I pushed myself up, desperately, "Give it back," I croaked out. My voice barely went above a whisper.

I lunged for it irrationally. Terrible mistake.

My dad shoved me back, and this time, when I tried again, he drew his arm out and drove a fist to my ribs. The force knocked all the air out of me. My side is on fire at this point.

Before I can curl away, another punch lands me just below my chest—then another. One after the other. Each hit a brutal, calculated strike, aimed at hurting but not leaving marks where people can see.

I folded in on myself, preparing for the next hit. Each one brings me closer to the numbness that calls out to me. My arms are covering my face, but it never mattered—he wasn't aiming there. It was more of a way to shield my expression; the betrayal I felt every single time.

A fist to my stomach had me retching, choking out for air as a gasp leaves my lips with no permission. Tears spring to my eyes, not from emotion, but from the sheer, unbearable ache radiating from my core.

Still, he kept going. A fist to my thigh. A forearm slamming against my hip. I hear him muttering to himself more than to me. The sharp jolt of pain made my vision blur around the edges, making the world fray and come apart.

Through the haze, I hear the same words repeatedly.

"Ungrateful," hit. "Just," hit. "Like," hit. "Her," numb.

Finally, he staggered back. Still holding my notebook in his hands, clutching onto it like it is his. He disappeared into the kitchen once again, the sound of the beer bottle clinking against the counter echoing through the silent household. He passes me as he heads to his room, on the other side of the living room.

I laid there, curled myself onto the couch—the same couch that once had been my shield against the world. Now it feels like a slab of ice on my dead, battered body.

Each breath was shallow and sharp; every movement sent fresh pain ricocheting through my ribs, my stomach, and legs. Despite the pain, my mind was in my notebook. The one taken away from me. My words, memories, and life.

I just layed on the couch, staring at the ceiling, feeling myself drifting away with each heaved breath. I feel myself leaning away from the little girl that once sat on this couch, laughing between my parents as the world outside fades away.

*Don't move.* I think. *Just breathe. Be...quiet.*

~~~~~~~~~~

It was late when I stirred. The world outside had melted into black, the only light in the living room coming from the flickering streetlamp just beyond the window.

My body screamed the moment I shifted. A stabbing, radiating pain bolted through my ribs, stomach, my legs—at this point my whole fucking presence.

I stayed still for a while longer, breathing through my nose, my teeth clenched together against the whimper I wouldn't let escape. Every inhaling scrape against my chest was like sandpaper, feeling the burn consuming me.

Through the muted walls of the house, I heard it—the faint slam of the door earlier. Heavy footsteps dragging down
~~~~~~~~~~

the porch steps. The sputtering ignition of the old truck my dad drove told me he was gone.

*Perfect.*

Maybe for an hour. Maybe for the whole night. *I can care less.*

I pushed myself up, every movement warned against my body. *I really am his punching bag. At least he noticed me this time.* It took longer than I am willing to admit, holding myself together like cracked porcelain. I clutched my side as I shuffled toward his bedroom, the house groaning under my weight like it pitied me.

His door was waiting for me, taunting me to come in. The darkness swallowed me whole as I pushed the door open. The smell hit first. Thick and oppressive, a sour smell of whiskey, sweat, and something rotten clinging to the air—stuck to the walls. The room was a wreck—clothes piled like bodies on the floor; broken picture frames face down on the dresser; stale beer bottles on the nightstand.

I covered my nose with the sleeve of my sweatshirt, wincing as I limped across the room. *He could have done so much worse.*

There—half-hidden in the drawer of the nightstand, I saw it. My notebook. I reached for it, my fingers trembling. As I tugged it free, something else clinked against it. I froze.

Inside the drawer, shoved to the side beneath crumpled receipts and cigarette packs, was an old flip-phone. My mother's phone.

I snatched it without thinking, not worried about the consequences. I cradle it against my chest like a wounded bird; *except I am the one wounded.* The plastic was warm, too warm, like it had been touched recently. My heart rattles in my ribcage.

Notebook and phone in hand, I backed out of the room, closing the door with a soft click. The hallway stretched in front of me like a tunnel. I willed myself upstairs, one slow, agonizing step at a time. Each movement sent lightning bolts through my side. Nevertheless, I forced my body to obey.

Finally, I collapsed onto my bed, curling into the blankets without caring for the pain. My hands scrambled to flip open the phone. The screen lit up, dim and grainy. Battery: one bar. *Great.*

I worked fast, ignoring the way my fingers shook. First photo. There she was—Mom.

Smiling at me through the years, holding my younger self in her arms, frozen in a thousand little moments, I forgot I even lived. I can feel the warmth radiating from the screen. I let out a small, broken smile slip onto my lips.

Swipe.

More photos—except this time it was her around my age now. She wasn't alone. Two boys. Teenager. One with shaggy hair, one wearing a crooked grin. Both draped casually over my mom's shoulders like they were there.

My stomach twisted. They look familiar to me, but I don't know them. Then, the battery icon blinked urgently.

I dove into the messages. Most were junk—old, years-old messages—but one stood out.

No contact name. Just a number, same area code.

```
She deserves to know, Astrid. You can't avoid
this.
```

A message sent on October 1, 2014. Just a few days before my mom's death.

The screen flickered. Panic rose like a tidal wave inside me, choking off my airflow. The room tilted, the walls pressing closer.

"No, no, no," I whispered, frantically scrolling, trying to find more—anything—but before I could open the rest, the screen went black. Dead.

I sat there, clutching the useless device to my chest. My body hurt, my chest heaved, and my mind spiraled faster than I could stop it. *Who was that? Why? What happened to my mother? Who is "she"? Was it me? Was it my mother?*

*My mother. My mother. My mother. Dead. Dead. Dead.*

*One...two...three...four...five. This. Is. Not. Working. Six...Seven...*

Thoughts continued to collide int one another, disjointed, frantic. *Who was after her? Did she do this to herself? Why was she scared?*

I had to move. I had to leave. I tore open my drawers, stuffing my notebook into my bag, yanking at the first sweater my hands could find. My hands were numb, working on autopilot. I didn't even bother tying my sneakers. *It's a good thing you lace them correctly. One thing you're useful for.*

Before I can think I am outside, feeling the cool wind, like a slap as it was cold and heavy. Down the streets, the one I once ran down as I was crying, screaming, concerning my neighbors. I pass the houses with dark windows, past the familiar cracks in the sidewalk.

I walked fast, faster, my feet pounding against the pavement, but inside I was slipping. The world blurred at the edges. Streetlights melted into smears. Every breath continued to burn. My mind raced—*her face, the boys, the letter, the message. Lies. All fucking lies.*

I didn't know where I was going until the park came into view. The one where I cried for her for the first time. The place had once been a wound and a salve all at once.

It is midnight now. The swings creaked. The trees whispered secrets I couldn't understand. The grass was wet under my shoes.

I stumbled to the bench, dropped my whole tiresome body, and let the weight of everything I have been carrying crush me.

# *As the World Caves in*
*Matt Maltese*

November 7, 2023

Depression is unconventional. It is hard to measure something that many people have a shitload of symptoms for. People take a razor to their skin one night and then smile at their friends the very next day; sweaters and bracelets being worn as a cover-up, distracting them from anything and anyone.

Then you have people with no physical scars, only for the mental ones to get worse. Though people can't truly know because they can't measure the pain when the mind attacks its host.

A whole generation can have depression; would it still be ruled as a sickness if the jobs get done and the world keeps spinning?

The swing chains moaned in the breeze as I curled tighter on the bench, trying to stay small, invisible. *Not possible.* My hands were clammy and cold around the dead phone, my mind still spinning in frantic circles I couldn't slow down.

Footsteps scuffed against the gravel path. I didn't lift my head up, I couldn't. Out of the corner of my eye, a figure climbed down the old slide—the one while a kid I would play all day on. Too big for it now, all long limbs and hunched shoulders, the figure came closer. D.J.

He didn't say anything at first. Just walked over with that same heavy energy, one dragging us both down in the dark. His hoodie was wrinkled; hands shoved into his pockets. He dropped down onto the other end of the bench like it hurt him to move.

For a second, we just sat there. Two broken pieces too jagged to fit together. D.J. pulled out a blunt from his pocket and offered it wordlessly between his two fingers. I take it reluctantly, hands trembling that I try to ignore.

I just held it, staring at it, as tear stains lay on my face like they were attached to me. I imagine not lighting it, as if I clung onto it a while longer then it wouldn't fall apart. *Not like my sad case I call life.*

"I don't have a lighter," I say nonchalantly. I breathe in hard, wincing quietly.

"Here." D.J. muttered, his voice rough like he hadn't used it in a while. He passes me a small red lighter, one that looks impossible to hold in his enormous hands.

As I started to light it, the heat from the lighter spreading towards my hands, D.J. leaned back. He is sprawled out over the bench behind him, staring at the black sky like he could punch a hole through it with his mind. Once lit, I take a big hit, desperate for the pain to wither away, physically and mentally. My lungs refuse the drug intake, but my mind is much more powerful.

"You are not home," D.J. says after a while, almost like it wasn't a question. I hand him the blunt that he takes remotely.

"Home is a generous word for where I barely sleep." I breathed out, shakily.

He made a small noise, almost like a laugh but with no humor behind it. I stare at the ground, watching the shadows stretch and warp under the streetlight. The phone weighed itself in my pocket. Heavy. Burning. My fingers itched.

Wanting to have it in my hands, the blunt replaces the tingly feeling. The effect of the weed slips into my body, disguising the pain that spreads.

*I should tell him. No, he is here, too. Why? What happened?*

My words are caught in my throat, thick and heavy. *What good does it do by telling him? How can he help? I am just destructive, waiting for someone else to bury me.*

"What's wrong?" I asked, my voice barely above a whisper.

For a moment there was silence as D.J. takes a hit from the half-blunt, the light hitting his face exactly right to see the purple streak in his jet-black hair. It falls to cover part of his eye only for the rest to rest right above his shoulders. He leaves the hair covering his face, not bothering to move it as dark, emerald eyes look out on the other side of the park.

"I can ask you the same question, River." He responds, mainly to himself.

I just stared at him, trying to understand the storm behind the silence. Only for a second he looks at me, his eyes captivating as they drip with pain. His eyes are low, and his shoulders sink into his body. His jaw flexes in the dark, shadows shape his face but also hide it in the right places. *Two wounds of the same cut.*

As if he can read my mind, D.J. shakes his head before passing the blunt back. "I will be fine River," he huffed out, like he was trying to convince himself more than me.

"Aren't you the one who always says you don't have to be?" I question, catching D.J.'s attention. I lift one eyebrow, blunt in mouth, finishing off the blunt before throwing it away from us.

I turn my face back to him, thinking about the struggle he must endure.

"Not around me," I say. D.J. nods slowly, but surely. I don't push him further, I just need him to know that I'm there for him, like he is there for me. Someone he can trust. *Can he though?*

I squeezed my eyes shut, feeling the old familiar fear curl around my ribs. Trust wasn't something I handed out anymore. Trust got me hurt. D.J. didn't say anything, but his hand brushed against mine on the bench. Just a moment, reminding me that he is here, present.

If there was anyone...anyone at all...

My voice cracked when I spoke. "I found my mom's old phone."

D.J. didn't flinch, just stared, waiting. He didn't press me; he was just there. He turned his head slightly towards me, waiting for me to continue.

"There was this message...before she died. Someone said," I pause, trying to catch my words before they fall out. My breathing picked up, hands found my necklace unconsciously, the same routine.

Still D.J. waited patiently; he moved closer to me on the bench. His arm wrapped around my shoulders, lightly not suffocating.

I find the strength to continue, "Someone said that she deserved to know, but it wasn't directed towards my mother. As if they were talking about someone else. I don't even know what it means," I said, the words tumbling out too fast, like if I stopped, I would drown.

My hands cling harder to my necklace, shaking harder, thinking back on the day I just endured. *My dad. Hit. Hit. Hit. Cellphone. She deserves to know Astrid.*

"It's like—I don't even know anymore. Who was it for? Her? Me? I don't know if she was scared. The letter, now this? Was someone after her? Did someone- no, D.J. this insane." My throat is closed. I swallowed hard, forcing it down.

D.J. stayed silent. He just held me, listening to my words. I can see his mind puzzling, trying to put the pieces together. Though he never opened his mouth, no, he never tried to make the situation neat. He always lets reality be what it is: painful, disturbing, and endless.

When I finally ran out of words, when the anger and fear burned down to ash inside me, D.J. sat forward. He lifts his shoulders from around me. His elbows rest on his knees, looking like he is in deep thought.

"You ever give tattoos to people spiraling out of their heads?" he asks quietly. I blinked at him, the sudden shift catching me off guard.

"What?"

He flashes a tired, crooked grin. "Could use some fresh ink. Distract the both of us."

I stared at him for a long moment before a shaky, reluctant laugh broke out in me. I see D.J.'s grin turns into a genuine smile. "You're an idiot."

"Never claimed otherwise," he said, standing and offering me his hand, "Come on, Picasso."

And just like that we left the park, where we once again held each other emotionally against the cruel world.

~~~~~~~~~~~~~~~~~~~~

I'm in D.J.'s room, one I haven't been in since I was a mere child. His room smelled like smoke and worn-out cologne. A hint of lavender, just merely. So faint and familiar.

D.J. slouched into the desk chair while I rifled through the small tattoo kit. We stopped by my house, very briefly, before heading to his. My kit opens like a suitcase, one that is filled with gloves, needles, stencil paper, and my machinery.

D.J. shoves his left hand towards me.

"Side of the ring finger," he said. "Small dandelion."

I looked at him as I pulled over an extra chair. Getting my tattoo things in place; my black, latex gloves clinging onto me like a second skin. "Why a dandelion?"

He didn't answer right away. Just shrugged, eyes trained somewhere over my shoulder, like he was watching ghosts pass through the walls.

"Something I would rather keep to myself."

I smirked, placing the stencil carefully on his finger. "What fun is that to keep from your tattoo artist?"

He chuckled lowly, almost to himself, then rolled his eyes without looking at me. "Someone close to me...I have not seen them in a long time. They always liked dandelions." His voice dropped at the end, something tender and sad stitched between his words.

I can only think of his father, the parent he had lost many years ago. A stab that was never stitched and only a Band-Aid placed.
~~~~~~~~~~~~~~~~~~~~

I didn't push. Just nodded and started working. I can feel D.J. stare at me the whole time, like if he looked away, he might lose something. For 15 minutes the air was comfortable, like two long lost souls intertwined with one another once again. No words being spoken to utterly understand one another.

When I finished wiping the ink away gently, D.J. flexed his fingers to see the tiny, fine-lined dandelion on the side of his finger. His mouth lifted with the barest hint of a smile.

"You are sleeping here tonight," he said. Telling, not asking.

I opened my mouth to argue, but he was already texting Shaya to stay at Lio's, already moving like it was decided. I sighed, heart heavy but light at the same time.

"Fine," I muttered. I move to clean up, only for D.J. to clap his hands on my shoulder.

He pointed towards Shaya room, "No. I will clean up, you crash."

As I shuffled out of the room, something small and fierce bloomed in my chest. Not hope, not yet. But something like it. Maybe something close.

I followed the soft hum of voices down the hallway, the warmth of the house clinging to my skin like a blanket I don't deserve. When I opened Shaya's door, it creaked—faint, familiar, like it had its own secrets.

The space inside is layered in lemon and dusk. Pillows spilled over one another on a wide bed pushed against the wall. Fairy lights strung haphazardly across the ceiling, flickering like tired stars. Candles—unlit—sat on a cluttered desk beside a mirror scribbled with old lipstick messages.

The air smelled like body spray and incense, traces of comfort and girlhood.

I didn't say anything, mute as always, my limbs lazily carrying themselves over to the bed. The moment my shoulder touched the bed, I was already sinking—into the mattress, into the stillness, into the weight of my body. I feel the darkness take over me, my thoughts still rambling about like there is no off switch. Nevertheless, I let it consume me, drifting in and out, until there was nothing left.

*A crack.*

*A voice, "Look what you've done."*

*Darkness folded over me, sharp and sudden. My father's face rose from the shadow—not shouting, not angry—empty. He raised his hand, and when it came down, it hit with the sound of a shattering plate. And with that blow, a memory fell from my mind: my father lifting me onto his shoulders at the carnival. Gone.*

*Another hit. Louder. Closer. My father is clapping at my third-grade play. Gone.*

*Another. Tucking in, kissing my forehead, whispering "I'm so proud of you," Gone. Gone. Vanished.*

*Each strike erased another version of him, every loving echo replaced by the man he became. Until nothing remained but the latest version—breath sour, hands unsteady, eyes wild with hate.*

*A black figure appears in the corner of my eyes. Then the voices.*

*"Not him. Not him. Not him. Never him." So distorted, so mechanical. Goosebumps spread across my body, more images of my father gone, turned into a monster. Until all I could remember was fear. Then suddenly, I heard a piercing scream, making my ears ring.*

I woke up with a gasp, lungs tight, and heart hammering. The fairy lights buzzed above, one flickering in and out like a faulty pulse. For a second, I didn't know where I was--only that I was still there.

I can't breathe in this room, one that was meant for comfort. I can't lie here and pretend that I was fine and go back to sleep.

The house was dark, cloaked in silence except for the faint hum of the fridge downstairs. Only D.J. and I were here. I moved slowly, my bare feet whispering against the cold wooden steps, hands slightly shaking as I found my way to the kitchen. Sleep clinging to my bones like wet clothes. Remnants of my nightmare still attached from behind my eyelids.

I open the kitchen cabinets quietly, finding the cocoa mix. My hands moved automatically—heat the milk, stir the powder, watch the swirl, only a few marshmallows. The cup warms my palms, grounding me in the present.

I wandered to the living room, curling into the couch like I belonged to it. *Another foreign home.* Coraline played on the TV, the blue glow soft against my skin. I sipped the hot chocolate slowly, letting the sweetness coat my throat. I smile at the images in front of me, seeing Coraline instantly bringing me relief.

I heard footsteps appear, seven steps, before looking up to see D.J.; a fitted black tank top cling to his torso, black shorts hanging low on his hips. He rubs the sleep from his eyes as he steps into the glow of the television. His curls were a chaotic mess, and they hung low, falling in front of his eyes. His purple hair streak poked through. It felt like a D.J. only I had the opportunity to see—unguarded, not trying. *Not mine.*

"Some things never change, huh?" His voice scratched through the quiet as he nodded toward my mug. Without asking, he took it from my hands and sipped it.

I roll my eyes, reaching for it. "Seriously?"

He grinned faintly, not letting it reach his eyes, "It is nostalgic."

I snatched the mug back, sinking deeper into the couch. "You're insufferable."

"And you are still up at 4 a.m. watching Coraline. Old habits die hard, I guess." He stood above me for a moment, then slowly lowered himself beside me.

The room was dim, but I could feel his eyes lingering on me.

"Why are you really up, Charli?" I didn't answer. I didn't want to.

The silence stretched until he spoke again. "I have been meaning to ask you something. Something I have been wondering about for a while." My stomach twisted at the level of seriousness his voice held.

"Why did you leave me?" he said, voice softer than ever, but still sharp with something unspoken. "Why did you disappear?"

I didn't look at him. I couldn't. It felt like my wounds were being stabbed with the same knife repeatedly. "I couldn't bear to hurt you," I hushed out, trying to move the conversation and move the pain away.

I looked at him for a moment, seeing his expression darkened. "Who told you that?"

I hesitated, "It doesn't matter. I was true."

"No, it was not," he said flatly. "That is not your truth. That is someone else's bullshit."

"Was," I stated again, staring at the screen as I placed the mug down. "Was true."

"What changed?" His voice turned low, almost whispering.

I stood up, turning my back to him, "Nothing."

"Do not give me that crap," he said, rising. "You show up in my life again like none of it happened and expect me to act like I am fine?"

"I never asked you to be fine," I snapped, spinning around. Words being thrown at each other like knives. This is what I wanted to avoid, the hurt in his eyes as they looked at me.

"I would have waited," he said, "I *did* fucking wait." His eyes cling to mine, breathing heavily, face full of despair. *I did this, I should've stayed away.*

"For what?" I bit back, "For a girl who ruins everything she touches?"

His face twisted. "You did not ruin anything. You *ran*. That is what you do."

My jaw clenched. "Because staying meant hurting you. Tearing you down with my own grief, my own problems. It would've broken you like it broke me," my voice rising slightly, every word laced with venom and hurt. Like a perfect potion for betrayal.

"You do not get to decide that!" D.J. shouted. I don't dare to flinch, I just stare at him, taken back. "You have no right to decide to those who break me!"

"I do when it concerns me, I do when I have already done so."

Our words punch each other like fists. Dying down, letting it sink in. The eerie silence surrounds us, something that used to comfort both of us as we breathed heavily.

"You think I would not have noticed?" D.J. continues, distress etched all over his face, like he was reliving the pain I caused. "You think I did not wonder every damn birthday why you stopped showing up?" He breathes heavily, his hands sliding in his hair, pushing it away from his face. I hold his hard stare.

"You *promised* you would be there Charli. You promised when no one else did," he choked back a sob.

His voice is thick, full of sorrow. I can feel the tightness built in my chest, seeing the only person I tried not to hurt break down his walls, begging me to do the same thing. The only thing I can focus on is anger. The anger I felt when I was twelve years old, the anger I felt since my mother's death.

"I. Was. Fucking. Twelve!" I cried out, fuck the walls. "I was just a kid who just lost her mom and didn't know how to breathe without guilt choking me. All I knew was to not bring you down with me."

"And I was a kid whose dad left, saying he wished I never was born. Erased from existence!" he fired back. "You were the only one, the only one I *fucking* care about, who understood me—and then you vanished." D.J. stares into my eyes, holding defeat, despair, deception.

I turn around, try to look away, trying to *run away*. I start walking to the kitchen to get space, to breathe, to feel less like an egg about to break open. I feel D.J. right on my toes, not giving me the distance I desperately need. *No, what I desperately deserve.*

He stood in front of me, so close that I could feel his breath. His chest was nearly brushing mine. The counter on my back, nowhere to go.

"Why, River, why?" he asked, voice low and desperate. "Why are you trying so hard to push me away?"

I didn't answer for a moment, hoping to ignore the question, but by the look of D.J.'s face it was no use. "To keep a promise," I whispered.

"What promise?"

I didn't answer. I pushed past him, darting back into the living room and collapsing onto the couch. My chest is rising and falling too fast. I didn't want to cry. Not now, not in front of him. That doesn't stop the feeling of nails being punctured in my throat climbing up.

Nevertheless, he followed; he always did. Sat right beside me, like a string pulling both of us towards each other.

"Do not shut me out again," he said, quieter this time. "We were supposed to be...more than this."

I laughed. Laughed in the face of destruction. "Is that why you started hanging out with Quinn?" I murmured.

D.J. blinks, surprised. "This is about Quinn?"

"No, but since we are on the subject don't play dumb, D.J., you know how that bitch treated me. Even from the sidelines of my life." I say, spitting venom on the last line. *Nobody's fault but your own dumb shit.*

D.J. did not miss a beat. "What about Philo?"

"Don't." I say, stung at his remark.

"Why not? You think I do not see it? He is a fucking void, Charli. One you go to when you are afraid, of me, of your friends, of reality."

My first curls into a fist, feeling nails puncturing my skin slowly.

"Because he doesn't look at me like I ruined him."

"I have never looked at you like that."

"You do now," I say, shaking my head in disbelief.

D.J. scuffs under his breath, leaning closer on the couch.

"Tell me why you hate Quinn so much."

"Hate's a strong word."

"So are your fists. Do not dodge the question, River." He huffs out, locking eyes with mine.

"Then why do you hate Philo?" I spit out, seeing an unfamiliar emotion radiate from his body. The same feeling I feel when he is with Quinn.

"Because he *uses* you."

"And maybe, just maybe, I use him too!" I shouted. "Maybe it's to feel *anything* other than agony," I whispered to myself. I look away from D.J., towards the paused screen with Coraline's other mother's button eyes. A soulless creature. *Just. Like. Me.*

Silence. Thick. Tearing.

"I do not understand," D.J. finally answered. He grabs my chin, turning my focus towards him.

I see his emerald eyes dawn on me. "Why run from the pain when I am *right here*?"

I stared at him. He wasn't hiding anymore; he couldn't. Not behind sarcasm, behind silence.

"Do not lie to me, River. We have felt this since we were kids. From our adventures, since our overnight stays in Lio's backyard. At least I have." He sounds genuine, like he was trying to convince me of his own feelings. Pure.

I look down at his wrist, at the bracelet, tears stinging in my eyes. The compass charm catching on the TV's light, its silver edges simmering like a reminder of everything I've kept buried. My heart is racing—my mind is screaming "No" repeatedly, like it's trying to sabotage the one thing that could finally make sense of all this mess.

I pressed into D.J.'s wrist, over the bracelet; he stares at me with those questioning eyes, his expression shifting like he's trying to make sense of what I'm doing. I want to say something, anything, to explain—but no words come. *He doesn't need them anyway.* Yes, he does. I fought back my thoughts.

"Quinn told me to stay away from you. On your twelfth birthday. She said I didn't belong. This was my gift that I kept all these years, trying to keep you as close as possible without torturing you."

His eyes widened, looking down at the bracelet in his hands. He instantly put it on and then looked up at me. "Why did you *listen* to her?"

"Because it was easier, D.J." I was exhausted.

"Easier for who?" He yells out, feeling every ounce of pain in his question from the stacking years. I, the person who left him, caused him to blame himself for everything that had happened.

"For me, easier to see you choose someone else rather than have me as a burden." A single tear streamed down my face before I wiped it away quickly. I break away from his glance, my chest begging to break open, tears spilling, my body wearing down.

D.J. lifts my chin up once again, shaking his head, eyes softening. "I would not choose anyone else over you, River. *Nobody.*"

"I didn't know that." I said softly. He leaned in slowly, his soft finger still under mine. I looked at him—truly looked—and something inside me cracked open. The wall broke, and the dam let the water pour out.

There were no more words. He looked at me with such awe. This time, I chose not to look away.

Our lips met, like promise breaking and reforming at once. He crashed into me with the force of everything unsaid. The kiss was desperate—his hands in my hair, frantic, like he was trying to remember the texture of the loose curls. Mine clung to his shirt like I could stitch us back together by force. It tasted like the years we lost, the memories that were buried. Like grief, want and hope tangled into one breathless moment.

Years of silence. Years of "almost". Years of pretending like we didn't ache for each other in every crowded hallway, every stolen glance, every sarcastic remark. D.J.'s hands found my waist, my back, my face—wiping away the residue of tears. It was almost like he was trying to take everything of me in, trying to live in the moment before it was gone. We share the taste of hot chocolate. Neither of us pulled back.

We kissed until it hurt, our lips swollen from the passion, only to be healed again. When we finally parted, breathless and shaking, he rested his forehead against mine. He looked at me like I've never been gone. Like love had waited quietly behind his eyes, accommodating all this time.

Without a word, he guided us back to the couch. We collapsed together and tangled up. D.J. curled around my body protectively, one hand on my waist, the other cradling the back of my head like I was something fragile—something he would die to protect. I buried my face in his chest, a whiff of lavender hitting my nose instantly, anchoring myself in his solid weight.

The movie played again, but neither of us really watched it. The sounds of my comfort movie play in the background as D.J.'s fingers threaded into mine under the blanket he tossed over. His thumb traced circles around the back of my hand. Like a silent promise. Like the dandelion etched onto his finger, a commitment.

Just as my eyes began to flutter closed, I hear D.J. whisper below me against my hair, his voice hoarse, "No pain can amount to anything if you are not here with me, Charlotte."

That. My name, one I was bound not to hear again until it held solace and security.

My name lingered in the air like a vow, and I didn't run. Not this time. The ship finally returned—no longer adrift at sea.

# *Stay* *Rihanna, Mikky Ekko*

November 7, 2023

The way our bodies are built tells us a story that everyone is prone to experience at least once. Our hearts are protected by the barrier of our ribcages, shielded, and unable to be penetrated since it is the most vulnerable organ. It feels like it ripens; it beats.

Our mind, on the other hand, is trapped, like a prisoner. It must stay accountable, stay persistent, and stay in place behind the walls of the cranium. Two distinct functions that enable a human to live a life where they meet and clash.

Imprisonment and protection; eventually the heart bleeds from a certain angle, and the mind escapes.

Growing up, I always thought about love. To experience it, to feel it, to be suffocated in it. I always thought I had good role models to look up to, to see the love pour out of my parents' hearts, their bodies, their minds. I always said I wanted what they had; to laugh with a person until your ribs hurt, to cry when sharing the pain worth every moment, or to even sit in silence and enjoy the company of one another.

I pictured this, even dreamt of it, and now I think it is finally within reach. Despite the efforts to push the thoughts out; to push any moment of happiness, it always lingers in the air. Love. Something many people try so hard to find in life, and many people do so. I saw love turn people into the most precious pair there is, I also saw how it can damage a person.

*So where will I fit in when I am faced with the idea of love?*

"I can feel your gears turning rapidly," D.J. says as I lay on him. His eyes were still closed, his hands still wrapped around me.

I woke up about ten minutes ago, not wanting to move an inch as I embraced the warmth I felt. The couch, the blanket, the comfort—none of it compares to the safe feeling when I am next to D.J., the one person who can stop me from drifting in space.

I look up to D.J., seeing his soft expression as he looks down at me. I am lying on his chest, the same position we fell asleep in. For once in my life, for a while at least, I had no feeling of dread waking up. The constant nag that pulls at my heartstrings every time I open my eyes. In the back of my mind, pain still resonates, questions still form, but in this moment nothing else matters. I am with my person, one I yearned for, one I tried to exclude from my life.

"I'm just taking everything in," I say as I move my head to rest on his shoulder, the pocket between his arm and chest.

D.J. peers down at me, emotions stirring behind his eyes. With his other arm he cups my face, pulling me in for a kiss. So sweet, sincere, and soft. D.J. pulls back just an inch, his hand still resting on my cheek.

"Will you tell me now? I can see the deep thoughts begging to come out, River," D.J. says, his voice rough and strong.

I think harshly. The moments from yesterday were tragic, full of pain, but as night fell, I was comforted and held. Though I have as much empathy and consolation, I still have questions, and I still have a feeling of doubt within my life.

The letter, the phone, the pictures, the death of my mother. It still surrounds me, lingering like a dark cloud waiting for rain. I am waiting for the new beginning, for the rain to clean everything and let go, but it can't until I understand.

I know in my soul that something happened to her, nothing adds up to her committing suicide. Her being scared, but leaving my father and I from something she was running from? It's not her. *Do I even know her?*

*No. It doesn't add up, who hurt my mother? Worse, who killed her? Who stripped her away from me, from my life with her?*

"Hey, River, come back to me." D.J. says, he sits us both up, with me cradling his hips, his hands holding me at my waist. "What is it?" he asks as he wipes the tears from my cheek. I didn't even know I was crying.

"I think," I hesitated, looking down at his hands, at the bracelet. Even when I don't have it, I unconsciously play with it. D.J. lifts my head, making me look at him. *My compass.* I take the chance to look at him, truly; I see his purple strand in front of his eyes as they stare back at me.

"I think my mom was murdered." I said bluntly, unable to connect to the pain that I felt for so long. My body reacts but my mind is numb, just persistent. I felt D.J. wrap around me. Tighter but his eyes never stray away. My body still hurts, but I ignore it. I don't want anything to ruin this feeling.

"What do you need?" he asks, never second guessing me, believing me.

I held a questioning look, in response to his question. "You believe me?"

"I believe you would not think of this unless something is not adding up." D.J. stroked my hair out of comfort, letting me relax instantly at the feeling of his touch.

"But I always believed that she didn't commit, ever since I found out the police ruled it as a suicide." There was a moment, one where we acknowledged each other's thoughts.

"I know. That is why I want to help you, River. Let me, please." He yearns. His whole face contorted to sympathy, one that is not agonizing to look at, to feel.

I hugged him tightly. I never want to let go. "Do you happen to have a flip-phone charger by any chance?"

D.J. pulls me back; confusion in his eyebrows. "Maybe. What for?"

"My mom's cellphone. It has pictures and that message I was telling you about." I say as D.J. nods.

"I do; I can grab it from my room when we get ready for school." He says nonchalantly. He lays us both down on the couch, arms curling, heartbeats matching.

He plants a kiss above my eyebrow, then my nose, then lifts my chin to reach my lips. No words can explain this feeling. Only a person can truly understand when they have the privilege to experience it. *One I still don't deserve.*

"What time is it?" I ask, not wanting to get up.

"Six in the morning, get some sleep Charlotte." He says my name gracefully, like it always belonged to him. It reminds me of a young D.J., calling out to me on our adventures, challenging me in any way, shape, or form.

"I want you to call me Dario," D.J. says, peering down at me. I look at him, surprise written all over my face.

"Why now? After all these years? You've beaten people up for calling you Dario."

"That is because it never belonged to them. I only like you calling me Dario," Dario says. He pushes his head back down to his chest. A small smile lingering on my face. "I would do anything for you to smile all the time, River. Starting with giving my name to you."

He kisses my forehead and starts stroking my hair.

"Dario?" The name tasted foreign to me, but it was so familiar to me.

"Hm?"

"Can we not go to school?" I asked. I think about it; him having football practice, me being dragged through meaningless classes.

"I thought you would never ask." He pulls me closer to him, as if it were possible. We lay there, two souls healing each other. Two energies that meandered, now aligned. A match that was found and sparked years later.

For now, I will reel in this feeling. For now, I will be with Dario. For now, my questions will have to wait. Only later will I find the strength to pick up what I have been searching for, but for now, I will lie with Dario as Charlotte. As someone who has been begging for the damn universe for this moment. I am damn sure I will take my time to prolong this.

~~~~~~~~~~~~

The car hummed smoothly along the road; the soft sound of tires against grains filled the silence between the two of us, Dario and me. It was nice, like sleeping on the cold
~~~~~~~~~~~~

side of a pillow. I glance over at D.J... Dario, finding his hands steady on the steering wheel. My mind races, as usual; at this point it should become a track star.

"Almost there," Dario mumbled. His eyes flickered to mine for a brief second before turning back to the road.

The world was blurring past, but in this moment, I was still. Like a statue, I stay grounded for once in my life. I needed this time—to prepare, to think, to breathe, to live. *To survive.*

When we pulled off from the bridge, the one over the river, I at once got out of the car. I didn't wait for Dario; I knew he would follow. If he doesn't then he is just giving me the space, both of which I am accustomed to.

The air is soft out here, like it's a different dynamic. The sky is wide and streaked with pale gold. The river moves with a low, endless sound. *Inviting.* I walk ahead until the ground turns damp and the current hums underneath my feet. I stand still, waiting, like my mother is going to jump out of the water. *Always waiting, never making a move.*

My arms wrap around me loosely, trying to hold myself together. To find the strength for what is about to come. The truth. I don't speak at first, I just take it all in. The left-out conversations that were stolen, the kisses I will never have again, the events we will miss with each other. I just breathe, letting the weight of my mother's closeness here, but at the same time feeling the distance.

*I was here once, and so were you.*

*You walked this earth before me.*

*Carried me, loved me. I wish I was able to return the favor.*

*I wish I could ask more. I wish I had known how to ask.*

*But if my wishes came true, then your goals wouldn't be met.*

*I see you now, even though I am years late.*

*I always knew I just never had the courage to dig.*

My eyes flickered down to the baby book in my hands. Clutched, secured. I don't open it. I don't need to. All of it is inside me—the nurture of the memories, the pieces that made up the puzzle of my mother's life.

"I'm trying," I whispered to myself. So low, that I don't think Dario could hear. "For once, I truly am. I don't have a rat's ass on what to do, but I'm still here mom. For you." A single tear, one of many that I allowed to fall before. I wiped it away but still feel it resonates in my skin.

The river answers with silence. Something I never thought I needed. After a moment, I heard Dario's footsteps behind me. He doesn't say anything at first. He just gives me my space but announces himself. Two sides of a coin. Dario's here; always has been.

I turn towards him; my face is now soft. Not unburdened, but lighter.

Dario gives me a small smile, lifting an eyebrow. "You know she is happy to see us together again, right? I can feel her here." He says softly, looking out to the stream ahead of us.

I return the raised eyebrow, which Dario caught. The smile turns into a smirk as he faces me, his requited attention.

"She used to pick on us," he continues, "Teasing us that we were cute together, but not you. No, you swore I was disgusting." He laughs out.

"Must have been playing hard to get," I say shrugging, huffing a laugh through my nose.

Dario steps closer to me, basically diminishing the space between us. "Trust me, River," He grins. "I had you since the very beginning."

I shook my head, but nevertheless, I didn't deny it. Dario snakes an arm around my waist, pulling us back to the bridge. The gravel beneath us crunching every step of the way, the river fading behind us.

18 steps until we meet with the car again. Dario pulls the passenger door open for me.

"You should sleep," he says gently. He grabs me with one hand and plants a kiss on my forehead, then nose, and finally on my lips. "You never really sleep. I will wake you up when we are at Wilma's," he continues as he pulls back from the kiss.

I don't argue against him as I slide into the seat. I leaned my head against the cushion, feeling the other side of the door open and close. A familiar lavender scent fills my nose. I close my eyes, taking in the senses around me.

The engine starts, and for now, I let myself rest before the propaganda.

~~~~~~~~~~~~~

I woke up at a sudden stop. One that pulled me out of my dreamless sleep. I wipe my eyes, wipe my mouth. I look ahead of me, seeing we're at Wilma's.

"I knew you would drool over me," Dario announces with a smirk. I roll my eyes and shake my head.

"Maybe over my favorite chips, but I don't know about you." I say as I let out a yawn.

"Takis, huh? That is what it takes?"

"How do you possibly know that?"

"Do you forget that we are the same person? You used to steal my bag all the time." Dario laughs. His head leans back on the headrest. His smile is still lingering.
~~~~~~~~~~~~~

"That is because my parents wouldn't allow me to eat them. Say they were bad for my stomach." I retorted, nudging him to the side.

"They are bad for the stomach."

"Didn't stop you though."

"Well luckily it did not. Otherwise, you would have never got Takis by stealing from me." Dario squints his eyes towards me; I roll my eyes once again. Dario turns off the car, and his seatbelt as well. I follow his movements up to the point where he turns to me.

"You ready?" His voice changed from teasing to sincerity. Softness lingers in his voice along with concern.

I ignore the ache in my body, like I have been doing all day. "No," I say as I open the door and hop out.

"Let's go," I say before closing the door. I am waiting for Dario. He took my hand instantly, knowing I needed comfort. My grip on my baby book makes my hands cramp, my mother's charged cellphone weighs down in my pocket.

*For her. For her. For her. Answers. Answers. Dig. Dig. Dig. Dig. Dig. 1...2...3...4...5...6...7...8...9...*

10 steps and we are in front of the door to the lobby. Motions set, my feet moving before me. I clutch harder onto Dario's hand. My breathing was harsh, rapid, and my chest was pounding. Bursting, threatening to come out. I am not worried about Wilma. I am just worried about what she will say, what she will answer. Or worse, *she won't answer.*

*Dario is here. He is here. He is here. I am here. My mom isn't here. My dad isn't here. The answers aren't here. Here. Here. Here.*

Dario pulls us towards the motions, talking to long nails. Seeing her flirting with him. I smile at her until it turns into a glare. I can sense when Dario is uncomfortable, and it is because of the bubble-gum popping bitch in front of me. I can't say anything, Dario is pulling us towards the stairs, past the security guards.

He pulls us into the stairwell, leading me up the stairs, never letting go.

"I love to see the jealousy radiate off you, River." Dario says stepping one step at a time ahead of me. He turns for a moment, flashing his annoying ass smirk.

"I wasn't jealous, more like annoyed." I say, pushing at his side to wipe that grin off. It didn't work. Well damn.

"Annoyed? Why is that, Charlotte?" I'm not used to hearing my name, but every time he says it catches me off guard in an effective way. A reminder of the past that is not hurtful.

"Because I can tell long-nails was making you uncomfortable."

"Long-nails?"

"Yes, long-nails."

A laugh echoes on the staircase. I joined Dario. Just us two, hearts beating with one another. Like we are children again. We made it to the floor where Wilma's place is, but neither of us moved. I don't want to. I move closer to Dario, letting go of his hand to cap his face.

I pushed back the purple strand to see his eyes. Haunting, compelling, and captivating. I push myself up to him, landing my lips on his. He connects to it at once, moving with each other instead of against. He grabs me with the waist to pull me closer, engulfing me with his scent. I pulled apart, just a few centimeters from his face. My lips are still brushing against his, our breaths still tangling with each other.

"I love you, Dario." I say confidently. It is the one statement I have not overthought or regretted. It is the only statement where words are put together that enables the truth.

The only truth that I know is in my heart, my will, my body, everything. I always have, but I never want to miss the chance to say it to someone I genuinely love again.

Dario is just staring at me, not with surprise, no. With a look that I have only seen in moments of time. Moments where our eyes would be locked, like children and strangers. Where we can feel each other from across the room. He brushes my cheek, breaking the space between us again. Three kisses: my forehead, the tip of my nose, and the longing kiss on my lips. It is deep but soft, empowering, but controlled. He pulls apart, my lips tingling.

"I love you with my soul Charlotte."

And with that confirmation, we are together as one. Taking on any problems ahead of us. With him by my side, I can find the courage to continue.

So, I do. Stepping my way towards Wilma's, waiting for new questions, old ones, answers fading, and answers coming to light.

# *So Hard to Find* Ben

*L'Oncle Soul*

November 12, 2023

I think of the younger version of myself at times. How carefree she was, untouched by the agonizing thoughts that now attack me daily. Every day was something new; a mission to be completed, an adventure to scale, a life willing to live. I think about the goofy grin that I used to have, only having the smile lines be a remnant of the past.

I imagine what I would say to her, or worse, what she would say to me. Would she be proud? Disappointed? Scared? Confused. Would she look at the older version and not recognize herself? It is questions like these that make me want to figure out my life, but at the same time to be swallowed up, never to be seen again.

A wish too fragile for any number of manifestations. A wish I know even if the universe won't answer.

I close my mushroom notebook slowly, feeling the smooth cover as I hesitate to move. The pen trembles slightly in my grip before I tuck it in my pocket, my notebook in my bag. The library around me is quiet, a little too quiet. The kind of quiet that makes your thoughts the main source of entertainment.

186

I get up and wander through the aisle of the town's small library, fingers trailing along the spines of the books until I reach the local history section. I'm not sure what I'm looking for, anything that jumps out at me. Anything that spikes my curiosity, quiets my questions, or something that leads me to more questions.

Really, anything that can bring focus towards my mother's story. She is speaking out to me, warning me to stop digging. To stop looking, but that is like telling someone not to push the big, red button.

Old yearbooks, newspaper clippings, dusty photo compilations. Lives piled up of those who stood in the same place I am right now, those who went to the same school, even sat at the same desk I dissociated at during class. My hand grazes over yellow pages until I find a worn binder labeled "Town Highlights—Early 2000s". I flip it open, scanning articles of school plays, sport victories, honor roll lists.

Then I saw it.

A colorful image, full of light beaming from the camera. Faded, but clear enough. Three teenagers stand side by side on a basketball court. Smiles wide enough, arms thrown around each other's shoulders. My dad, unrecognizable at first, but young and proud. *Something he once said to me.* My mother was beside him, beaming. And--

I froze. The third person, his face was so familiar in a strange way. I didn't recognize him at first. Though the name underneath the picture brings my breathing to a halt.

**Seniors Astrid Farah, Lloyd Riverson, Mykel Cardiner—Track and Field State Champions 1998.**

My heart skips a beat. Mykel? The name spins in my head like it's trying to fit into a shape it no longer resembles. I flip through my bag, pulling out the old photo, bent and bruised, but still useful. A picture I took from my mother's photo album—my mother between two boys, all three of them making silly faces.

Tongues were stuck out, eyebrows raised, and eyes popped out. One of the boys, who I know now is my father, is holding the camera out like a selfie.

The same three people. But younger. Freer.

I couldn't help but think about Wilma, about what she told me. My mind plundered as the thoughts moved around like boulders threatening to hit me.

*"You should've called. You can't just show up on people like this—we might be dead by the time you knock." Wilma's said.*

Mykel is my mother's friend, or is he, my father's? Why was his arm around her in the picture? The picture that I am gripping onto for dear life. I pull out my phone from my back pocket, opening the camera app.

*"I know, Wilma, I'm sorry," I said quickly. "I just—I just need to know if you recognize anyone in this photo." I stumble on my words, having it fall out before my mind can grasp it.*

I snapped the picture in the binder. Looking closer, compare two pictures of the same people. I looked at the photo in my hand, the photo I showed Wilma a few days ago, when I barged into her time.

*"Oh yes," Wilma said, a slow smile spreading across her lips. "That's Comet and her friends. The one with the arm around her shoulder was that rowdy boy who rushed out of the house to give him band aids. Such a sweet soul."*

Such a sweet soul, indeed. Comet, my mother, the same person. A person who died because she had so much care in the world. *That's Comet and her friends. Comet and her friends. Rowdy boy. Comet. Comet. Comet. Astrid Riverson.*

My mind continues to race, running away from problems it can't escape. The library's silence presses in on me as my thoughts whirl. I didn't recognize the "rowdy boy" Wilma pointed out was Mykel. *Why didn't he say anything?* My hand tightens around my phone. *Why lie?*

My phone buzzes in my hand, yanking me out of my thoughts

Shaya: Camping trip today. You in? Lio's bringing some smores. You better come.

I let out a breath I didn't know I was holding as I typed on my phone.

Me: Do I have a choice?

Shaya: Do you want me to answer that? Meet us at Lio's house. His parents are letting us borrow the van. Dario's coming ;D.

I rolled my eyes at the last part of the message. Neither she nor Emilio know that we are together. *Are we? Yes. We are. Did we say we love each other too soon? Too late? Too much?*

I shake my head, trying to stop the doubt from our relationship. We waited too long, everyone did. *Fuck off.* I scroll through my messages, clicking on Dario's name before sending him a text message.

Me: Can you pick me up from the library?

As I wait for a response, I stare back at the article. I stare at the names once again. Then I focus on my mother's smile. Her youth in her eyes, the smile lines appearing.

About five minutes later my phone lit up again.

Dario: Outside.

I don't waste any time. Grabbing my bag, I rush out, pushing through the library's heavy doors and into a soft hazy late afternoon. Dario's car is parked along the curb, the engine humming low. I slid into the passenger seat, my thoughts still caught in that picture, the names.

"Were you stalking me?" I say jokingly, trying to calm down my mind. It didn't work though, kind of obvious.

I can feel Dario's eyes on me. "You look flushed, River." He reaches over and gently pulls my chin towards him. He examines my face closely as I look at him. The light freckles on his brown skin shine with the sun.

His eyes search mine, "What is going on?"

I hesitate. Taking a deep breath and just letting go.

"I don't know," I mutter. "I don't even know how to piece it all together."

I start rambling about everything. Before I can even stop myself, my mouth takes account of their own. "I found this newspaper article with my mom and dad in it—back when they were in high school. It was after a track and field championship or something. And Mykel..." I hesitate. Looking up at Dario, seeing him giving me his undivided attention.

"He was there too," I continued. "His arm was around my mom. He looked...close to her. Like family, but he never said anything." I can feel my throat getting restricted, choked up on words that threaten to come out.

My voice trembles, "It's the same people from the photo I found in her things; the one Wilma recognized. But now seeing Mykel's name written like that, like they were normally together, like how we are with Shaya and Emilio. It's just...I don't know. I'm confused Dario."

"Maybe they were close? But what is bothering you about friendship? "Dario asks lightly.  His hands are now resting on mine over the center console.

"My mother's letter was written about two people, best friends. Wilma said that the rowdy boy is Mykel, yes? But my question is why Mykel? Why not--" I choked at the thought of my dad. *Why not the man who lays his hand on me?*

He let the silence hang, waiting. My eyes wander from all over the car to match my mind that never sticks to one place.

"I think," I hesitate. My throat thickens against my will. "I think my dad has something to do with my mother's death," I whisper suddenly, my eyes fixed on my lap. My fingers trace over the bracelet on Dario's wrist. "I don't know what Mykel's role is, but--"

I cut myself off, heart hammering. My mind flashes to my father's voice, his fists, the last time I saw the swelling on my ribcage.

Dario's voice is soft. "Why do you think your dad did something?"

My mouth part. The truth rises, but I choke on it.

*Because he beats me. One punch after the next. The kick to the ribs created fire through my whole body. Because he looks at me like I am a ghost.*

*A remnant of my own mother. A reminder. A reminder. A reminder. Shoot me, suffer the same fate. They say, "Like mother, like daughter".*

*Because I'm starting to think he killed her, and I'm next.*

"He's been distant ever since she died," I say instead, hushing the lingering thoughts. "It's almost like he looks guilty. Like looking at me reminds him of something he can't live with."

It's a half lie. It makes my stomach twist, but it's all I can give.

Dario's gaze stays on me, warm but heavy with concern. He doesn't press me, which I am grateful for. *Not yet. Not now.*

We pull up across from my house as I am still lost in thought when he parks.

"Why are we here?" I blink at my front porch.

"To pack," Dario says gently. "Camping trip. Remember?"

My shoulders drop. "I don't feel like going..."

"I know." He leans in and kisses my temple. "But it might be one of the last times we all hung out before college starts. Just us. Before life gets in the way."

I swallowed hard. The ache in my chest swells.

"We will always be around, Charlotte." He murmurs. "We have been friends since before we could spell each other's names. I just meant...it would be nice to be this young again with Lio and Shaya."

I nod, eyes glistening.

Dario kisses my forehead. Then nose. Then my lips. A repetitive remark. One I would never get sick of. I take this moment to look at him. The purple streak started to grow towards the end. I smiled at him, and he returned gracefully.

When I step out of the car, I feel like I am floating. Everything hurts and nothing makes sense, but at least I have Dario, Shaya, and Lio. I walk towards my front door without looking back. -

~~~~~~~~~~~~~~~~

The low hum of conversation and occasional clang of dishes filled the warm space of Lio's house. I sat curled into the end of the couch, my knees pulled close, a soft throw pillow tucked under my arms. Shaya was cross-legged beside me, scrolling through a playlist on her phone.

"They got a cabin," Shaya said, eyes still flickering across the screen. "Three rooms, one bathroom, and a fireplace in front. Pretty basic, but it's nice. Tucked up in the
~~~~~~~~~~~~~~~~

trails, about three hours away from here." Shaya puts her phone down and lays her head back on the couch.

I nodded slowly, trying to picture it. I imagined tall trees, full of greenery trying to poke through the blanket of snow. Silence thick enough to choke on, I'm not sure if that excites or terrifies me.

"The boys are almost done packing up the car," Shaya added, glancing toward the open front door. "Hopefully."

Just as she said it, Emilio walked in with a burst of cool air, hauling a duffel bag over his shoulder. "Do *either* of you have the speaker?"

"D.J. has it," Shaya said without missing a beat.

He grunted, turned around, and disappeared again.

I let out a breathy laugh. "Like clockwork."

Shaya smirked, "This always happens. They do the heavy lifting, as they should, but forget everything else." She finishes as she rolls her eyes.

A moment later, Dario came through the door with a backpack half-zipped, a bundle of tangled chargers hanging from his hand. His eyes instantly met mine, my heart does a corny ass flip.

"You good?" He asked softly.

I gave him a small nod, lips curling into a smile that didn't quite meet my eyes. "Yeah."

Emilio came back in and dropped the last bag by the door.

"Okay. We're all good. Let's head out." He leans down to kiss his mom on the cheek, then claps his dad on the shoulder. "Thanks for the food, old man."

Mykel chuckled; still buttering sandwich bread while his mom loads up containers. A pin of jealousy hits my chest as I look over the normal scene ahead of me. Something so close but too far to grasp.

"Be good," Persephone called after him. "And *don't* forget to stop at the gas station before the trailhead."

"Yeah, yeah," Lio muttered, before shooting his mom his cheeky smile. He grabs Shaya's hand and tugs her towards the door. "Let's go before it gets dark."

Shaya looked back at Charli, "You're coming?"

"I'll meet you guys in the car," I said, rising slowly. "Just need to use the bathroom really quick."

Shaya nodded and stepped out with Emilio, the front door creaking open and then thudding shut. Dario lingered. He stood just inside the doorway, still holding the backpack. His fingers are tapping against the zipper. His eyes search my face.

"You sure you are okay?" Dario asked, his voice low.

I met his gaze and forced a softer smile this time. It doesn't matter since D.J. can see right through me. "I'm good, Dario."

I wasn't, not really. But I would be. Maybe. Hopefully.

Dario hesitated but finally nodded. "Okay, I will be in the car." He walks out, the door closing gently behind him. I stood in the middle of the hallway for a second, staring at nothing. I shook myself out of it and padded to the bathroom.

I locked the door behind me and leaned over the sink. My hands braced the porcelain as I looked in the mirror. My eyes looked darker than usual, like they held something I hadn't yet let surface.

*Just go talk to him. It's just a conversation. Just ask.*

My breath fogged the mirror. I rubbed it clean with the back of the sleeve of my hoodie. I turned off the light and stepped back into the hall. The house is quieter now. The kitchen still buzzed faintly with the radio and the hum of the fridge.

I peeked around the corner and saw Mykel standing in the corner, phone pressed to his ear, nodding slowly at whatever he was hearing. His back was to me. I swallowed.

Outside the window, above the sink, I spotted Persephone lying in the hammock in the backyard. Book in hand, one leg hanging off lazily. The wind played with a strand of her hair as she flipped the page.

I linger in the hallway, my heart beating just a little too fast. Then I took a step forward. On cue, Mykel turns around, his phone now in his hand. He is still looking down until he can feel my presence.

"Charli? What are you still doing here? Everyone is waiting," Mykel said, confusion written all over his face.

"I'm going soon, I just needed to talk to you." I say, pulling a chair near the island table across from Mykel. I don't want to meet his gaze, but I do, and once I do, I hold it. To the best of my ability.

"Alright, what's going on? Is something bothering you? Is this about *Dario*? God, I haven't heard that name in a while." Mykel said, putting his phone in his pocket and then leaning on the island with his elbows. Curiosity swirls with amusement in his eyes.

I forced a low laugh, "No, I--I was thinking of something...my mother's necklace. The one was found in your house. Why was it there?" I can seek Mykel flinch at my question. His casual attitude is wearing off, but he tries to cover it with a laugh; his eyes darting away briefly.

"Your mom's necklace? I don't know, Charli. Maybe she left it here when she was here with your father one day. Probably one of those things she misplaced. She was always...moving things around. You know how she was." Mykel answers, his voice going higher in some sentences, he tries to cover with nonchalant.

My gaze sharpens. I don't believe him. My mother was going to give this necklace to me. She doesn't *misplace* things.

"Really? I thought it was special to her. She always talked about it like it was important." I press, not showing all my cards. I don't say anything about the pictures, letters, the messages. None of it, unless I have a direct answer.

Mykel's smile fades for a moment, and he shifts uncomfortably. The forced casualness in his voice is a little too noticeable. He shrugs.

"Maybe. But things get lost. I don't know, Charli. She was in and out of my life, and you know...I guess I never gave it back. No big deal." *No big deal my ass*. No, this is just paranoia. *No, your mother died.*

I watch him carefully, picking on the small cracks in his story. I don't let him see my thoughts; my face stays neutral, a mechanism I have built over time.

"You said you weren't that close to my mom, but...I don't know. From what I've been told, you two were pretty good friends. What's the deal with that? Why lie?" I asked casually but pointed it out.

"I didn't lie. Your mother and I were friends. I was closer to your father than her if anything. Never really knew hung out with her until after college, but in high school she was just around." Mykel expression tightens; his eyes narrowed a little bit but quickly forces his face into a neutral expression. He spoke with a slight edge, avoiding my eye contact. I let him speak, not disrupting him one bit.

"We were friends. Nothing more. People like to exaggerate relationships. I don't know why Wilma or anyone else would say we were that close." Mykel finishes before grabbing his phone. I nodded and muttered a thank you before heading out the door.

Eight steps made before I reached the back door to the minivan. I open it up, instantly connecting my eyes with

Dario before seeing Shaya and Lio filling the car with their out of tune vocals. When they notice me hopping in, they turn the volume down and turn towards me.

"Well God damn, did you take a shit or something?" Emilio asks, earning a punch on the shoulder from Shaya. Since it wasn't enough, I decided to punch him as well, then high fiving Shaya in the process.

"Just drive," I roll my eyes, and then glancing over to Dario. He wears a smirk as he pulls me closer, clasping his arm around my shoulder, and pulling me into his chest. Shaya catches us, and I have not seen a smile this big from her in all my years being friends.

"Well, it's about damn time you guys got together." Dario and I both responded by sticking the middle finger at her simultaneously, causing her to hold a fake shock on her face before turning around.

Dario plants a kiss on my forehead, letting it linger, as Lio is pulling out of the driveway.

"Oh, you guys belong to each other," Lio says, looking in the rearview mirror, his fingers dancing on the steering wheel. I can only imagine the smirk that he has on his face.

The car ride is smooth; music playing in the background, Shaya and Emilio holding hands, Dario holding me as he leans against the window with his back. He traces small circles on my bicep. I trace the dandelion on his finger softly.

The November chills run through my body, which causes Dario to place a blanket from his bag over us, mainly me. Though his body heat is more than enough.

My mind drags with everything that has been clouding my mind for the past month. *Dig. Dig. Dig.* What Mykel said to me was a lie. *He lies. He lies. He lies. Dig.* I never mentioned Wilma to anyone but Dario. Why would Mykel know Wilma if he were never around my mother, *Comet,* during high school?

*Because he lies. He is fake. Fake. Fake. He was nervous. Friends of a friend. Stop digging.*

"River," Dario whispers in my ear. The music almost drowned out his voice, but loud enough for only me to hear. I look up at him, seeing the glint in his eyes—the color of a glow of quiet intensity of secrets buried beneath ancient trees.

He rubs my temple softly, nurturing. "Sleep," I was about to shake my head when Dario held it in place. He gave me stern eyes, one that makes me want to go back to my decision.

"Get some rest. I will be here when you wake up." Dario continues before leaning down to kiss my forehead. Soft and warm. One that made me close my eyes.

A feeling that I yearn to last, the same one that leads me to the comfort of sleep. Only do I wish it would still radiate when I wake up from slumber.

~~~~~~~~~~~~~~~~~

I can feel the warmth from the fire against my skin instead of consuming it for once. Dario and Emilio are getting more wood for the fire, leaving Shaya and I to fight off the bears. Knowing the two of us, we would try to keep the animals as pets. *Shaya would get eaten first.*

Playing with my fingers, I look out to the fire. The heat stings my eyes and for a moment I wonder if I should just let the tears fall. The hot coals glow like half-dead stars. My shoulders are hunched out, mirroring Shaya as she pushed a stick into the ashes, turning them repeatedly until the smoke curled around us.

"Charli," Shaya broke the silence. I just stared at the embers, pulsing gold and red like they were alive but tired.

"Do you remember," she started again, the small voice lingering in the air, "when we used to pretend the backyard was the whole world?"
~~~~~~~~~~~~~~~~~

A ghost of a smile tugs at my lips. I want to push the idea out of my head. To reject the painting being pictured as the memory unfolds, I turn towards her, taking in her presence as she looks at the fire still.

"Yeah," I whispered.

"You made me wear that stupid blue cape," Shaya nudges my arm, her smile illuminating through the night. "You called me 'Shaya the Slayer' fighting off dragons and warlocks. Meanwhile you were "Queen Charli of the Castle."

"I was a terrible queen," I said, snickering at the thought.

Shaya joins in and before you know it, we sound like hyenas. She poked the coals again, watching the sparks up into the dark.

"We really believed nothing could get to us," she murmured. "Just us against everything, well besides the dumb ass guys that we can't get rid of." We laugh together again, bellies going up and down, warmth filling our chests. It was like drinking cold water with mint gum. Refreshing.

Though once the laughter died, the night felt heavier, like the memory itself weighed. I hesitated to speak up; to be more open to what is going on with my life. From my mother's necklace to Wilma's story, to the picture I found in the library. All I know is that I do not know my mother. *I don't know if I ever did. I never knew of her mistakes.*

*Was I one?*

"It felt safe," I admitted. "Back then." Shaya's eyes softened, and she turned her whole body to face me.

"When did it stop feeling safe?" Shaya asked curiously. Not accusing me. *When was the time I felt I had no one else in a sea of people?* I hesitated, looking at the fire. The flames blurred around the edges.

"Charls," Shaya said again, soft and low. Careful. "I know it hurts, but it's worse when you try to keep it inside." The fire cracked, sending sparks swirling.

"You used to tell me everything," she whispered. I can hear the pain lacing her words as she spits them out. "Silly things, scary things...we swore to never lie to each other."

I swallowed hard. My voice felt caught behind my ribs.

"I haven't forgotten," I whispered. "It's just...harder now."

Shaya just looked at me, like I was this person in her eyes that only mattered. "I know," she said, her voice cracking just a little.

"But you're the strongest person I know. I just want my best friend...to need me. Like she needed me before."

For a second, it was just us again—like when we were little girls teasing Lio, sneaking off to prank the boys. Happy. I thought I was chasing the truth to feel that again, but really, it just gave me something to hold besides the emptiness of these nine years.

So, I took a deep breath. Manually, physically. I took my best friend's hand, not for her but for me. For my own sake. "I think my dad...no I can't."

Shaya squeezes my hand. Giving me a sense of clarity to continue. No words from her, just understanding.

"I think my dad did something to my mom." I finally said it out loud. I look over to Shaya and see she's holding a confused look.

"Is it because he's not around? Why would your dad do this? I'm confused Charls." Shaya waited. The firelight caught tears in her eyes. I shook my head and let go of Shaya's hand.

"Look Shaya, over the past month I have been doing my own research on my mom. You've been asking me what has been wrong with me, and the answer is this." I can feel my hands glide through my hair, wanting to pull at my scalp.

"Between the messages I found in my mom's phone, the letter in her shit in the attic, I don't know what to think. Even Wilma recognized the kids in the picture, the one with my mom."

I open my notebook again, but this time I open it to the back of the notebook that has a slip. I pulled out the two photos from earlier and passed them to Shaya.

"Wilma is someone who used to babysit my mother. Dario took me to her building for service one time. Ever since, she would tell me stories of this young girl named Comet, a nickname she had for my mother." I reached into my notebook again and grabbed my mother's letter, the one where she was desperately looking for help.

I passed it to Shaya and studied her as she looked at the bits of information I collected over the past month or so.

I look over to the fire, the house behind it, and the trees. I took a deep breath, feeling the elements around me. I smell the fresh wet leaves even in the cold, November air. Only a few more minutes of this until Shaya finally shared her presence again. *I could burn everything and make it disappear.*

"Charls...why didn't you share this with me?"

I smiled at her, a genuine one. Looking down at my hands, I rub them together harshly. "I just didn't want to see my best friend thinking the same way I was. The same reason I stopped being friends with Dario all that time ago."

"And which way was that?"

For a heartbeat, everything stopped. The fire, the breeze, the noise in the trees. I can feel my body slow down as time passes by.

"That if my dad didn't do this then..." my throat gets thick, making it hard for words to come through.

"Then what Charli?" Shaya voice is laced with concern. She hangs onto every word I say, do, or feel.

I wait. Waiting for the answer to come for my own question but nothing ever came. I waited for the clues to make sense, but nothing came. I waited for my dad to be there for me, but he never came back. Just like mom.

"Then why does he hurt me Shaya?" I choked out with a sob. My hands find my mother's necklace as support. I can feel my chest ache with pain. Tears are coming down before I can catch them.

"Why does he hurt me if I'm his little girl? I'm still his baby girl, right?" I can feel my breathing pick up, my hands grabbing my chest as I hyperventilate.

I was so focused on myself, barely registered that Shaya wrapped her arms around me. It felt tight, secure, welcoming, and present. After a few minutes I calmed myself down, with Shaya soothing my back. She pulls us apart and wipes my eyes.

"You're holding onto a ghost Charli," Shaya whispered. "And you're letting go of us. The people still here."

I pulled back. The words landed like stones in my chest. Heavy, true. I shake my head, tears still brimming in my eyes.

"I don't mean to. I just—I just want my parents back. I keep trying to hold onto them," I confessed. "I see you, Dario, and Lio so happy with your parents and I remember a time when I was just like that. But with every punch my dad landed on me was just another reminder of what I lost."

I can hear Shaya take a deep breath beside me. I look over to her and see she is close to the fire. I wonder if she feels the burn in her chest as I do.

"How long?" She asks. The pain in her voice is not hard to miss.

"Since I was twelve Shaya," I whispered. "The very first time was right before my birthday, a couple of months after I stopped being friends with Dario."

I close my eyes to the memory. "I was walking back from therapy, but that day was when I didn't go straight home. I knew my father was drinking, so I just went to the park, to the basketball court." I held my breath, trying to make the memory keep going, but it didn't work.

"When I got home, he was holding a belt. After the 10th hit, I just lost count, and from that day I swore I would keep count of everything. Anything to pass the time." By the time I finished my sentence, numbness had started to take place.

The choking sob that was once stuck in my throat is now replaced with insensate feelings. We sat there, hands locked, breathing hard like we'd run a mile. The fire burned low, heat kissing our faces.

A branch snapped in the dark. Dario stepped into the light, arms full of wood. His eyes locked on me, unreadable. Pale and hard. He didn't blink.

"Where's Lio?" Shaya asked, voice hoarse.

"Pissing," Dario muttered, eyes never leaving mine.

For a moment, Shaya's gaze darted between us. Then she stood, wiping her cheeks with the back of her hand.

"I'll go find him." She disappeared into the dark, her steps fading. The silence left behind was thick, like smoke you couldn't breathe through.

I couldn't look at Dario. My heart pounded so loud it felt like it might break me open. In my head, I counted Shaya's steps. Ten...fifteen...twenty...thirty.

Only then did the tears fall, burning down my cheek.

"I'm sorry."

I apologize again, repeatedly, for the pain I caused. A habit that will never die.

The wood slipped from Dario's arms, hitting the ground in a dull thud. He took three fast steps and was in front of me, close enough to steal my breath. His arms came around me, strong and shaking, pulling me so close it hurt. His hand cradled my head; his lips pressed warm and firm against my forehead.

Our hearts slammed together, beating wild and scared.

"My strong girl," he muttered.

"Never say sorry to me. *Ever again.*"

# *Killer and The Sound*

*Phoebe Bridgers*

November 17, 2017.

"Come on, Charlotte! We're gonna miss the sunset!" Dario yelled. He was already halfway up the hill, and I was so slow behind him.

My legs burned and sweat stuck from my shirt to my back. The wind felt nice though, like a hand on my shoulder. I kept thinking about Mom. Even up there, I couldn't stop missing her.

Dario wanted to do this hike to make us feel better, especially on Thanksgiving. At the top, he waited for me with that dumb grin he always makes. Like he really believed we could forget how bad this year has been.

When I finally got there, out of breath, he teased, "Took you long enough!"

I stuck my tongue out at him.

"You dragged me up here... for what, Dar— D.J.," I said. It still feels weird calling him that.

His smile got smaller for a second. I know it's been hard for him, too. People keep calling him Dario and he gets so mad, yelling until his face turns red. But sometimes with me, he lets it slide.

"I'm glad you came, Charli," he said, quieter this time.

"Like I had a choice," I said, but I smiled a little.

We looked out together at the sea of green below. The forest felt endless, bigger than our hearts. The sight hugs me like a blanket, comforted by the art created by nature. I feel Dario's presence beside me, pulling me to look at him. His eyes mirrored the view.

"Can I ask you something D.J.?" I see him flinch at his name. The one he chose.

"Charli, ask me anything, but only if you use my name."

"But you literally fought–"

"Only if you use my name." His harsh expressions do not change.

I bit the inside of my cheek. My eyebrows come together, trying to read the person in front of me. I nodded slowly.

Dario sighs, "This year's been really bad, hasn't it?" He said, kicking the dirt. "But we still have each other, right? You'll tell me when you're sad if I tell you when I'm sad?"

"Yeah. Of course," I said. And I held my pinky out.

He linked his pinky with mine. Then, before I could even laugh, he hugged me so tight it nearly knocked me over.

He smelled like grass and that lemon soap his mom bought. His arms wrapped around me like he was terrified I'd vanish.

"Charls, promise me you'll tell me when it hurts. Promise."

"Promise," I whispered back, my own voice shaking.

For a little while, it felt like nothing could break us. Just two kids on a hill, trying to keep the world away.

~~~~~~~~~~~~~~~~~~~~~

It's been almost a week since the conversation in front of the fire. Where I burned old habits and confided in my best friend. Where I was surrounded by the family that mattered to me. With my two best friends, and my lover since childhood, all together and being us.

A group that goes undivided. Still answers go unanswered, and thoughts still linger. My brain has itched countless times trying to figure out the missing piece.

Days would go by as I blank out of conversations. Dario would try his best to pull me through, but no matter what, nothing helped me. My friends would mess with me, distracting me from my own head for a few moments, but the thoughts always linger back. For the past week, I have not been home. I have not seen my father; I have not felt my mother within the walls.

Five days and now I sit on my front porch, waiting. Not for anything but just waiting. I sit cross-legged; my rolling tray balanced in my lap. I put one blunt to the side, the rest of it in the bag where the weed came in.
~~~~~~~~~~~~~~~~~~~~~

I picked up the crisp, rolled up blunt, and put it between my fingers. If I'm going to be held hostage for a week, I might as well smoke the devil's lettuce.

Heat spreads across my fingertips as I light up. The fire catches and smoke soon fill the air, joining the rainy smell that is faint. Thanksgiving. A day full of food and family, laughter and memories.

As I fill my belly with smoke instead of food, the memories over the years start to numb. Alone, not inevitably, but still alone. In the moments when the brain starts to think and no one is there beside me to catch it. The moments when the world would dim down and all that's left is how I use everything to get away from myself.

The porch light is on, the sun is setting, and another day is ending. A day where I did not do anything but smoke, journal, and regret waking up. A day where I remain clueless.

The smoke curls lazily from the blunt as I take a deep hit. I see my father approach the corner of our block, his figure walking slanted as it comes closer. I can hear him muttering in the wind, laughing at nothing around him. He makes his way to the porch after a minute or so, looking at me up and down. *Disgust, agony, disappointment.* Nonetheless, he took a seat next to me. I pass him the wood, not wasting a breath to spare.

"You ever think about her? About Mom?" I said bluntly, no pun intended. I can hear my dad exhale sharply, as if the question is a nuisance. He passed me blunt back, and I took it gratefully.

"What's with the questions? You already know all you need to." He coughs out.

*Except for the one where I wonder what happened to my father.*

"I was just curious." I look straight ahead of me, forcing myself to take a hit as the smoke burns my throat. I do it three more times, enforcing the drug to come take over faster.

"You always were good at that," I hear my dad whisper to himself.

"Good at what?" I had the courage to look at him. My father. His eyes are not filled with love but instead they are dim, tired, and empty.

For a moment he just stares. Like he is recognizing something he hasn't seen in a long while. The moment ended when he shakes his head, like he is trying to deny me.

"Nothing. Never mind." I pass him back bluntly, the effect slowly creeping on me. It was just us two, the remains of a portrait painted perfectly. Cause and effect of people who grew up with and without each other.

We sat on a porch that had known us for years, saw everything that happened to us. To see different versions of people who never noticed their change.

"She used to disappear. Sometimes. You remember that?" My dad broke the silence. Blunt between his fingers as it lays over his legs. His elbows rest on his legs as he stares out. I nodded slowly, urging him to continue.

"She'd say she needed air. That she needed to 'feel like herself again.' I never knew what she meant. Not for a long time until it was right in front of me." He looks at me sideways before handing me the finished blunt. I take it in my hands and spark it up once again, bringing it to life.

"She was on fire, you know. The kind th-that keeps you warm until it burns everything down." His voice is low. Not angry, just tired. "I didn't know how to love someone like that. I thought giving her space would keep her mine. But it only gave her room to forget me. To *use* me."

My dad leans back; a breath leaves him like a confession.

"She had so many versions of herself. I never knew which one I was going to get. But they were all better than me." The silence grows thick between us. The sound of rain making its' appearance as the silence continues to drown us.

"She loved you," he adds, suddenly. "That was the one thing I believed every time."

My chest tightens. My lungs ache, but not from the smoke. I look at him--at his sunken face, the stubble beard he didn't bother to shave. The man who once lifted me on the shoulders only to drag me to the ground.

The words slipped out before I could grab them, "What about me? Why do you *hate* me?" My voice cracked, sobs threatening to come out.

He flinches—barely. Not close to the number of times I did every time he lifted his arms. But it's still there: remorse. Guilt for what he had done eternally. This man in front of me killed my father.

"Charli..."

"Just say it." Whatever emotion was left in my system was drained out. I only feel the anger pump into my veins.

"You look like her." He says it is a fact, like a wound. "You walk like her, talk like her. You ask too many questions. You don't stay in one place. You want too much. You expect more." I'm still. My heartbeat echoes through my ears.

"Every single time I look at you, I see all the ways I couldn't keep her. All the reminders that don't belong to me. and now you're her shadow. But louder. Bolder." He shakes his head. His eyes attack mine.

"I don't hate you Charli. I just..." he says as his voice barely holding. "I hate that I lost her, and you keep making me remember."

I want to say something, anything, but my throat feels like glass. He continues to look at me, and for a split second, I see my dad that died with my mother. The one that called me baby girl. The one that carried me to bed after I fell asleep on the couch.

But it's gone just as fast.

"Sometimes I just think if I just...shut it all down, I won't feel it anymore. But then you walk into the room, and it all comes back." My dad stands, wobbling a bit. He drains whatever is left in his glass.

"I *love* you. I always have. *Always do.*" I breathed out harshly. My dad stops in his footsteps.

"I always wanted to understand, Dad. And I do, but you never see change. And for a long time neither have I. But I realized this hate anymore because it's not me, it's you." The sound of rain just hits the ground like bullets threatening to puncture. I hold my breath as my dad turns around, unrecognizable pain, but understandable.

"Be careful who you become," he slurs, "You're already halfway there."

He leaves. The joint is burned down to the filter in my hand. And I don't know if the tears are from the smoke or if part of me still wants to believe he still loves me.

I get up. *Keep moving. Keep moving. Don't look back. Breathe. 1...2....3...*

The rain doesn't feel like rain. It feels like a punishment.

Each drop is a slap across my skin. Cold. Unforgiving. But I keep walking, one foot after the other, because stopping means thinking. And thinking means remembering, and *remembering means I might not survi—*

It's just a lot. The porch light fades behind me. The smell of weed lingers in my hair. The ache from my father's voice sits like a stone in my stomach.

*Be careful who you become...you're already half-way there.*

I walk faster, not because I want to, but because the pain is pulsing through my legs now, begging for an outlet. The sidewalk blurs. I can't tell if it's the rain or my eyes, but I kept going.

Clench fists, unclench, and clench again. My nails dig into my palm, trying to wake me up. *I'm still here, I'm still fucking here. In front of you!*

It's not until I reach the river—20 minutes away, secluded, hallow, forgotten—that I let go.

I collapsed near the edge, knees hitting wet dirt. The sky above splits open harder, rain soaking my hoodie, jeans, everything. I feel my hands make their way up my body. Desperately trying to pull myself together. I grab my hair.

*Ripping the thoughts out.* I try. *Pathetic. You look like her. I don't hate you. You just remind me of her. Her. Her. Her.* My life is depicted by someone who hasn't breathed in years.

My fingers continue to claw at my scalp until it stings. I punched the ground. I scream—but everything is muffled.

"Why?" Hit. "Why?" Hit. "Why?" Hit. My hands are bruised with mud as band aid.

*You're her shadow. But louder. Bolder.*

I am nothing but all the dark parts of my parents. My skin burns with every scratch. My throat closes around the air that won't come. I shake. I tremble. I pull at myself like I can peel off the pain.

And then something—something glints in the dirt. Just barely. A faint shimmer beneath the mud. I froze. Stare. The rain pools around it, tricking slowly.

I dig. *Stop digging.* Dig, dig, dig, dig. *He always knew.* I have to dig. For her. My nails caked in mud, fingers shaking. I scrape at the earth as if it insulted me. Until it gives way.

A small plastic bag. A key inside. Silver. Dull, but not lifeless. The rain makes it gleam like a secret wanting to be found. I can't read it clearly, not in the storm, but I see two initials:

**M.C.**

My fingers curl around it like it might have disappeared. It could've been seconds, minutes, hours of me just sitting there. At least until my phone buzzes in my pocket.

Emilio: Where are you?

Emilio: Charls, where are you? It's pouring.

I hesitate. If he doesn't find me, maybe I'll stay here forever.

Me: The river.

~~~~~~~~~~~~~~~~~~~~~~~

His car pulls up ten minutes later. The headlights are slicing through the trees. I hear the door slam before I see him. His hoodie is up, but he's soaked anyway. He rushes to me, his breathing fogging in the cold.

"Charli, are you serious? What are you doing? It's not just a drizzle, it's pouring—Jesus."

I didn't answer. I just walked past him and slid into the passenger seat. He follows, shivering.

"Why?" Emilio's voice is strained. Like he's choosing anger over panic.

"Why alone?"

I stare out the window. "It helped."

I can hear Lio sigh heavily along with the drips onto the steering wheel.
~~~~~~~~~~~~~~~~~~~~~~~

"Whatever, Charls. I'm bringing you to my house. Shaya's there, Dario is on his way." That pulls something from me. I shake my head, fast.

"'No, I can't go to your house."

"Why not?"

"I just...I just want to be home."

Silence. The engine hums. The heat blasts faintly between us.

"No. You can't go back there Charls," he mutters. His eyes focused on the road.

"I can't just leave Lio—"

"The hell you can't. I'm not letting you go near that bastard."

I stay quiet. I just listened to my friend. My true family.

Lio sighs out loud, rubbing the droplets from his forehead, "Come to the house Charls, it's just my parents and I. Shaya and Dario are joining us too since they're parents are out of town."

I leaned back into the car, watching the rain pour against the windows. Clutching the bag tighter in my pocket, the key presses into my palm. I pull it slowly, like it might bite me.

"What's that?" Emilio asks as he glances from the corner of his eye.

I trace the letters with my thumb.

"Do you," I hesitated.

I breathe out, "Do you have anything locked in your house?"

"Like what?"

"A box. Something small. Something with a key."

Emilio scoffs. "No, what is going on with you?" He continues to drive smoothly. The pavement of the road makes no sound other than the raindrops hitting the windows.

"Nothing. It's just—never mind."

"Charli, you're being weird. You find a key, press me about it, and now you shut off again-"

"It has initials on it."

"And?"

"And I found it at the river, in a plastic bag, hidden."

"Why does that bother you so much Charls?"

"Why would a key be hidden by a lake? Especially where my mom was found dead?" Lio shrugs, clueless about where this is going.

"Why would you go dig around a river in the middle of the storm? What was you looking for Charli?" Emilio spits out. Concern was written all over his face. I want to laugh; he doesn't understand. Why should he?

"Charli, what is it?"

I swallowed hard. My voice is small. Broken.

"I have something to tell you, Emilio."

He slows down the car and pulls into his driveway as he parks.

"Okay. Tell me," Emilio demands. I grip the key. My chest tightens.

"Back in October, I found my mother's necklace. It was found in your house, downstairs in the living room. I was curious about it, and it bothered me." I started explaining, but Emilio's face continued to show confusion.

"I always said my mother's death wasn't a suicide. I still believe that. It was my gut feeling to tell me to keep searching. To find something that was hidden." I took this time to face him. I looked out of the window and took in his appearance. My best friend since diapers; his mother and mine were close, automatically making us as well.

"Lio, I found a letter in the attic with my mom's things. It was from her handwriting. I found it with Dario."

"Wait, what? Charli, why didn't you tell me or Shaya?"

"I don't know. I'm sorry, it was just too much for me, so I didn't want to put that on my best friends." I breathed out. Lio puts his hand on my shoulder and gives me a gentle squeeze.

"Is there anything else?" He says as he comforts me.

"Yeah," I try to get my thoughts together. "I found a photo in the library. It was my parents together, but also your father. Mykel." I try explaining to Emilio to the best of my ability. How Wilma helped piece everything together.

I explain that over the past month Dario has been there through everything, even when I wouldn't expect him to. I explain, explain, explain, but none of it adds up. People are still confused; I am still confused.

"So, let me get this straight Charli." Lio straightens up in his seat, facing me fully.

"For the past month, you and Dario have been on this mystery hunt for what happened to your mother. Found out that my father was friends with your parents during high school, and now what? You think he did something?" Emilio anger flared up. His usual cool demeanor vanished.

He was annoyed the moment he saw me, and now by telling him everything he can't stand me. Nobody can stand me.

All I do is stay quiet. Not knowing what words to say. Emilio takes his seatbelt off, grabbing a fist of his hair, and then taking in my appearance again.

"I mean seriously, Charli." He huffs, "You're so bent on finding the truth that you're losing yourself. What about your dad?"

This catches my attention. "What about him?"

"Why not him? Why not ask a question about him? Why, Charli, why? None of this adds up."

I can feel the heat rise on my face. *Why not my dad? He hits you, beats you, drags you, and manipulates you. Most of all despise you.* "It's not him." I said coldly.

"And what makes you so sure of that? You don't notice half the things around you, what makes you think you're able to detect…"

One…

I can barely hear Emilio still talking to me.

Two…

The key in my hand holds like an anchor as my mind floats in the sea of abyss.

Three…

*Dig. Dig. Dig*

"WHAT THE FUCK DO YOU WANT ME TO SAY LIO!" Silence rings in the air. Emilio just stares at me, but not in anger anymore. Recognition?

"That I can't concentrate in school because I am so tired of everything? That I can't stand being near people because they are not my parents I lost years ago?"

"Charli-"

"No, you know why I know it's not my dad? Because it can't be Emilio. It just can't be! Because that means I truly did lose both parents." I can feel the tears trinkle down my cheeks.

Sobs burst through my throat. Emilio reaches for me, but I push him away.

"No, don't you get it? I am destructible. Everyone I touch, love, they eventually fade away. They die, physically or mentally. Those who are still around are just reminded of how hurtful I can become." My chest becomes stone; I can't breathe. I feel like I am a fish in the air, needing water to replenish myself.

"I stopped being friends with Dario all those years ago because I am just going to drag him down. I don't engage in conversation because I am just a body waiting to be dropped. I stopped talking to you and Shaya about me because I couldn't even understand myself at first."

I don't know what came over me. Lio's stare? His confusion? His hurt? Everyone's hurt? I look out the window, staring at the house in front of me. *How can I step inside knowing that Mykel was the only adult left I thought I could trust? Is it bad to appreciate the love I have, even the spiteful ones?*

"Nothing can be as hurtful as the love I get from my father all over my body. Every other day it is just another reminder of why I can't be more than my mother in his eyes. I hurt him because he didn't do enough for her." It kills me to say that even in the loving moments, my father only looked at me with the love he had for my mother. Only she holds the truth that made love turn into hate.

Emilio pulls me into a strong hug, suffocating me with love I haven't felt in ages. "I'm so sorry Charli. I only wanted my sister back. *I'm sorry.*"

Lio's shirt smelled like pine grass, like nature. I grip on him for dear life, for my best friend. For my brother from a different mother. No matter what I think of Mykel, Lio never showed me anything but love. A brotherly love, a sibling I have yearned for.

"Charli," he pulls us apart as we face each other. His hands are on my shoulders, his eyes holding desperation.

"I need to know why my father, Charli? Why Mykel?" It burns me looking at him. To face the guilt of blaming everyone for my pain, I feel terrible. So, I stepped out of the car, rain hitting my skin automatically.

"Charli!" Lio yells behind me. More voices joined in, calling me in. I thought it was all in my head.

I turn. Dario is already moving toward me, jacket coming off, his voice urgent but calm. I can see Shaya behind him, reaching for Lio by car.

"Come on, head inside." We headed towards the door, hearing Emilio's footsteps behind us. He doesn't say a word, but I feel his eyes. Not accusing, just tired, but respectful, nonetheless. He understands that I understand him. His wants, his needs. But he never pushes my boundaries or my mentality.

Once inside, warmth greets us. The smell of thanksgiving food fills our nostrils. Shivers ran down my back. I look over to Dario, who has his face on me the entire time. I can tell he is worried about me, but only with care.

I look the other way to see Emilio holding a concerned look over his face. I read sorrow and empathy. Everything I tried to avoid but I succumbed to it.

"Lio, I am going to take Charli downstairs. Let her sleep." Dario explained. Emilio nods and I just stand there. I'm too drained to reply. To engage in conversation. Like I am just a statue seeing everything. *Everything my father was complaining about.*

I can only feel, and in this moment, the comfort of Dario's arm around my shoulders as he guides us downstairs overpowers everything else. It takes us one...five...ten...fifteen...eighteen steps for us to reach the bedroom downstairs. We pass by Persephone, who is still cooking in the kitchen. She greeted us shortly before going back to her business. *Queen.*

As we enter the room, the tension rises between Dario and me. I haven't been exactly for myself, and I don't want Dario to think it's his fault. I grabbed Dario's hand and led us to bed. I take off my wet jacket, along with my shoes, encouraging Dario to do the same. We peel off the soaked layers in silence, down to shorts and skin. My sports bra clings cold to my ribs. Still, there's comfort in the quiet choreography of survival.

We're sitting on the bed, side by side. Dario takes in my appearance, my bruises, my pain. He grabs my hand and places it in his lap; tracing my knuckles that have been cut from earlier.

"Do you remember how you asked me about the way I spoke? The reason behind it." Dario spoke softly, like he was trying to ease my mind.

I nodded in response. Too tired to speak. But I still cling onto his words, the only matter in this moment.

"The reason is because when my father left," he stopped momentarily. I press on his hands, encouraging him. "It was years until my mother got with Shaya's dad, and for those years it was hell." Dario clears his throat at the memory. He looks down at me, and plants a kiss on my forehead before continuing as he wraps his shoulder around me.

"I thought if I was like my dad I would end up like him; leaving his family behind and all. So as a kid I did the things I could to not be like him, even changing the way I spoke. It is something simple, but that very little thing carries a lot." I look at Dario with gratitude.

To witness a kid, turn out to be very mature at a young age. I envy how he does it.

"Is that why you started going by D.J. instead of Dario?" My voice is hoarse.

"Yeah, is it the same reason for you *Charli?*"

I roll my eyes at the name. A facade of who I was, a reality I must accept now.  "I guess you would say so." I yawn between my sentences, feeling slumber about to take over. "How come you still have your dad's last name?"

I can feel Dario breathe harshly as I lay on his chest. "I guess you would have to say we have another thing in common when it comes to our loved ones. We hold onto those who hurt us when promised unconditional love."

And that sentence alone taught me everything.

My father taught me to be patient with love while Dario taught me that love is patient.

# *Revenge* *XXXTentacion*

November 30, 2023

As people, we're prone to seek knowledge we never truly attain. We focus so much on what we don't have—what isn't in our hands—that we forget what surrounds us.

Sometimes we chase things that were never meant for us. We run toward the inevitable, even as we try so hard to avoid it. The truth has a way of shifting the course we thought we were on, reminding us of how fragile our sense of control really is.

In the end, we are measured, hypothesized, and painfully predictable. We believe in what we connect with, whether that is nature or salvation, but manipulated into lessons and abundance. How can we live if our love is taken as a token to pay for our gratitude?

In this society, what we love can easily turn into a lesson; a predicament that others can take advantage of. At what cost *does a person give until they realize that they have themselves first before others. Or truly a mother first before all.*

My heartbeat is heavy as I wake up. The room is dim, lit only by the last stretch of daylight slipping through the guest room window. For a moment, I don't know where I am—just that I'm alone.

The silence presses down on me, made heavier by the muffled sound of laughter above. It seeps through the ceiling: music, voices layered, the warmth of people who belong.

My head feels heavy, like I slept too deeply. I sit up slowly, pushing the blanket aside. The guest room smells faintly of laundry detergent. I crawl out of bed, dragging my limbs across the room in a sluggish manner.

When I open the door, the hallways greet me with stillness. The living room is empty. I look around anyways, and the drawer in the coffee table catches my eye. My hands naturally find their way to my necklace—my mother's necklace.

*He lied. Rowdy boy. Lied. Lied. Lied. He has always known.*

*Hit. Dig. Hit. Dig. Hit. Hit. You look like her.*

The sound of life floats down from upstairs, pulling me out of my thoughts. Laughter, the scrape of chairs, the low buzz of conversation. I follow it, taking the steps one at a time.

At the top, the house feels different; alive.

They're all gathered around the dining table, cluttered with mugs and open decks of cards, and plates with the remains of something homemade. Shaya is leaning forward, eyes bright, telling a story that I can't quite catch from here. Lio interrupts with something teasing, and Dario laughs, loud and open, the kind of laugh that fills a room.

Persephone shakes her head at them, half smiling, half scolding. Mykel sits beside her, shoulders slightly hunched, hands wrapped around a cup. He listens more than he talks, but every so often he adds something quiet that makes the others smile.

I stay back, half-hidden in the hallway. Watching. *Like the stalker I am. Like the betraying thoughts that keep me searching for what I shouldn't know.*

For a few minutes—five, maybe ten—no one noticed me. And in that time, I see them as they are when they forget for me: whole, stable. Their voices rise and fall like a tide I've forgotten how to swim in. Dario teasing Shaya, Lio and Persephone bickering softly, the steady undercurrent of Mykel's voice—calm, weighted, but not there fully.

They belong to each other. And for a moment, I let myself believe that maybe they're better off this way— balanced, without the quiet heaviness I bring to the room.

The thoughts sting in my chest, sharp and familiar. I could step forward, say something, and let them see me. But the thoughts feel foreign, like trying to force two pieces of a puzzle that don't fit anymore. Instead, I turn away, quietly stepping down the stairs.

The living room feels colder than before, the hush almost comforting in its emptiness. I sit on the edge of the couch, by the coffee table, where I found my mother's necklace weeks ago. From my pocket, I pull out the key, holding it tightly in my palm. Small, tarnished, but solid.

I'm so lost in memory of what I know and what I don't know that I almost never heard the footsteps behind me. Hair sticks to the back of my neck.

Then quietly, Mykel's voice breaks through, "Charli?"

I look up from the couch, my fingers still curled tight around the key.

"Hey."

He steps closer, taking a seat next to me as he has a mug in his hand. "You okay?"

"Yeah," I lied. *I don't know how to talk to him.*

"Want something to eat?" He asks, softer now. "Persephone made enough food to feed the block."

I smile at the thought. "Not really hungry."

He pauses, then nods, and leans back onto the couch. The cushion creaks under its weight, and the room feels quieter than it should; like the air itself is waiting.

"How did you know I was up?" I asked, breaking the silence. I could feel his eyes on me as I asked the question.

"I saw you around the corner, when you were heading back downstairs," Mykel sighed. "I was wondering why you didn't join us."

I shook my head more to myself than to him. "You were quiet upstairs," I said after a moment.

"Guess, so," he says with a low voice. "It's nothing, really."

"Doesn't look like nothing," I say gently. "You look like you were somewhere else."

Mykel laughs out loud, "You would know the feeling huh, Charli?" His gaze drifts past me to some places I can't see.

"Old memories," he says after a bet.

"About her?"

His lips parted, then pressed shut again. "Yeah," he breathes out. Like he is relieved in a sort of way. "About her."

I look closely, studying the man in front of me. Trying to put the puzzle pieces together. My dad said I reminded him of what my mother did to him, her mistake.

I see the truth and the lies confirmed as one.

"You always say you weren't that close," I say. My voice isn't sharp—it's tired, almost sad. "But I know you were. You wouldn't look like that if you weren't."

He looks down at the mug, black with a little panda on it. Cute. "She was...complicated."

"Tell me," I say; desperate for any version of my mother.

His shoulders dropped a bit. Then it is his turn to shake his head.

"No," he takes a sip out of the panda mug. "Not anything worth sharing." He looks so relaxed, but I can tell his nerves are twitching.

As mine are boiling with anger. I try to cool down before letting my words slip.

One mistake I don't regret.

"*Any* topic of my mother is worth sharing." I said coldly. Seeing Mykel take a physical pause makes me take a breath. In and out.

"I was watching you all," I go on, my voice catching at the edge. "All of you around the table. Laughing, teasing, the noise filling the room."

He listens, silent.

"It reminded me of how it used to be." *Road trips, movie nights, game days.* My voice trembles. "Before everything fell apart. You ask me why I hold on, and it's because that very house...that special house is the last thing I have left of my parents. Even as hurtful as it is now, it's familiar. It's home."

Mykel catches a breath. His fingers are rubbing together against the mug, and his face is content, almost too much. It was like an act, like an entity consuming a distinct face. It was gone as soon as I noticed it.

"Charli--"

"They were once good," I whispered, almost to myself.

"Weren't they?" His shoulders stiffen at my question.

"It wasn't what you think it was," he says as he shakes his head. He places the mug down on the coffee table.

I look at him fully, taking in his whole appearance. His beard has grown out, he has eyebags building up, lips chapped. He looks exhausted. "What do you mean?"

His gaze drops—landing on the key still clutched in my hand. His voice comes out low, rough at the edges. "Give me the key you found."

*How the fu—*

"What are you not telling me Mykel?"

His eyes meet mine, tired and sad. *What is going on? The key. Dig. Dig. Dig. He knows. He knows. He knows.*

*"Give me the key you found."* He repeats, "And I'll show you."

I didn't move at first. How can I? Do I trust him? How does he know? *Was he watching me as I watched him?*

Something though told me otherwise. I uncurl my fingers, one by one. I handed him the key, slowly and shaking. Mykel takes it swiftly, his hand mirroring mine.

He stands, walking over to the coffee table. I watch every movement, like my life depended on it. Breath still. Silence fills the room. A pin could drop, and nothing would break the tension.

He soon lifts the tabletop, revealing a hidden drawer I'd found but could never open. Mykel reaches inside, pulls out an envelope and folded letter. The edge worn soft from years of being opened, closed, and opened again. Without a word, he turns and holds them out to me.

My heart slams so hard it hurts. I take them. I open the envelope first. The paper rattles in my hands. I see my name, Mykel's name, and Lio's. My eyes skim through the paper, darting to the bottom.

Probability of paternity: 99.97%.

Nothing. Numbness. I was not prepared for this. For my world to split open once again. Mykel. My dad. He is my father, not mine. Not drunk. Not the abusive asshole. I have another parent. I still have a family. I still have blood.

My hands shake as I unfold the letter next. Mykel doesn't say anything. He just observes quietly. Only the sound of the soft music upstairs, the relaxing chatter and laughter continuing through the floorboards.

*10.04. 2014*

*My love, my heartbeat.*

*I don't even know where to begin with you. Maybe I never did. Maybe that was always the problem. You've been the center of everything in me since we were kids.*

*Every fight I picked with you — it was just me begging you to see me. Just for a second. I knew if I made you mad, you'd talk to me. If I made you laugh, you'd touch my arm. And sometimes you did.*

*Eventually, it was more. And for those moments, I got to feel like I mattered to you. For fuck's sake, I lived for those moments. I lived for you. And even when you walked away — when you picked my best friend again — I never stopped. I told myself love means patience. Quiet sacrifice. That maybe one day, you'd turn back around, and I'd still be there.*

*And you did, Astrid. I thought I'd say this at our wedding, not our goodbye. You came back, but not for me. You came back with a child — my fucking child — and you looked me in the eye and let me believe she wasn't mine.*

*For eight fucking damn years I had another child. Do you know what that does to a man like me? One who would have given you everything? One who did?*

*I would've died for you, Astrid. A part of me did tonight.*

*You knew that. You used to laugh at how serious I got whenever you cried — remember that? And I would've raised Charli no matter what. I would've loved her even if she wasn't mine.*

*I loved her thinking she wasn't.*

*But you lied, and not just once. Every time I saw her — every time I wondered if maybe she had my eyes — you just smiled and let me stay silent. Let me stay small.*

*You took the one thing I never asked you for. You took fatherhood from me.*

*And I still... still I love you. I love you now, even while I'm shaking writing this. Even though I feel like I'm coming apart.*

*I don't want to hate you, Astrid. I cannot. But tonight, all I feel is something crawling up through my chest. And I keep thinking: if you could do this to me — you, the only person I've ever truly loved — then maybe I never meant anything to you at all.*

*And that's what breaks me. Not a lie. Not the years. But the thought that maybe all that time, you were never really mine.*

*—M.*

A single tear. More follows down the trail. My hands are trembling. I tried to reach for comfort in my mother's necklace but even that didn't work. My breathing becomes shallow.

*He always knew. Mykel always knew. Dig. I dug and found hell.*

Words burn in my lungs.

My voice tears, out, ragged and shaking, "*What did you do to her?*" I can't even look at him, but I must. Because she is the very last thing she saw before being stripped away against her will.

His head jerks up, eyes wild, mouth opening like he's choking on something that's been buried too long. "Why are you asking me--"

In a second, I picked up the mug on the coffee table and threw it towards the opposite wall to us, the one by the staircase. Coffee splatters on the walls and the stairs, staining the picture-perfect atmosphere.

"WHAT. DID. YOU. FUCKING. DO. TO. HER?" I said slowly and slyly. My eyes trained on the man in front of me. I can feel my body shut down, becoming numb to the situation. My mind is on autopilot.

The music above has turned off. The whole house is now silent. I wait for an answer. Mykel hands claw through his hair, tugging so hard it looks painful. "Don't--Don't ask me that--"

"WHAT DID YOU DO TO MY FUCKING MOM! WHAT DID YOU DO? WHAT DID YOU DO? WHAT DID YOU FUCKING DO!" My voice is strained.

I can feel the burning sensation in my throat as it roars through the basement. My words bounce off the walls, sharper, louder. My chest aches for rest, air coming in broken gasps.

I hear footsteps--two...four...six...eight--Lio and Dario appear first, eyes wide and terrified. *I would be, too.* Persephone and Shaya are right behind, faces white with horror.

"Charli, *hey love, hey,*" Dario's voice shakes as he moves towards me, his hand out like he might catch me. "Look at me—*breathe. For me.*"

But I couldn't look away. Mykel's face twists, rage crawling from somewhere deep and old.

"You're the reason," I sob, the words spilling out faster than I can stop them. "He hurts me now because of you. Because of what you did to her, right? Tell me, how did you kill my mother?"

He shakes his head; I can feel everyone's eyes on me.

"Charli, stop." Dario hisses, for once I can feel his anger towards me. I look at him confused, taken aback.

I look all around, seeing multiple pairs of eyes lingering around mine. A pair of hands grabs my face, pulling directly into a forest.

"Charlotte," Dario softly says this time. I shake my head in his comforting hands. I pulled away and looked down at the papers in my hands. I turn to Lio. His face contorted, but he was worried.

"Here," passing him the papers, I wait for his reactions. It took him thirty seconds for each paper, a minute to get what I was looking for. The same desperation look I wore whenever I looked at my father; to seek the truth in an image we cannot accept.

"No!" Mykel yelled out. "Your father hits you because he always took what he had for granted!"

"Mykel, stop!" Persephone voice cracks desperately. Lio's arms shot out, pulling her and Shaya back behind him.

But he doesn't hear her. His eyes are locked on me-- wild, shiny with tears that won't fall. "I gave him *everything.*" He shouts, voices shaking the walls.

"His lover, his daughter, his fucking life. And for what? To drink it all away and lay his hand on *my* daughter. All of it should have been mine. You should have been mine. You *are* mine."

I look around at the people sharing this moment with me. Lio pushes Shaya and Persephone upstairs, telling them to call the police. Dario is in front of me, his eyes never leave Mykel's. His back covers me, but not enough to hide *daddy dearest.*

*"You. Killed. My. Mother."* My knees buckle, but I never hit the ground. Dario's arms are around my waist, holding me back from going to Mykel. "You are the reason! The reason why I limp going to school, the reason why I am so fucking depressed I quit everything I have loved."

I can feel heat rise to my forehead, sweat forming, and a headache coming to the surface. Dario is still holding me, whispering in my ear the whole time.

"You are the reason why I can't do shit without thinking of her."

I tried hitting myself in the chest, to push the ache in my heart that was starting to cramp. Instead, I am met with Dario's hand over mine. I can feel his strength carry me and protect me.

"She lied, Charli," Mykel starts making his way forward. One step, two steps, and three.

"Back *the fuck* up Mykel," Dario threatens. In seconds, he takes a pocketknife out of his jacket and flings it open.

Mykel put his hands up against Dario, Lio taking his place next to me. He places a hand on Dario's shoulder but does not make eye contact with his father.

"I would never hurt her, D.J." Dario doesn't move. His only movement is the grip on the pocketknife; his one hand wrapped around my waist.

"Is that what you promised Astrid?" Lio spoke out. I watch him and Mykel stare at each other, neither of them breaking eye contact. I see the similarities in them, which now pertains to me. I feel lightheaded. "What happened to you, dad?"

And this is where I finally saw him truly break. Mykel's face contorts—the fury slides off him all at once, leaving nothing but something smaller, shaking, destroyed.

Human.

His chest heaves as tears finally spilled. His breath hitches like it hurts to breathe. "I loved her," he rasps, so low it cracks apart. "Charli, I'm sorry...I'm so fucking sorry."

Lio's face twists — half fury, half horror — as he looks at his father crying like a child. "*What did you do?!*"

Mykel's hands slide down his face, eyes red and raw. "Charli, please—" But I'm already moving — trying to shove past Dario, my chest heaving, lungs screaming. "Let me go! That's my dad, Dario!"

His arms snap around me, holding me back even as I thrash. "Charli, no—stop—"

"*LET ME GO!*" I sob, the words tearing my throat. "That's my dad — the only parent I have left, Dario!"

My vision blurs, tears streaming hot and blinding. But even through the blur, I see him: Mykel — wrecked, crying, mouth open around words that won't come out.

And something breaks open inside me.

For the first time, I see him *truly*: His vulnerability, his mistakes, the darkness that swallowed him whole. The love that turned into something rotten when it was denied for too long.

I think about every time my father's hand struck me — and how he *knew* I wasn't his, and still never told me. Never told anyone. The truth was buried with my mother. And now, in the wreckage, all that's left is this: a ruined man crying for what he destroyed, and a daughter trying to reach for something she can't save.

Dario's arms tighten, voice shaking, "*Charli, please...*"

But my voice cracks around a sob, raw and desperate: "He's my dad, Dario. Please, he's my dad..."

I should hate him, but I see half of me.

The boy who loved too much, who stayed small for love.

His guilt. His love. His darkness swallowed him whole.

The truth, at last, doesn't save us.

It unmakes us.

And in that ruin, I see myself.

"Why... why did you never tell me you were my father?" His gaze drags up to meet mine. For a breath, the rage drains away — and all I see is ruin.

His voice cracks, barely a whisper, but it cuts deeper than any shout, "Because... despite everything... I didn't want to give you another parent to look down on."

The words don't fix anything. They didn't change what he did.

But they tear something open inside me. In that breath — the room blurs out. Faces smear into color. My chest keeps seizing, lungs burning with every ragged breath I try to drag in.

Dario's arms lock around me, holding me so tight it almost hurts, but it's the only thing keeping me from shattering across the floor.

"Breathe, Charli," he keeps whispering, repeatedly, voice shaking so bad I barely recognize it. "Focus on me, I am right here."

My vision of tunnels, edges black and swimming. My chest seizes, lungs scraping raw air in and out.

In.

Out.

The room blurs at the edges, colors bleeding into each other. Dario's arms are jarred around me, voice shaking, repeating my name over and over — but it sounds like it's coming from underwater.

In.

Out.

Mykel's face dissolves into tears and rage, Persephone's cries crack like glass somewhere behind me. Shaya consoled Emilio.

In.

Out.

Lio's stare — wide, hollow, stunned — floats in the haze.

The walls breathe in and out with me. The air feels too heavy to swallow. Flashing blue and red lights against

Mykel's eyes; soft hues resonating against my soul as I look at him one last time.

In...

~~~~~~~~~~~~~~

And I'm outside on the porch steps, knees pulled to my chest, the cold biting through my jeans. Lio sits beside me, elbows on his knees, eyes red-rimmed and unfocused. Neither of us says anything at first. Just breathing the same cold air, the space between us is heavy and fragile.

Finally, I swallow hard, voice raw, "I didn't even know I had an ugly brother."

His lips twitch like he wants to laugh, but it dies before it gets there. "Yeah," he says, voice hoarse, "turns out I had a horse for a sister this whole time, too."

I turn my head to look at him, tears stinging fresh behind my eyes. "It doesn't feel real." No matter how hard we try, our jokes cannot even lift spirits. Not this time.

He nods slowly. "Yeah. Feels like the ground just... split open under us." The porch creaks beneath us as we shift, both of us smaller than before. "But" Lio says, voice lower, steadier, "none of it changes what we've been, Charli. You've been my sister my whole life, even when we didn't know it. Even when Dad... even when he kept it from us."

My voice cracks. "And you've been my brother. My stupid, annoying brother."

A small, broken smile pulls at his mouth. "Still am."

"Yeah," I whisper. "Still are."

For a second, the silence feels softer. Warmer. I rest my head against his shoulder, breath shaking out of me. "Everything else is fucked. But us... we were never a lie."
~~~~~~~~~~~~~~

His shoulder rises and falls with shaky breath. "Yeah. We're real."

And in that moment, with the cold creeping into my bones, my chest still raw from screaming — I let myself trust it.

We're real.

# *July* *Noah Cyrus*

December 10, 2013

Today Mommy said that I could open my eyes and see the kitchen and there was a chocolate cake on the table with candles that had rainbow stripes. Daddy was still in his PJ's, and he had flour on his face. So silly. He tried to put sprinkles in my hair, but they spilled everywhere, and Mommy laughed so loud it made me laugh too.

Shaya gave me a bracelet she made, all pink and green beads. She said it was magic so if I wore it, no monsters would get me at night. I believe in her. I want to wear it forever, even in the bath. Dario and Lio only teased me through the whole day, giving me their stupidity as a gift.

After the cake we went outside, and Daddy spun me around on his back. I felt so high I could see the top of my house.

Mommy took a picture and said she was going to put it on the fridge. She called us her "two babies."

I told Daddy I wanted to be seven forever. He smiled but then looked sad for a bit. I didn't know why, maybe he thought seven was really big. Later, I sat by the window and watched the lights on the porch. They look like stars. I wished they would stay on all year so it could feel like my birthday all the time.

I love today so much. I don't want it to end. I'm seven now.

Love, Charlotte.

December 10, 2017

Dear journal,

Shaya came over after school with a little cupcake she made. The frosting got smushed together in her bag, but it still tasted sweet. We ate it on the porch.

After, she dropped me off at the rec center. Coach Lawson said happy birthday and asked if I wanted to work on some drills. I tried. I really did. But my legs felt heavy, like they weren't mine. Every shot bounced off the rim. Every dribble felt wrong, like the ball was too loud in my hands. I used to feel safe on the court. Like Mom was still watching.

Today it just felt empty. Like it didn't belong to me anymore.

Dad wasn't home yet when I got back. When he did come in, he smelled like that drink he has now. The strong one that makes him quiet and nonexistent in the house. He kissed my head, but it felt fast, like he really didn't see me.

There's a pile of envelopes on the kitchen counter. Some have red writing that says, "past due." I don't think I'm supposed to know what it means, but I do. Sometimes I hear dad on the phone late at night, his voice is all low and angry.

Dario texted me after dinner. He asked what I did for my birthday. I almost told him nothing, but I didn't want to sound sad, so I told him Shaya came over and I went to shoot around. He sent a heart and for a moment, my heart felt soft instead of stone.

It didn't last as I kept thinking of mom. What she'd do if she were here. She'd probably dance with me in the kitchen like she used to. Complaining that I'm getting so big but beautiful. I tried to remember what her voice sounded like when she sang but it's getting fuzzy. That makes me scared.

I am eleven years old. It doesn't feel special. Just feel like another day without her.

Charlotte

December 10, 2021

I didn't plan to write tonight but I can't stop watching it.

It was in the cafeteria. I heard her voice before I saw her face. I don't even remember what she said exactly—something about mom. A joke that made her friends laugh.

My hands were already curling before I thought about it. Then I stood over her. She was still laughing, but her eyes flicked up to me and then--

One punch to her cheek. I remember how it felt: soft and sharp at the same time. The noise it made, like hitting a locker door. My fists came down again; I wasn't counting. Just punching. Her head jerked back, and blood came out of her nose, bright red against her skin. I watched it spread across her lip, dripping onto her shirt.

I don't even know her name. That's the part that scares me. That I am like him. The victim turned into the perpetrator.

Someone's hands were on my shoulders, dragging me back. My legs felt heavy, like they didn't belong to me. I've been getting into fights a lot recently. My chest hurts from breathing so fast. The principal's voice was shouting. Suspension. Dad had to come and get me. He barely looked at me the whole ride home. Something I was so used to.

Now my knuckles are split and swollen. They sting when I open my hands and when I write on this page. But it feels distant. Like it happened to someone else.

I don't know why it felt good. Just for a second, like letting something out that's been burning inside for too long. Then afterward, all that's left is the ashes.

Fifteen feels like rage that never turns off.

Charli

December 10, 2022

Seventeen. It is the year before adulthood. The last year as a minor. Many people rush through their childhood to get away from their families, to make their own life. To adventure life on stilts as they wander through lessons, trying to balance it all together.

Not me, I want the opposite. I woke up in an empty house. Dad was gone, probably to a bar. I haven't checked my phone yet. Just the thought of it feels heavy. Like it would take too much out of me to open a message and pretend to care.

I sat in the kitchen for a while; the chair felt hard and cold under me. The house was quiet, I could hear the refrigerator humming, the pipes clicking somewhere deep in the walls.

I kept waiting to hear dad's keys, but it never came. The sun moved across the floor in slow lines until it got dark again. The cold got worse after sunset. I didn't bother turning on the heat. It feels right to be cold.

I thought about lighting a candle for mom, but it felt stupid. Like it wouldn't change anything. Like it would only make the room feel heavier.

The walls feel further away at night. The house is breathing around me, waiting for me to say something. But I have nothing left to share.

Happy Birthday Charli.

Charli

# *Waiting Room* *Phoebe Bridgers*

December 10, 2023

Everything comes full circle eventually; the colors start bleeding into one another and before you know it you have a full painting. No matter which brush stroke was the first, the last one is the one that initializes the end of the journey.

Paint drips from the paths that are carved into a canvas, embodying the idealistic standards from an artist's mind that was made into reality.

Though despite the work being unfinished, the hardest part is saying goodbye to the token that has always kept someone going. A painting is worth sharing with the eyes of the world, just like a story is meant to be read.

The end is inevitable; the lessons and structure of art would always leave a feeling toward the individual seeing it, especially during the process of its creation.

The end becomes only the beginning of a new painting.

Fifteen seconds. A mere few seconds measure one's life. That is how long it takes until the truth is spoken out loud. Or how long life can flip a coin.

Fifteen seconds, multiple of five and three, is the bridge that connects two worlds; two contradictions that go against one another. A cupid and its devil maybe, or a hole that was never meant to be filled for one to get stuck between.

I try to blink my eyes, wanting to grasp a memory while it's there…

*I feel the sun on my face, my eyes closed. Soft warmth enters my pores as I lie half naked, wearing Dario's oversized shirt and undergarments, in the embrace of the mattress below me. Smelling the fresh air that surrounds me as my hands glide through my covers.*

*I search and search for the familiar body or try to smell the familiar scent that surrounds me every morning. Instantly I get up, my eyes still closed as I rub them, trying to make the constant sleepiness go away.*

*As I was trying to pull the covers off, I felt a hand on my calf, making me finally open my eyes to see the familiar emerald orbs. Locked in a trance, my smile grew instantly.*

*"Stop," Dario said as he lifted his hand from my leg to finish tying his shoe.*

*Once he was done, he made his way around the tan frame that held the bed and sat right next to me at the edge of the mattress. He lands his hand on the back of my neck and starts pushing me down to the bed, following me as I let him guide me.*

*"Get some more rest River," Dario said, now inches away from my face.*

*"I love you," I say softly as he smiles.*

*He pecks my lip again, whispering the same words back to me.*

*I can feel his minty breath against me; his eyes locked onto mine waiting for my answer. For once, my mind is quiet, therefore no words can be expelled out of my mouth; instead, I just nod with a smile on my face.*

*Dario returns the smile as his lips connect to my forehead, soft and quick. He then connects to the tip of my nose, very faint that it almost tickles. My eyes are wide open, not wanting to miss any moment of the exhilarating sensuous being that sits before me.*

*Dario hovers over my lips, licking his own as he momentarily makes eye contact with me before connecting him to mine. Only then do I close my eyes, only then do I enliven in the moment with the boy I always loved, turned into the man I will forever cherish.*

*The kiss is soft, safe, as we move as one unit against each other. Our energy drips off from one another, envisioning an aura that clouds us like cushions every time our skin connects. I can feel Dario's tongue slip in, mine circling him as we dance in each other's mouths.*

*Clinging onto each other like our life depends on it--- the feeling of his heart beating against mine momentarily. The kiss dies down and the nourishing sensation fills our bodies as if we are one person. Like every relevant story, the kiss ends after it has lingered more than usual.*

*"Sleep, Charlotte, sleep." Dario announced before breaking away. He doesn't get up as he strokes my head, his fingers tracing my face like he is memorizing a painting before he leaves.*

*It was only a few hours he would be gone for, along with everyone else. A new reality was painted in front of my eyes, but I do not have the strength to bear it. But those few hours do not compare to the ache that has been rotting for years.*

*I stare into his eyes, like a forest that one can get lost in, as he stares right back. Energy matched. Dario then gets up from the bed, the mattress instantly lifting from his big ass.*

*I watch as he picks up his bag from the closet across the room and turns to the door, sunlight pouring in like fire sparking onto wood.*

*He opens it, ready to leave but doesn't until he turns and sees me one last time. Dario puts his lips together and sends me an air kiss, to which I return before he ultimately leaves.*

It took 267 seconds for Dario to make his way into my front yard. His car roared as it took 26 seconds until it faded away. That was an hour ago.

I stare at the words I have written as I dropped my red pen onto the mushroom notebook as I filled up the last page. The last memory lingering in my head from this morning. I look through the book, filled with red ink onto the cream-colored pages; like blood bleeding and spreading as the story comes to an end. My mind is finally silent, clarity at last.

I pull out the ripped pages from the notebook, on the back cover, with a little slip. I read all the childhood memories, old journals from younger me handwriting. It was like seeing a world where I am a ghost in my own story.

Laughing, crying, gasping, and cringing all over my bed. Alone in a house that had no one existed in for years. I see the energy pouring in from the window, bringing light to the subject. The soft haze brought a sense of solitude to my room that was not there before.

I look up to the side of the bed to see a picture of the core four: Shaya, Lio, Dario, and I in the tent we spent almost every weekend in one summer. Smiles as bright as the moon that plays in the memory captured forever. The last time I truly felt purity.

"One final sleep," I breathed out as I lay back in the empty bed.

I am met with tenebrosity as the empty pill container is in one hand and the notebook in the other. I am met with a sensation of tranquility as everything comes to an...

Dario's P.O.V.

A year later

I could not move on. I did not even try because I did not wish to. Even if a knife were pressed against my throat, I would meet its edge with a smile, welcoming the end to be reunited with my love once more.

Yet here I am without her; the absence of her presence settling deep within my bones, as they tremble in quiet despair. My heart, incomplete, skips its beat, for the other half is lost to a world where I cannot follow.

Today is not a day of farewell; it is a day to say, "see you later," as she would have wished, urging me to cease holding onto the past. I must stop reliving the moment her cold body lay against mine, her breath fading as the ambulance arrived.

Her room, once yellow and warm, was now consumed by suffocating grey. I did not know then that it would be the last time I felt her warmth; the last time her smile locked my heart in place. If I had known, I would not have left. I just got her back. *I just got to hold her again. My river,* nothing hurts more than this.

But that was her wish.

Who am I to be angry at a battle she could not win?

I blurred everything as I saw people passing by, talking to each other. They feel normal, like they are still whole. But I am in pieces, never to be mended.

Charlotte's absence is a space I cannot fill, no matter how many smiles or coffee cups are offered around me. Half of the people here have not talked to my River once in their lifetime.

My River, my flame burned out way too soon. I had to leave her in my teen years as I turned 20 a few months ago, something we both had planned to spend time with each other.

Nonetheless, I will carry River for the rest of my adulthood, spending it as she should have been right by my side. I feel her energy lingering around me, I like to believe it is her way to let me know she is okay, as okay as she can be with the final rest she took. That she is with her mother, enjoying the love I could not provide for her.

I could not even make it to her funeral a week after, seeing the love of my life without her usual chaotic energy; with her cloudy grey eyes searching in mine like she had the answer already.

That is why I am hosting the event today, in her favorite cafe that she did not enjoy enough of. On the day the world was not ready for Charlotte Riverson to walk the earth, bracing every challenge thrown at her.

 People are swarming in and out of the door, with books and coffee in their hands constantly chattering. I can smell the caramel in the air along with mint as I stand by the bookshelf next to the fireplace, observing the strangers among me. And I see her in the corner seeing it all.

Only then do I recognize the light brown locs that matched my sister with her idiot fiancé right alongside her. Shaya and Lio make their way through the crowd, coming towards me with love all over their faces. It took a few seconds for them to reach me, Shaya instantly hugging me tightly; a sister's love.

"How are you doing D.J.? Seriously?" Shaya asked with concern in her voice as she released from the hug. Emilio matches the same expression as Shaya, only he is more distraught. He lost his sister, and so did Shaya. My throat thickens and the air seems to be hard to gather at this moment.

"The same as you right now, I was not the only one who lost Charli." I responded, looking downwards to not meet their gaze.

My body eternally flinches at her name, the taste on my tongue leaves poison as it is only used to describe her now. Not to talk to her until we meet again. I want to scream and run out of this place, but I must stay for her. For her only.

A strong grip lays on my shoulder, making me look up to the person connected to it. Lio has a stoic expression; one he wears when he is trying to mask his pain.

"We lost our best friend, my sister, yes, but you lost a version of her that only you knew, a version she was able to be vulnerable to. You had that luxury D.J., so no you are not feeling as we are. We just want to let you know we're not going anywhere. You are family D.J." Lio says, his voice shaking towards the end.

"Besides, we want you to tell you something, anything to help ease the pain a little bit," Shaya continues, looking nervously and avoiding my eye contact.

"What is it Shaya?" I asked impatiently, rolling my eyes.

Shaya breathed out, before handing me a picture of what looks like to be an ultrasound.

"You're going to be an uncle D.J., I know this isn't the best time to announce this, but we found out a few months-"

I cut Shaya off and at once hugged her, not too tight so I didn't want to hurt the baby. I want to cry, laugh, scream, but most of all I want to share this feeling with my River. I am sure she is smiling with her beautiful smile nevertheless with her mother.

"No, do not do that. This is huge news, and I am happy for both of you," I announced, stepping away from the hug to see Lio and Shaya together, a family in the making.

I understand now why Charli had these two idiots in her life all this time. It took everything in me to not reach for my phone, wanting to hear the voice of my girl to share the news.

"That's not all D.J.," Emilio said.

"What else? Are they twins?"

Lio laughs, "I think I would have a heart attack if that were the case, but no, the name of our child is going to be River Cardiner, after Charls."

I just stare at them, not knowing how to react. My nephew or niece will carry on the name Charli, my forever love, their best friend. For the first time since I found Charli, cold and who was asleep peacefully, have I felt tears brimming in my eyes. For the first time I did not fight it off and just let them fall.

More came down and until I realized it, two pairs of arms embraced me; feeling love and sorrow in one. Like rain and sun, I can feel a rainbow grow towards the future ahead of us, the family that Charli left behind, but one she would never dare to forget.

I clear my throat, making Shaya and Lio break the hug.

"Thank you for everything for the past few months. I have not been myself but today makes me realize that I still have her, not entirely but in glimpses," I said, my voice breaking as I wiped the tears from my eyes.

Shaya nods and Emilio passes me the microphone before they both make their way towards an empty table.

Holding the mic in my hand, I headed from my corner where I had been hiding and moved towards the center of the room. There is a table next to a podium that was placed for the memorial today. Shaya helped me mostly set the event together, props to her.

Once I was in the view of everyone, people started dying down, and conversations were still going on. I cleared my throat in the microphone to grab everyone's attention, which instantly does as the whole cafe is now silent; a pin could drop to break the tension, besides the coffee makers brewing and the wind hitting the windows outside.

"Good afternoon, everyone. I am Dario Black; those who know me only calls me D.J. and Charli was my lover before her sun has set a year ago." I broke the silence.

Looking around I see all types of people together, from different friend groups, even Quinn herself. I took a deep breath and let it out before continuing.

Coach Lawson nods at me, along with Mrs. Cailo. Without them, I would have no idea how to help Charlotte the way I did today. To bring a room like this together.

"I want to start off to explain my final tattoo, one that Charli tattooed herself. You see, on my wedding ring finger lies a dandelion. When Charli tattooed this image, we hadn't graduated yet. She asked me the meaning of it, and why I got it. I just told her someone I used to know loved dandelions.

Back in middle school, my friends and annoying ass sister decided to camp in the backyard of my house one weekend in the summer." I paused to look up at Lio and Shaya; she was already flicking me off. I see some people around them laughing and smiling at the story I am trying to convey.

"We decided to go around one by one to talk about what their favorite things were in the entire world. Being nine years old and all, of course my best friend Emilio said his hot wheels collection and my sister saying her endless amount of cheer bows." I hear the crowd laugh together; despite the reason we are here today. "I do not remember what I said at the time but-"

"He's lying! He said he couldn't choose between his video games or his books!" Lio roared out, making the crowd laugh once again, me laughing right along with them.

"Okay, okay, yes, it is true. Can I get back to the story or would you like to tell it instead?" I smile at my dumbass friend, gratefully, who puts his hands up in defense. I shake my head before continuing.

"Anyways, Charli said something different. She said her favorite thing in the world was a dandelion." I look up to see the crowd in awe, witnessing my story like it just happened yesterday.

"She said dandelions were delicate enough to scatter with breath, yet strong enough to grant wishes," I said as my voice cracked. I could feel myself starting to choke up, tears threatening to come out but not yet.

Not until I finish this for her; I owe that to my River.

"Not everything beautiful can last forever. Charli always reminded me of a walking dandelion: so powerful that she did not understand it herself but instead showed everyone else the wishes she could grant," my voice broke out as I fight to let out the next sentence. "She had no idea how strong she was...but I did. I could only love her more for it. *I still do.*" I fight back a sob, wanting to make it through this damn speech.

I look up towards Shaya and Lio, "To her best friends, she granted trust and admiration every time she spoke of them. She would go to war for those two, and in her mind, it was in fact a war."

I look around the room, continuing my speech, "To her mentors and peers, most of you folks did not give a fuck about her and should not even be here. Regardless, she granted patience and gratitude as she would smile to see the group of people gathered here today." Some of the crowd murmured, others laughed, and others were already crying.

Charli's presence is felt by all, not only by the people she had in her lifetime. But by those who understand her, who she stands for. She is touched by those who cry in silence but smile in the morning to the best of their ab

I cleared my throat before I carried on, "As for her grant to me," I paused, looking down and taking a breath, "to me, a friend before and after a tragedy she endured, and lover to all her scars and wounds she tried so hard to cover up. She granted me love and perception." Flashes of her smile come to my mind. Her laugh lingering in my mind.

"She granted me my only wish since childhood and that was to be loved by Charlotte Riverson. It is only fair that I would return the favor and grant my River her final wish."

That said, I stepped away from the podium, putting the microphone in its holder. I move towards the table alongside, one with mountains of books. I grab one on top and read the cover of the novel in my head.

I can feel the harsh spine in the palms of my hands as I open the fresh, printed book. I make my way back to the podium, adjusting the microphone. I open the book—her book. It is strange, like holding something that should not exist anymore. But here it is, her heart laid bare for the world to see.

I ran my fingers over the pages, the ink, the weight of everything she gave me. Once I was ready, I cleared my throat, ready to speak in place of my River, my flame. For her, I granted her the final wish and started reading.

The crowd is silent, but my voice is strong, for Charli,

"Riverson, by Charlotte Riverson. Chapter 1." I took a breath before continuing.

"1...2...3...4...5. Time is all about counting."

# *About the Author*

## LAILA ISLER

Hi! First, thank you for choosing to read this book.

*Riverson* has been a part of my life since I was about eleven years old. Over the years, friends, teachers, and classmates read early versions of this story. In many ways, it became my journal. Charlotte Riverson is not me, but she carries a great part of me — as well as pieces of people I've met and grown close to.

Many of the characters are inspired by real people, though their actions and experiences are fictional. Writing this book was my way of trying to understand my own youth and feelings. I've been fortunate to have family, friends, and love in my life, but I still experienced deep vulnerability and depression, especially at a young age.

This book is for those who struggle to understand themselves, who fear causing pain to others, who hide their hurt and find it hard to ask for help. It wasn't until I was sixteen that I told my mother the truth. A year later, I published my first piece at school about my adolescent depression.

Now, at nineteen, I am learning to let go of my youth — the pain I once held so tightly, the embarrassment I felt towards my younger self. Through writing *Riverson*, I've learned to love myself. I've discovered the power within me to create and to be disciplined, even when I felt alone.

*Riverson* will always be part of me. As I enter a new decade of my life, I carry forward the lessons it taught me: that vulnerability is strength, and that healing is possible.

Love kills. Especially for Charli Riverson — the epitome of a mountain bowing to the storm.

At just eight years old, her world shattered when her mother's death was deemed a suicide. What followed was a future heavy with expectations and bright dreams that faded into despondency, corruption, and tragedy.

Only broken souls can find other pieces to fit into their fractured lives — a puzzle forever missing parts stolen by the past.

Love kills. It always has. But sometimes, the dead don't lie in graves with headstones. They remain among us, waiting to be mended by the very hands that broke them.